Copyright © 2022 by Loren Leigh

All rights reserved.

No part of this book may be reproduced in any form or by any electronic or mechanical means, including information storage and retrieval systems, without written permission from the author, except for the use of brief quotations in a book review.

Edited by Cassie's Book Services

Paperback cover by The Raven's Touch, Insta: @the.ravens.touch

ALWAYS

1

Inertia
Noun
1. a tendency to do nothing or to remain unchanged unless acted on by an external force

Dex nudges my elbow with his beer cup. "That girl you came with is looking for you."

"Okay." I don't move from my spot, just reach down to grab the keg hose and top off my cup. I promised her I'd be back in five minutes. And now I've been here—in this suffocatingly hot kitchen—for an hour.

He laughs, shaking his head. "This one didn't even last a night, J."

I step back from the keg. "Nah, I'll go find her soon."

I'm not sure if that's the truth.

It's not specific to the girl. I'm not *trying* to be a dick.

I'm just weary. It took Dex a lot of convincing to even get me out tonight. Last year, parties like this held some interest for me. I'd have a couple beers, chat with Dex or whomever, and get lost in a girl for a few hours. All good stuff. But now I'm five years into a four-year degree and putting off whatever comes next. I know I should get my ass in gear, especially since classes start on Monday, but everything just feels...tired.

And I've got to admit that I don't have much interest when it comes to hooking up with girls recently.

"Sure you're good?" Dex bumps my forearm with his beer again. His olive-green eyes flick around my face with concern. He's got a slight drawl, and it always comes out more when he's had a couple of beers. "I know I dragged you out tonight, man. I've just been kinda worried about..."

Me. And the permanent impression my ass has made on our couch lately.

"I'm good." I scrub a hand through my thick hair, which is always stupidly unruly, but even more so in this inferno of a kitchen. I can actually see the strands sticking out from the corner of my vision. "Probably a good thing we came out. I need to get out of this funk."

But what I *know* and what I *do* are often two completely separate things.

"Damn right it's good." He flashes me a wide grin, making his dimples pop out under the scruff he's been growing this summer. "What's her name?"

He cranes his head toward the living room door, probably trying to get a glimpse of my date on the cramped dance floor. She'd be easy to spot, wearing a silvery, shiny tank-top-thing that drew just about everyone's attention to the compact body she's got underneath.

"Michela." I take a drink, my tee sticking to my bicep as I raise the cup. I'm not sure why he's pushing about her so much. Likely hoping to brighten me up. He's a good friend.

Dex and I were finger painting together in kindergarten, riding our bikes off homemade ramps in sixth grade, blowing shit up in *Call of Duty* in high school, and now we share an apartment on the far side of town, both finishing up college. He's more of a brother to me than my own brother is, although we look like complete opposites—him with those dimples and, other than the scruff, a boy-next-door kind of thing with shorn sandy-colored hair. And me, Korean-American, with the uncontrollable hair, ink covering both arms, and a couple of piercings that aren't considered family friendly.

"Michela? Nice name," Dex says.

"Yeah, she's smart too. Last year, I had an ethics class with—" I groan in relief as the sliding door into the kitchen opens and a waft of crisp night air blows in, cooling the sweat on the nape of my neck.

I glance over my shoulder at the door, then freeze.

Holy fuck.

I didn't know *he* was here. I clench my cup so hard it pops, beer jumping out over my knuckles and dribbling on the floor.

Kepler Quinn steps into the kitchen, his smoke gray eyes shifting over the room like he's looking for someone. Towering and stupidly confident, he's got a cup in one hand, and the other sinks into well-loved jeans as his focus halts on me, and it's like a bolt of electricity zaps up my spine, hitting every single vertebra on the way.

He raises a single brow in my direction like he knows exactly what he does to me. Like he knows . . . everything.

He does know everything. Kepler is the smartest guy I know. Fiercely intelligent, he was the valedictorian of his and my brother's high school class. The guy who set the curves and was supposed to go off to some East Coast college instead of languishing in small-town Colorado where the most popular majors are business and forestry. Now he's earning a PhD in physics, while still partying on the weekends apparently.

And I'm pretty sure he *can* see right through me. That he somehow knows about that zapping hum still quivering low along my spine. That he can sift through my thoughts and categorize my deepest secrets. Which is the last thing I want him to see.

My heart's pumping about a million gallons per second, my stomach tightening, and my apathy disappears in a *whoosh*. Just swallowed right the fuck up as I stare back at him. The music from the other room pounds through my entire body, reverberating in every damn muscle and cell.

Simkung. It's Korean for that throb you get in your chest with some people.

It definitely describes whatever this fucking response is to Kepler Quinn.

He swivels away and says something to the guy stepping through the door behind him. Then he pulls his hand from his pocket to take the guy's cup before heading toward the keg.

Toward me.

Shit.

Take a breath, J.

With every step he takes, my throat dries more. The hum in my spine multiplies. There's no normal when it comes to him. My response to him is a sudden onset of flame that always gets hotter. It never burns out. It never goes away.

It's not attraction. It's something else entirely. Too intense to parse out or put a name on. And it doesn't happen with any other guy.

It's just Kepler. He messes me up.

Which is really freaking inconvenient because he's also my brother's best friend. The same way that Dex and I are friends: lifelong, inseparable, more family than friends.

Which makes Kepler and me family?

I shake my head sharply. *No.*

Dex says something, so I turn toward him, my stance widening as Kepler stops next to the keg. Kepler's to my right, and I can just see him out of the corner of my eye as he shifts two cups into the same hand, his forearm flexing, long fingers stretched out to hold them both.

Why does the way he's holding those cups make my breath hitch?

I try my damnedest not to notice the way his light-gray tee pastes to his shoulders with the sweltering heat. His dark-blond hair falls across his high forehead. His sharp jawline clenches slightly. His thin lips stay in an unforgiving line.

I haven't seen him smile in a long time.

Why is that?

Thinking back about it, I'm hard pressed to picture him with a smile *at all*. From either across the room or across campus. I can't remember him truly smiling since we were kids.

Dex frowns, glancing behind me toward Kepler and then fixing back on me. "You were saying?"

"Uh," I mumble, fighting to remember. "Michela. Yeah. We had an ethics class together last year. She's pretty damn smart."

Which is the reason I struck up a conversation with her when I ran into her at the library this summer. We partnered on an assignment for Kant's Rational Basis of Morality and sailed through it. She also seems like a good person, always with a bright smile. And Dex isn't wrong—she's pretty. Or "hot as hell" in his words.

She shouldn't inspire indifference in anyone. She deserves a lot more. Maybe I *am* being a dick to her.

In my peripheral, Kepler shifts his hand to fill the second cup, those long fingers tensing.

I scrub through my hair and then quickly shove my hand in my jeans pocket, not sure what to do with myself. I'm hotly aware of the way my tee's stuck to my chest, the pinch of the metal barbell in my eyebrow, the sweat covering the ink along both forearms, and the chafe of the thick leather band strapped around my wrist.

Why does he make me so aware of myself? I rarely think about myself like that.

"You'd like her," I say, trying to stick to the subject. Which is Michela. The girl I'm here with. The girl I should be more interested in.

"Okay," Dex says, squinting at me.

Shit. Am I acting weird? Do I look normal on the outside?

Because I sure as hell don't feel normal on the inside.

Kepler reaches out an arm to pump the keg, up and down, up and down. He peers into the second cup as it fills, his cheeks sucking in slightly.

Christ. *Don't look.*

A girl with long, looped-up braids stops by the keg, and he straightens to talk to her. I can't hear what they're saying.

I shouldn't care what they're saying.

I swallow hard and focus on Dex as he chats about getting the landlord to come over and fix the cheap-ass windows at our apartment. Like that'll ever actually happen. We mop up water every time it rains.

I even say a few things:

"Yeah."

"Okay."

"I'll do that."

Do what? No clue.

When the girl steps away, Kepler pivots toward me, lingering for a moment like he's debating.

"Hey, Jin." His voice is soft and low, and he lengthens my name like he always does.

He's the only one who calls me by the second syllable of my name, Jae Jin. Everyone else sticks with Jae or, like Dex, an even more basic *J*. But for some unknown reason, Kepler started calling me *Jin* when we were still kids.

"Hey, Quinn." My voice is rough, and sticking with his last name seems like a good idea.

His gaze falls to where beer *still* drips off my hand because I've been too freaking distracted to wipe it off. His lips arc in the faintest echo of a smile. It can't even really be called a smile, actually. It's that faint, and it disappears almost immediately.

"Need some help with that?" he asks. "A towel, perhaps?"

I shift the cup to my other hand before wiping my knuckles on my jeans. "Think I'll manage."

His eyes narrow, but then he turns to upnod at Dex, who returns the gesture. A second later, Kepler strides back toward the guy he came with.

That's the extent of our exchange. Kepler and I aren't friends. We never have been. Never will be. He's always been Shin's friend, not mine.

He crosses back to the other side of the kitchen and extends a cup to his friend. Some dude I vaguely recognize with chubby lips and a cleft in his chin.

Their fingers brush as Kepler hands him the cup, and the guy's chubby lips break into a smile.

My mouth dries, my stomach twisting hard. Is Kepler here *with* him?

I'm numb. Sounds muffle. The only thing left is my pulse hammering in my throat. I know the music is still thumping in the other room, but to me, it feels like the kitchen is *silent*.

I've never seen him with anyone before. Friends, yeah, but not a date.

Is he on a date?

Doesn't matter, J. I don't care who Kepler dates.

Besides, it was nothing more than a brush of fingers. Hell, Dex brushes my forearm all the freaking time, and it means nothing.

Dex itches at his scruff. "J? You still in there?"

"Uh, yeah." I take a sip of my beer and then cough when it gets caught in my throat. "Think I might go dance."

He gives me a look like I just told him I've got a trip to the moon planned for this weekend. Two hours ago, he had to threaten me to get off the couch and now my hands are shaking, my pulse is racing, and the need to *move* pumps through my chest.

Kepler sidesteps away from the guy he's with . . . his date? . . . and runs his palm over the back of his neck, bicep flexing as his elbow points at the ceiling. Then he suddenly pivots with a jerk, his back to me, gray tee glued so tight across his shoulder blades that I can see his delts, hand still cupping his neck, jeans low, one pocket faded with the outline of his wallet.

There's something uneasy about the way he moves.

Stop staring, J. I need to get out of this sweltering heat that's making my jeans chafe against my thighs. I drag in a breath and turn to Dex. I'm making a bad decision. And I fucking know it.

I do it anyway.

"I'm gonna go find Michela," I say.

MICHELA ISN'T hard to find. She's in the middle of the dance floor with three other girls, all holding light-green shots above their heads. They cheer over the music before throwing them back.

She waves me over. Her pink lips broaden into a smile as she tugs me onto the dance floor with her small hand in mine. Her other hand settles on my chest, and we start to move, my t-shirt sticking to my skin under her palm. She sways her hips in perfect time to the music, smiling up at me. Her curly hair bounces and flashes of pink and green lights reflect off the silvery tank-top-thing she's wearing.

I grin down at her and shove away any and all thoughts of Kepler Quinn. The beat thumps so loud it compresses in my chest. One song and then another. More shots come around, but I don't drink one—I've already hit my self-imposed two-drink limit. I don't need the liquor anyway. I *move*, sweat thick between my shoulder blades. The jitter in my hands fades as I grip her hips and pull her against me. I don't usually dance, but it's like I have to get out that damn vibration that Kepler started in me.

Kepler. His long fingers pumping that keg.

No. *Don't think, J.*

The skin just above the waistband of Michela's shorts is soft against my fingers, and when I feather my thumb over it, she wraps her hands around the nape of my neck and brings me down into a kiss that tastes like butterscotch and liquor.

Her tongue darts in and out of my mouth too fast, but I kiss her anyway, my hands roving down to cup her hips, hauling her against me. Her shorts-clad ass fits in my palms.

Kepler.

"Fuck," I mumble as I break off the kiss.

Her lips pitch into a frown, but she starts grinding against me, and I go with it. Another song, and I'm able to shake him off. Before I know it, Michela's tugging me up a darkened staircase, stumbling backwards in front of me, her deep-brown eyes flitting down to my crotch and then back up again.

This is what I need.

Right?

I back her up against the wall, and her legs wrap around my hips as she scales me like a rock climber. Right here, where anyone could see us.

Fuck it.

I don't care.

She's soft and warm, and she moans into the kiss as her tongue flicks with that too fast pace along mine. She grinds against me with her shorts directly over my zipper, and my dick's definitely not immune.

I close my eyes and try to focus on kissing her, getting into the weird tongue rhythm and letting myself go, the music pounding, the heat simmering, that mystifying gray gaze pinning me, his long fingers cupping the back of his neck as he pivoted.

My eyes flash open.

Michela's tongue is deep in my mouth, tasting like syrupy liquor. Her legs are still clamping my hips, her soft breasts jammed against my chest.

I'm not unaffected. I'm hard as fuck, my breath is uneven. But there's only one person who is rolling through my thoughts. It's not her.

He's like a monster under my bed. Roaring into my brain the second I try not to think about him.

Is he still in the kitchen? It's directly below us. My feet might be over his head. Or maybe he's gone off with the finger-toucher. Maybe Kepler's doing the same thing I am now. His hands on the dude's ass, pulling him flush against his dick.

For fuck's sake. *Get a grip, J.*

Michela's weird kiss continues, her tongue sliding along my teeth.

No. This isn't right.

I push back from her, breaking mid-kiss and practically shoving her off me. *Shit.* That was a dick move.

"Jae?" Her expression laces with confusion.

I backstep so I'm across the hall from her. *What the fuck am I doing?* Michela stares up at me with a pinched expression.

"Jae?" she repeats, louder this time.

I nod toward the stairs. "Uh, maybe we should head back? I'll grab you another drink."

She blinks at me. "I don't understand. That's . . . *it?*"

I take another step back, and my shoulders hit the far wall. "I'm sorry. I'm not trying to be a dick."

"Then don't be so confusing." She closes the distance between us, her fingers brushing the solar system ink that wraps my forearm. "Just tell me what happened. Was it a bad kiss?"

"No, it's not that. You're a great kisser." I pull away from her and run my wrist over my forehead. It's still a million freaking degrees in this house. "You're great. Everything was great." *Christ, J, stop saying* great. "It's not you."

"Then what is it?" She stares up at me, not letting me off the hook. "I really like you."

I stiffen. Head to toe. She must see because her eyes widen.

"But you don't like me," she concludes.

"No, you're . . . cool." I drag in a breath, willing myself to stop saying stupid shit. "You're an awesome person, Mich—"

"I'm a big girl." She sets her chin. "Tell me what really happened. Is there someone else?"

"Yes." My answer slips out before I think. "I mean, *no*."

Her mouth drops open. "Are you cheating on someone?"

"No," I say firmly. Why did I say there was someone else? "I'm just . . . not in the right headspace to date right now."

I should have ignored Dex and just stayed on the freaking couch tonight. No Michela.

Definitely no Kepler Quinn.

I shake my head and get back on the subject—which is her. I know I'm messing this up, but I don't want her to leave thinking there's a single thing wrong with her. Because there's not. She really is a cool person. And she deserves a hell of a lot more than a guy shrugging her off in a hallway.

I meet her gaze head-on. "I'm just not here with you right now. I really wish I was."

"Now *that* I believe." She reaches up to tap my chest with her fingertips. "I wish you were too. It's not everyone who gets to hook up with one of the hotty-pants twins."

I blink. "What?"

She shrugs one shoulder. "You know. What they call you and Dex."

I shake my head. "I have no idea what you're talking about."

"How could you not know?"

"I guess I'm in my own head a lot." *Understatement.* "Dex and I get called the hotty-pants twins?"

She rolls her eyes. "It's stupid. But kinda true."

"But *twins*?" I'm trying to stifle a laugh, but I let it out when a small smile darts to her lips. "We look nothing alike."

"I swear I didn't make it up." She shakes her head, her shoulders relaxing. "And I think the 'twins' is just because the two of you are together a lot. I don't know, I'm only a sophomore. Someone made it up long before I met you."

"That's hilarious." Wait until I tell Dex. He'll be belly-laughing for an hour.

I erase my smile, focusing back on her. "I'm sorry, Michela. I really do think you're a cool person. And you're smart and fun to be around. Anyone would be lucky to be here with you. I'm just not . . . I don't even fucking *know* what I am right now."

She blows out a breath, puffing out her cheeks. "Maybe another time?"

"Yeah, of course," I say, but I think we both know that's not likely to happen.

"Don't be a stranger, Jae." She pushes up to her toes and gives me a kiss on the cheek before turning and heading back down the stairs. I scrub a hand through my hair, staring after her. That could have gone much worse.

Except I'm still at a loss for what's going on in my head.

Kepler's a curse. Even just standing here, in the dark, music thumping from below, my lips still damp from Michela's, my abs tight and dick twitching, I'm thinking of *him* instead of the girl I just had wrapped around me.

What am I supposed to do about that?

A light flashes on at the other end of the hallway, and I startle, turning.

Gray t-shirt. Well-loved jeans.

Shit, shit, shit-on-me shit.

Kepler tilts his head, his smoky gaze fixed on me, light from the room to the side of him painting the curve of his left shoulder, then playing down his bicep to his forearm and those long fingers.

"What are you doing there?" I spit out. The hardness in my voice surprises me, but Kepler just stands there, calm as can be, not jarred by my tone.

He sinks the lighted up hand into his jeans pocket. "I was watching you make out with a girl, apparently."

"Christ," I mumble. "You were *watching*?"

"You're in a hallway," he says, voice so low I can barely hear it over the thumping music. "In a house crowded with people. And you didn't think that someone might happen by?"

He saw me kissing her.

I've got no freaking clue why that matters so much. I just know that it does. That it's rattling around in my head while I roll my shoulders and try to look like I'm not freaking the fuck out.

"Guess I wasn't thinking," I say. *Not about her, at least.* I drag my damp palms down the side of my jeans, which re-alerts me to my breath pooling low in my stomach and to how dramatically I'm tenting my zipper after Michela was grinding all over me.

Could this get any more awkward?

I take a step back, hooking my thumb toward the stairs. "I'm gonna—"

"Do you do that a lot?"

I stop in my tracks. "Do what?"

"Not think?" He dials into me with that intense gaze. "You said you weren't thinking. Do you do that a lot when you're kissing someone?"

"What kind of question is that?" I blurt.

He shrugs a shoulder. "Don't answer if you don't want to."

"I, uh . . ." I frown. Am I seriously answering him? "I guess I don't think about much. I mean, what should you think about when you're kissing someone?"

He arches a brow. "A hell of a lot, in my opinion."

"Like what?" I toss back at him.

A flicker of surprise races through his eyes, and his lips part slowly.

Sweat beads on the nape of my neck as I take in the six feet between us. The hallway didn't feel narrow with Michela, but with Kepler and his height, it feels damn near claustrophobic.

The song from downstairs ends, and in the sudden silence, I can practically hear my own heartbeat thumping up in my throat.

Why do I care what he thinks about when he's kissing someone? This is a weird conversation to have with your brother's best friend.

"That all depends," he says slowly, tilting his head so the light from the doorway highlights the sharp edge of his jaw. His voice is softer now that he doesn't have to speak over the music, and there's a deep husk in it that brushes a shiver over the nape of my neck. "I think about the man I'm kissing. How he tastes. The softness of his lips. The sounds he makes. The warmth of his skin. Among other things."

He.

Him.

I clear my tight throat. "Yeah, okay."

Freaking stupid response, J.

But I can't move. Can't think. Can't reason out what to say.

I'm just standing here, gripped by what *he* said.

Why am I so fixated on his answer? Why does it feel like it's flipping my comfy little world head over heels? Like the entire freaking planet just shifted off orbit.

"Jin?" The way he says my name jerks me back to the present.

"Yeah." I swallow and point toward the stairs. "I should, uh..."

"And there it is." His voice hardens a touch.

I frown. "There *what* is?"

"You avoiding me."

I stiffen. "I don't."

"You do." His eyes narrow. "Every time I enter a room, you're out of it in less than five minutes. You're ready to bolt right now."

Self-preservation.

And how the fuck does he know me so well?

I swallow. "It's nothing personal."

"You sure?" He takes half a step closer. "If I've done something to—"

"No."

His brow furrows. "I'll fix it. Whatever I've done. I know I can be ... off-putting."

"Off-putting? I wouldn't call you that."

"Most people would."

I shake my head, my forehead lining. Is that true? Maybe. "Regardless, you haven't done anything. Why this sudden interest?"

"It's not sudden," he says smoothly. "My interest is a constant."

"What does that mean?"

He watches me intently. "How about this time, you don't rush away. And instead, I'll show you something."

I blink. "What?"

"You'll like it." He turns, striding back down the hall toward a far door. "Come on."

My eyes narrow on the darkened room behind him. "You want me to follow you into a dark room?"

"Exactly." And then he disappears into the doorway.

2

No fuckin' way.

I stand there, lock-kneed, in the hallway, breathing in the scent of too many drunk bodies packed into the house. College party cologne: sweat, cheap beer, and weed.

I swallow hard, trying to calm the vibration in my chest.

Following Kepler into that room is a bad decision. I should turn away, like I always do. Get out before he sees the way he offsets me.

But I'm going to follow him anyway.

I can't *not*. I'm drawn forward, moth to flame, and I follow him into a bedroom with a carefully made bed, a wall of snowboards, and a place for everything.

Kepler's at the window, hands on the frame.

"Do you know whose room this is?" I ask.

"Not at all." He pushes up on the window.

"So, what are we doing here?" My gaze falls on the bed. Which is *not* where I should be staring when Kepler and I are alone in a room.

"Just wait." He slides the window all the way up, and a cool breeze plays past him.

I lift my chin to the fresh air. "*Fuuuck*, that feels good."

He hitches a brow at me before snapping out the screen and setting it against the wall. Outside, there's a stretch of roof that extends out just below the window.

"Follow me." He hunches to fit through the opening, his jean-clad legs bending, his ass to me, and my eyes fall on that square outline of his wallet in his back pocket. Once he's out, he crouches and looks at me from the other side.

I shake my head. "This wasn't what I expected."

"What did you expect?" He extends a hand toward me back through the window, long fingers stretched out. A braided cord of brown leather is tied around his wrist. A vein crosses underneath it, wrapping up and around his forearm. It's *masculine*.

Of course it is. He's a dude.

I stare down at that vein, swallowing hard against the rush of heat that's clawing up my throat. I can't touch him.

"I'm good." I set my hand on the window frame instead of taking his.

A muscle in his jaw ticks once, but he drops his hand and steps back so I can duck my head under and pull myself out. My untied Chucks plant on dark-gray shingles as I straighten up on the other side of the window, dragging in a deep breath, and—

Holy fuck.

The night sky's *stacked* with stars. Bright and dim ones. Constellations and clusters. There's only a thin sliver of a moon and not a single cloud in the sky. It's too late in the evening to see the planets, but those are out there too. Entire far-off worlds.

"It's beautiful," I mumble. The cool breeze skims across my forearms, chills my sweat-dotted tee, and filters through my hair. I rake a hand through the unruly strands, pulling them back from my face. The music is muffled out here—feeling as far off as those hidden planets.

"It is beautiful." Kepler takes one small step farther down the steeply sloped roof. His head tips back as he points above us. "There's a shooting star."

I look where he's gesturing, but I already missed it. "Where was it?"

"Just south of Andromeda." He slips his hands into his pockets, attention flicking to me, and that almost-smile skirts his lips. Never a full smile.

I avoid his gaze by looking toward Andromeda. Its brightest star, Alpheratz, is brilliant tonight. Next to it, the four stars that make the square shape of Pegasus stretch out. Pisces is below that, which is one of the most interesting constellations with a colliding galaxy pair.

I walk to the edge of the roof, not stopping until my toes are at the gutter. The lawn slopes away from the house, tidy green grass far below. The mountains roll up in blacks and grays to make a jagged edge along the bottom of the star-laden sky.

It's breath-catchingly gorgeous. And infinite. Some people say it makes them feel small, but looking up at a star-stacked sky like this, I've always felt part of something.

Maybe that's why I've inked it all over my body. Or maybe it's simpler than that: I just like this shit. *The possibilities of the night sky.*

"I knew you'd like it," Kepler says quietly. He's still behind me at the window.

"How?" I ask, turning back to him.

"For real?" He shakes his head. "You were always hovering over that telescope when we were kids." He studies me from his place on the roof. "Not to mention the tattoos."

I laugh. "Yeah, I admit I was—*am*—obsessed. Always

trying to map out stars and shit." I spent hours behind that telescope that I got from . . . somewhere. I can't remember anymore. But I loved it. I haven't seen it in years. My mom probably sold it for fifty bucks so she could go out drinking for a night.

Back in the day, Kepler always humored me by listening to me ramble on about galaxies and black holes and dwarf stars. He'd listen to me chatter endlessly until my brother would call him, and then they would jump into Kepler's Jeep and head out to do whatever high school shit they had going on.

I shake off the flash of Kepler leaning close to me, shoulder brushing mine to see through the eyepiece.

He's Shin's best friend. For so many, many years. Hell, he's had a better relationship with my brother than I've ever had.

I inch forward until my toes are over the gutter. From here it feels like I could launch up into the universe. Somewhere new. Somewhere *different*. "I probably annoyed the fuck out of you. Always begging you to look in that telescope."

"You do realize I'm a grad student in physics and astronomy?" His low voice carries from over my shoulder. "And I'm named after two astronomers?"

"Kepler," I find myself saying. I never questioned where his name came from, but I suppose I've never met anyone else with that name. "Kepler's Laws of Motion."

"That's one."

I can't think of an astronomer named Quinn.

I twist toward him. "The other one's your middle name?"

He tilts his head, his gray eyes impossible to read in the dark. "Perhaps."

"What is it?" I'm struck by how little I actually know about Kepler.

"Not telling." He clears his throat. "And, fuck, Jin. Is it necessary for you to stand that close to the edge?"

"Why not?" I shrug, still rolling through the names of astronomers in my head.

He nods past me. "Because it's likely a long way down."

"Not that far."

"Far enough to hurt?"

My smile is quick. "Come on."

"Playing my own words against me." He takes a few careful steps forward, stopping a foot from the edge. He leans forward to glance down at the trimmed lawn, and that muscle in his jaw tenses again. "That's awful."

I rock forward on my toes, my heart double-beating at my nearness to the edge. Kinda like *simkung*. "You're scared of heights?"

"Not scared, no. *Terrified*." He leans back, rubbing his palm along the back of his neck.

"I like seeing your nerves, man." I shove my hands in my pockets. "Reminds me you're a real, live person."

He frowns. "Why wouldn't I be?"

"I don't know." I shrug a shoulder, then swivel to look down at the grass. "Just saying random shit."

Stop talking, J.

The wind kicks up and I drag in a deep inhale through my nose, trying to clear my head. Out here, it smells like evergreen and night. So different from inside.

There's another smell too. Complexly spicy. A smell that reminds me of a tea my father used to make out of dried omija berries from the Korean market over on Snake River Road. It tastes like a hundred different flavors all mixed together. Like lemon dipped in honey, sweet berries and cinnamon, the taste changing on your tongue even as you drink it.

Kepler. That's *him*. As he shifts another few inches closer to the edge—closer to me—I smell it again.

Why does he smell like that? And what's his middle name? Why do I always have to wonder shit about him? Why can't I shrug him off like I do with anyone else?

Instead, questions keep coming like an out-of-control wildfire leaping from one treetop to another. *Why did he really want me to follow him out here? How many men has he kissed? Is he here with that freaking finger-toucher?*

"Who?" Kepler leans closer to me.

Shit. Did I just say that last question *out loud*? I blink myself back into reality.

I did not.

I did not.

He's staring at me. "You're talking about Smith?"

I totally did.

"Uh . . ." I'm already in for a penny. "Maybe? The guy you brought a drink to in the kitchen. The, uh, finger-toucher."

Both his brows rise. "Finger-toucher?"

And here I go, making shit worse. "Yeah, he touched your fingers when you handed him the cup."

"I didn't notice."

I shake my head. "Not sure I buy that, Quinn. It was practically a fondle."

"A finger-fondle?" Humor flits in his voice. "I guess I was thinking about something else."

"What?"

"Molecular quantum mechanics," he says, totally deadpan, then he leans back on his heels. "Regardless, I'm definitely not here with him in a finger-fondling way. He's not . . ." He frowns, then shakes his head. "I work with him. Which is actually something I wanted to talk to you about before the semester starts." He rolls his shoulders, gray tee pulling across his chest. "I'm a TA for physics. More specifically, I'm your TA for physics. I got class lists last week, and you're on my roster."

Whatever I thought he could possibly say, that wasn't it. Kepler as my TA? There's no freaking way.

"It's a lecture style class," he continues. "You won't deal with me much there. Except you've been assigned to my lab."

"I'll take another class," I blurt out.

One beat of silence turns into two. Then three.

He stares across at me with this dark expression I can't even begin to read. "If that's what you want to do, but I don't think it's necessary."

It's really fucking necessary.

I rake my fingers through my hair, my skull still damp from the heat. "You'd grade me, right? Isn't that a conflict of interest? Considering your friendship with my brother."

"You wouldn't be the first student that I've known." His jaw clenches. "I'd be fair."

"I'm not questioning your fairness. It's just . . ." No. This is a hard *no*. It's difficult enough seeing him across the room in a packed house. Or standing here with him on a roof. There's no flipping way that I'll be able to sit in a lecture and take notes if he's there.

I can't think when he's near. I'm like this spastic, brain-riddled kid with a . . . *crush*.

A sudden coldness hits me at the core.

That's what this is.

I have a fucking crush on my brother's best friend.

I don't know why it took me so long to recognize that. It's obvious now that I think about it. How I used to covet every second with him back when he'd be over at our house. How he sets my blood pumping. How I want to *smell* him.

Fucking *simkung*.

How did I not realize this sooner? I'm an idiot. That's the only explanation.

That and I've never had a crush on a guy before.

Wait . . . have I?

"Jin?"

"I just don't think it's a good idea to—" We both flinch at a sharp ringtone.

He pulls his phone from his pocket.

Shin's name lights across the screen.

My brother.

I step away from the gutter, my shoulders tightening at just seeing his name.

Kepler looks up at me. "I'm supposed to meet him."

"Now?" It's got to be one in the morning.

He shrugs a shoulder. "He's usually just getting off his shift around now, and I don't sleep much."

The phone stops ringing and then pings a second later with what I assume is a voicemail.

He looks me up and down. "Do you want to come?"

"With you and Shin?"

"Why not?"

I lick my lips, emitting a low, humorless laugh. "You know that we'd just argue the entire time. Besides, if Shin wanted to see me, then he'd call."

The phone rings again, which doesn't surprise me because my brother is persistent. It helps him be a good cop. But it also made him an annoying brother growing up.

Kepler silences it. "Shin's just—"

"You don't need to step into this." Or maybe I don't *want* him to step into it. My relationship with my brother is like two boxers dancing. Back-and-forth, neither quite willing to take a swing, but we both know that's what it's coming to.

Kepler doesn't need to be in the middle of that. And it all reminds me of who he is: Shin's best friend.

And he's right. I avoid him. And there are smart reasons for that. My neck heats to a million degrees just thinking about him and Shin finding out about this ridiculous crush.

Kepler's lips part with a beat of hesitation before he speaks. "I've been around your family for fifteen years. I don't mind being—"

"I've gotta catch up with Dex." I don't give a shit that I just interrupted him. This conversation is finished. I turn and walk back to the window, squeezing myself back into the house, and telling myself I don't need to look back.

My conviction lasts all of about five seconds, and I turn to find him watching me, and not moving from the edge, like he's forgotten how high up he is.

"See you in lecture," he says evenly, not a hint of emotion in his voice.

Fuck no, he won't.

3

THERE'S GOT to be another freaking class.

I scan through the course catalogue on my phone, the morning sun highlighting the breakfast bar from the leaky skylight.

The class just needs to fulfill my last science requirement. I'll take *anything*. Introduction to Beekeeping? The Biology of Sperm Whales? I don't care. I can't be trapped in a room with Kepler Quinn at regular intervals.

I'm still jittery from seeing him last night, my foot bouncing on the rung of the barstool, my thumb jabbing at my phone.

The microwave beep makes me hop off the stool. I grab the warmed-up bowl of ginger soup and bring it back to my spot at the counter.

It's quiet in our cheap-ass apartment without Dex. Other than the faint sound of traffic from the gas station across the street, there's nothing except for the thunk when I set my bowl down.

Dex talks a lot. And I begrudgingly miss it when he's gone.

I grab my phone to scan the catalogue one last time and dig into my breakfast.

Soup for breakfast is the usual in my family. At least until my father died.

Mani muguh, he'd always say as he spread out more than either Shin or I could ever hope to consume—Korean pancakes for Shin, and soup and kimchi and rice for me.

It's hard to believe he's been dead nine years. Feels both longer and shorter at the same time.

After going through the catalogue again, I send off a quick email to my advisor asking for a meeting—maybe he can do something about the class—and then my thumb hovers over the screen.

I shouldn't do it.

But that didn't stop me last night, and it doesn't stop me now.

I set down my spoon, type *Kepler Quinn* in the query box, and hold my breath as the results load.

The first listing is for the Physics and Astronomy Department at Indigo Falls University, "the IFU" as we call it.

I click on the link for teachers' assistants. His name is second on the list, and a picture of him stares at me. My foot stops bouncing on the stool, my breath cages in my chest, and I just *look* at him. In a way I never let myself do in person. All out *staring.*

I study him—smoky grays, high forehead, straight nose, thin lips, sharply angled jaw, a small mole on the rise of his cheek.

My fingers twitch. Even a damn photograph sends a jolt of energy down my spine that tingles in my dick.

The sound of the front deadbolt echoes through the apartment, and I take a calming breath and set my phone face down on the counter as Dex strolls into the room. He's wearing the same wrinkled t-shirt he had on last night. His hair's askew, eyes bloodshot, and a wide smile is plastered on his face.

"Looks like you had a good night." I pick up my bowl and walk around the island to rinse it in the sink before stacking it into the dishwasher. "Hungry?"

"Yep." He stops on the other side of the kitchen island. "Last night's not why I'm smiling. All that happened was Brady and I had some beers after you bailed, then I crashed on his couch since I didn't want to drive."

"You've been crashing over there a lot," I say offhandedly as I grab some bread out of the pantry and stuff two pieces in the toaster for him.

"Uh, sure. No big." He drops on a stool next to the kitchen counter. We don't actually have anything as complex as a table, so we just sit here. It's where all the food is anyway.

"Okay." I shrug. "So why the big-ass smile?"

He winks at me. "Because I came home and found out that you've rejoined the living."

My chest tightens a little. He's grinning now, but I know he was worried about me. And I sure as hell know what it's like to worry about people.

"Yeah." I clear my throat. "I figured our couch could use a break from my ass."

"Truth." He nods. "Also, this was on our door."

He smacks a Post-it Note between us on the counter and then points down at it like I'm not already staring.

KEPLER is inked across the yellow Post-it in black Sharpie. All caps. Certain, heavy strokes. Self-assured and towering letters, just like him.

I swallow back the lump in my throat as I stare down at it.

The Post-it wasn't on the door when I got home last night. I'm sure I would have noticed it. So, when was he here? Middle of the freaking night? After he hung out with my brother? Why would he leave this for me?

Dex studies me. "You know what it's about?"

"No." The toaster pops and I grab a plate from the cabinet. "Juice?"

"Sure." Dex shrugs. "I hadn't seen Kepler in forever before last night."

"Me neither." I drop the toast in front of him, turn to the fridge, and pull out a carton of orange juice. After filling two glasses, I slide one across the counter to him.

Although that's not really true. I'd seen him across the Quad when I was registering for classes. I remember because I'd veered off toward the student center, curious where he was headed. Wait . . . had I been following him?

No. I had to go to the student center anyway.

It was just coincidence.

Right?

Dex takes a huge-ass bite of dry toast. No freaking clue how he eats that stuff. "I'd thought you'd run into him because of Shin?"

"Nope. I haven't seen Shin in a while either."

Dex downs half his orange juice. "Because of your mom?"

"Yeah."

"How's she doing?"

"Always the same." I put the juice carton back, leaving it at that, and Dex doesn't pressure me. It's not that I don't want Dex to know. He's the kind of guy you can say anything to. He understands how things are with my mom. I just don't like talking about her.

I drain the rest of my juice. "How'd the student teaching go?"

I'm not asking just because I want to change the subject —although that's an added benefit—but also because he's been talking about his upcoming student teaching job for months, while passing by my ass on the couch. Last week, he finally started his job at the middle school we both attended when we were kids.

The smile vanishes from his face at my question, worry lines appearing around his olive greens in record time. "It's okay."

"You sure?" I lean back against the counter, crossing my arms over my chest. "Doesn't look so okay."

For as long as I've known him, Dex has wanted to be an art teacher. His mom taught at Indigo Falls High School until she had to take unemployment for multiple sclerosis, and he's always wanted to follow in her teaching footsteps.

He empties his glass in one huge gulp. "The classes are good. Kids are cool, of course. It's just that I spent all summer drawing these lesson plans up, but they're all for shit when we don't have much more than broken crayons, dried up watercolors, and computer paper."

"Can you put in a funding request?"

"Not one that's gonna be granted." He sighs, itching at the scruff on his jaw. "You remember what it was like when we were there."

"Yeah, I do." Our eyes lock for a second. We both remember what it was like, growing up in the neighborhood we did, the way we did. Things were better for me before my dad died, but after . . . all the life insurance went to medical bills and funeral costs. It was only by taking out a reverse mortgage that we were able to keep a roof over our heads. Dex lived the same life I had.

Kepler . . . I'm not sure what kind of life he's lived, but something tells me from the Jeep he drove in high school and the leather trimmed messenger bag he carried that things were different for him.

Dex wipes his mouth with the back of his hand. "I gave this eighth-grade girl my pencil set because she likes drawing comics, but I can't keep doing that." He shrugs a shoulder. "It just feels fuckin' hopeless."

"Can we do something?"

He squints at me. "Like what?"

"I don't know. Fundraiser or something? A raffle? There's gotta be a lot of people around the IFU that would donate a couple bucks so that some kids can get some art supplies. I can help organize."

His eyes narrow on me. "Who are you and what have you done with J?"

That's a good question. I glance down at the Post-it, and before I can think too much, I grab it and crumple it in my palm. "Do you want my help or not?"

His grin is huge. "Hell, yeah, I do. Just happy to see you back, man."

He says it like I've been in another freaking country. Was I really that out of it?

WE SPEND Sunday doing shit around the apartment. A bit of cleaning, some epic brainstorming about this fundraiser idea that's taken Dex by storm, and a three-mile jog—which is something I should be doing much more often as evidenced by the exhaustion in my legs after the first hill.

I text Michela too, and we chat back and forth about classes a bit. I'm hoping that means we'll be on cordial terms whenever we run into each other again.

But by Monday morning, there's a second **KEPLER** Post-it left on my door. I've still barely slept for over twenty minutes, and I haven't left the apartment other than that jog and a trip to the gym. No matter how much I throw myself into shit around the apartment or at the gym, my brain still keeps circling back to him. And that TA picture doesn't help. I keep *staring* at it, like I'll see something else in his face I haven't seen before.

Actually, I have. He's got a light scar on his chin. His bottom lip is slightly thinner than his top. And those smoky grays have a few flecks of brown in them.

Fuck me. This is ridiculous.

I'm a spring about to pop as I toss my backpack into my little shitter car for the first day of classes. Dex slides in next to me for the four-mile drive to campus.

I've got a meeting with my advisor in twenty minutes, and Dex needs to submit his lesson plans for student teaching.

I tuck a tumbler of omija tea into the cup holder, and the scent fills the car.

Not reminding me of Kepler.

Not at fucking all.

Although the smell isn't *exactly* the same. There's something warmer about Kepler. Something more masculine.

Get him out of your head, J.

Dex grabs his phone as I'm pulling out onto the street. "Check this out." He pulls up an Instagram page. "I found this artist when I was looking for ideas for the fundraiser. Eli Reynolds. He's a street artist in Atlanta, but he grew up here and moved back a few years ago. His work is in-fucking-credible."

"Yeah?" I stop for a red light.

"Look at this." He tilts his phone to show me a drawing of a man standing waist deep in a lake, ass to the viewer, droplets of water running down his biceps and shoulders. "Check out the movement of the water. The ripples and shading. It's *insane*."

I'm pretty sure I'm supposed to be focused on the artistry, and the rendering of the water is pretty freaking amazing, but my eyes flick over the man.

There's something about him.

Okay, a lot of somethings. The dimples above his ass, the long line of his spine as it curves up to the wide spread of his shoulders, the powerful muscles of his biceps and forearms, the way his wrists twist as his long fingers dip into the water.

Christ. That twist of those forearms, a vein running from elbow to wrist, those long fingers.

Kepler. His hand extended toward me through that window.

Heat prickles down my sternum and tightens my stomach.

A horn blares behind me, and my head bobs up to find a green light. I punch the gas too hard. "Yeah, it's uh . . . Good movement."

I stare out the windshield, trying to concentrate on not ramming us into the back of an old Ford truck as we cross from our side of town, with its cracked and pothole-filled roads, onto the clean, well-maintained streets around the campus buildings.

That man is fucking hot. Not just a little. A whole *lot*.

And there's something about him that reminds me of Kepler.

What does that mean?

You already know, J.

"Maybe it's a stretch," Dex continues, completely oblivious to the riot that's started in my head. "But I contacted him to see if he'd be interested in supporting the fundraiser."

"Good idea," I say as he chats about his other ideas.

Simkung. Even though looking at that painting didn't create a full-on Kepler-level response—until I thought of Kepler, that is—there's no question about what I just felt. And if I doubted it, then the way my dick is currently digging against my zipper would end the debate. I use my palm to push down on the thigh of my jeans enough to relieve the pressure. My stomach is tight, the back of my neck hot.

"Maybe this Reynolds guy knows some other artists," Dex is saying, his thumb scrolling through more posts. "It's pretty out there to think he'd donate a piece or anything."

I clear my throat. "There's no harm in asking."

"Nope," he says as we park. I slide out, adjust my jeans with a sigh of relief, and then grab my backpack. I walk next to him as he keeps scrolling and talking about art.

He hardly looks up to see what direction he's walking, but I'm staring at every dude we come across.

None of them create the same level of response in me as Kepler. Although I notice that more than once, my attention flicks down to a guy's ass, and I definitely feel a slight tightening in my stomach and balls. It's attraction, even if it's not Kepler-level. Same with the girls we pass, and thinking back, I've never responded to a girl the same way I respond to Kepler either.

He's singular. Like he's in an entirely separate orbit than everyone else.

I stare ahead as we walk, lost in thought. I've never held very tightly onto the idea that I'm straight. In fact, if I really think about it, I might have had moments of noticing a guy's ass here or there. I guess I thought everyone is like that—just this subtle, low-level attraction that can happen with anyone.

But it's still never Kepler-level, and maybe that's why I never gave it much thought before now. Maybe this thing I have for Kepler isn't just about his ass or the physical things I can see about him. Maybe it's intangible. Based on *who* he is.

I force my attention back to Dex and nod at the phone. "You should do something like that."

"Post on Insta?" He looks up as we head toward the Liberal Arts building. It's a warm day—sunny without a cloud in the sky—and the Quad is packed. Dex tucks away his phone.

"Yeah," I say. "You're good."

That's an understatement. What he does is unbelievable. Portraits—usually in pencil because that's all he had to draw with growing up—with emotion so real that it's like a punch to the gut.

I've always thought it might be his ticket out of Indigo Falls, if he ever decides he wants to do something besides teach.

"Nah." He shrugs, looping his thumb in the strap of his backpack. "I don't have that level of talent." He thumps my shoulder with his other hand before taking off toward the education building.

I wish he could see what I saw. We've got his artwork plastered all over our living room, and even though I've passed by his work a million times, sometimes I just stand there, staring at it all in complete awe.

He's that good.

I turn and head toward the far side of the Quad for the appointment with my advisor, smiling at the bustle of movement all around me. I've always enjoyed when campus fills up in the fall. It's desolate in this town over the summer.

"Jae," a deep voice calls across the Quad, and I turn to see Vain Henley peel off from his entourage and jog across the grass toward me, thick biceps stretching the arms of his IFU hockey tee. His dick bounces as he jogs in his athletic shorts. Which I notice, but it doesn't seem to create more than that low casual tightness in my gut.

I step off the sidewalk and wait for him to cross the grass. A navy beanie is pulled low over his shoulder length blond hair. He runs with a long stride, all cocky confidence and athleticism. He looks every bit the hockey jock that he is.

A few of his teammates stare after him longingly, and I almost expect them to trail after him like a herd of baby ducks following their hockey god.

"Hey," he says as he stops before me and holds out a fist that I bump. "I've been looking for you."

"Yeah?" I'm surprised. Vain and I have a couple beers at parties on occasion, but I don't know him all that well. "What can I do for you?"

He leans closer, smelling like the minty gum he snaps between his teeth. "I've heard you do that essay thing."

That essay thing.

So, what I do for money might or might not be considered shady. I got into it by mistake, but now it's my main source of income. I write essays. More specifically, people hire me to write their class essays for them. I'm damn good at it—I even enjoy it—and they sell for more than you'd think.

It helps that last year the university instituted a rule that every single class requires at least one written essay, so business is good. In combination with scholarships, I'll be able to graduate mostly debt free.

Not that I know what I'll do with myself after that.

I study Vain's worried gaze. I've written a lot of essays for athletes, but he's never requested my services before.

"Yeah, man." I nod, sinking my hand into my pocket. "What class do you need it for?"

"All of them." His eyes widen. "Seriously, dude, I'm screwed this semester. Between the team schedule and my course load, I'm gonna have to give up something."

I flash him a smile. "Partying on the weekends?"

Vain is well known for being a beast on the ice, bringing the IFU to two national championships in a row, but he's also known for rather legendary house parties, being constantly surrounded by puck bunnies, and never holding back what's on his mind.

He grins. "Funny. But no."

"So, you want my help then."

"I *need* your help. I'm thinking we can meet maybe once a week? If you can work around my practice and gym schedule. Late night during the week would be best. I usually do a lifting sesh until around ten."

I frown. "Usually people just give me a list of the classes, and I take care of the essay part. Faster that way."

He shakes his head, his hazel eyes fixed on me. "I don't want you to write the shit for me. I want you to teach me how to do it. I'm constantly struggling to pass, and I'm sick of it. I hear you can write any fucking essay on the planet and nail a good grade, and I want to learn from the best."

I frown, rubbing a hand over my mouth. "Teaching isn't really what I do."

He shrugs a meaty shoulder. "I'll pay you double. I'll do whatever it takes. You just tell me what to do. I grew up with a tough-as-nails military dad, so I know how to take orders."

"I believe that." I hesitate. I'm not a tutor, and it sounds like that's what he's asking me to do.

He leans closer, seeming to sense my hesitation, eyes serious as his hand clasps my shoulder. "You've got to help me. I've been getting worried about what's going to happen if I'm not scouted by the NHL next year. I don't want to be the dumb jock who's only good for scorin', fuckin', and drinkin'." He pauses, a grin spreading across his face. "Although I am pretty damn good at all those things."

"You're not dumb," I say, my forehead lining. I've never gotten a glimpse of Vain's insecurities. I'm not sure that many people do, but I know what it's like to want to change things about your life. "You probably just don't know what professors are looking for. How to play their game."

He shoots out a half-laugh as his hand falls from my shoulder. "That's the first time anyone's ever accused me of not knowing how to play the game."

"Yeah, I bet."

"You gotta help me." He itches at his chest with darkly tanned hands that are banged and scratched up. He's got a dark bruise along his jaw, probably from that pile-up fight I heard he started at the game last night. Vain lives big and loud, and I'm guessing that he puts in more time than anyone else on the ice. He probably just needs a couple pointers on how to make sure he's targeting the right topics and following the professors' rubrics. Maybe take a glance at past exams the professors are required to file at the library. There's no reason I can't help him out.

"Yeah, okay," I agree. "Throw me a text and we'll schedule. I'm good for most weeknights."

"Cool." He grins. "Thanks, man. Like seriously. I owe you."

I nod toward his hockey flock. "Do you want to keep this between us?"

He frowns. "Nah. Why?"

I shrug. "I don't know. If you're worried about what people think."

"I don't give a shit what people think." His eyes sail over my face, lingering on my brow piercing and my crazy-ass hair. "I'd gotten the idea that you don't much either."

I laugh. "I'm not really sure how to take that."

"Compliment, dude." He grins. "Completely."

"Okay, then thanks." Although, at least Vain seems to have a pretty clear idea of who he is. I feel like I'm just waking up and figuring shit out.

We both go our separate ways, and I'm stopped twice more to schedule essays. Repeat clients getting their orders in before my schedule gets too crowded. You've got to admire someone with the foresight to plan ahead on cheating. They could just write the essay. But I never tell them that.

Ten minutes later, I plop down on a chair in my advisor's office. I need to take care of this Kepler situation.

"There's nothing," my advisor says after staring at his computer for five long minutes.

I rake a hand through my hair. "You're sure?"

"Positive," my advisor says, stubby fingers flying over his keyboard. "Everything else conflicts or is already full."

Shit.

"What if I drop physics this semester and take it next?"

He tosses me a look through thick glasses. "It's not a

good idea to push a requirement like that to your last semester. Your GPA is impressive, but this is a challenging class for everyone."

"Please." I lean across the desk toward him. "I can pass any class you give me."

"Is there a specific reason you don't want to take this one?"

Yes. But I have a feeling my explanation wouldn't make him budge.

I sigh. "Nothing specific, no."

"Alright then." He flips a file folder with my name on it closed. "There's a slim chance I can move you into an evening section if you can get both professors and TAs to sign off on it and you're willing to go to lecture on Thursday nights. Otherwise, buckle down and take the class."

"Do I really need the form?" I ask. "I can't convince you to just slip my name onto the roster? Hell, I'll clean your house for a month. Walk your dog. I'm desperate here."

He gives me an appeasing smile. "Signatures are a requirement." He taps an index finger against the folder. "You really shouldn't have waited this long to finish up your lab requirement."

He's not wrong.

I groan and lean back in my seat.

"Get the signatures," he says. "And then we'll see."

I DON'T SEE Kepler when I step into the lecture hall. A white-haired woman with long braids is setting up an old-school overhead projector down in the lecture well. She's got on a trim red suit, so I figure she's Professor Lacher.

Not seeing Kepler does nothing to calm my nerves. I still

know he's going to be here, and that's enough to start the prickle across my shoulders.

I scrub a damp palm over my mouth and jog down the steps, digging the class change request out of my back pocket.

"Professor Lacher?" I extend the yellow paper to her, but she shakes her head.

"I'll look at it after the lecture." She goes back to fiddling with the overhead.

"Just need a quick signature," I press. I really don't want to sit through this lecture if I'm changing classes. Especially if Kepler is going to be here. Trying to sit still in a chair while he's in the room sounds like torture.

"After the lecture," she says flatly. "That's a nonnegotiable rule."

"Are you sure we can't negotiate a little?" I ask.

She glances up, and if a look could kill, the one she gives me would chop off my limbs and drop me off a cliff. It's obvious she's not gonna relent.

"Okay, thanks." I mumble and stuff the request form back into my pocket. I head up the stairs and consider slipping out until class is over, but I finally sigh and take a seat a few rows from the back in the theater style lecture hall. I debate for a minute, then pull out the flip-up desk and take out my notebook and pen. Feels rude to sit in a lecture and not take notes.

A couple of minutes later, people start to filter in, taking seats around me. I watch them lazily, not really noticing anyone until a guy stops at the end of the aisle I'm sitting in. He's tall—or at least he seems that way while I'm sitting down—wearing a black hoodie vest with a pair of lavender jeans. But the jeans aren't what make him stand out. It's the full lips that he draws his tongue nervously over, the thick black faux hawk, the deep-brown gaze that matches his warm skin tone, and the ring in his nose.

There's something about the guy that's intensely unique. Like he's the kind of guy who doesn't just walk to his own drumbeat but conducts the whole orchestra.

He's also pretty hot. Even if I wasn't going through this apparent sexual awakening, it's easy to see objectively.

He sits a couple of seats down from me and pulls up the desk before dropping a messy notebook on top. It's got sketches all over the cover even though the semester has barely started.

He flips open the notebook, and it's filled. Sketches, designs, lists. All in black pen. I can't help peeking at it as he searches for a blank page.

He pulls out a pen, and as soon as it hits the paper, it starts to move. In less than thirty seconds, an image comes to life of an . . . elephant?

That feels sorta random, but I like it. The elephant's trunk reaches back to scratch its shoulders, the lines long and clean.

"You're good," I say, nodding toward the notebook.

He looks over, startled, deep-brown eyes taking me in. "Thanks."

"You should meet my roommate," I say suddenly, watching his fingers hold his pen as he sketches. "He's got this fundraiser he's working on to get art supplies for kids. I don't know if you'd be interested in helping out?"

His pen lifts from the paper mid-stroke, like he's surprised by the sudden invite. "That would be really cool."

"Yeah?" My eyes flick down to his lips. They're nice. But when they twist up into a smile, I get a little pinch in my chest.

And a flash of Kepler, that faint trace of an almost smile ghosting his lips.

Christ. Does *everything* have to remind me of Kepler Quinn?

I shove my brother's best friend out of my thoughts, and I chat with my aisle-mate about artwork for a few minutes. He's been influenced by a lot of Chilean artists recently, and we talk about Roberto Matta and Eileen Lunecke while the lecture hall fills with everyone but Kepler.

His name is London, and he ended up in Indigo Falls because of the fine arts program here, but there's a catch in his words when he says that, and I don't think it's the full truth. Not to mention that the IFU isn't exactly known for fine arts.

There's some other reason he's here, but as much as I eye him trying to figure it out, I also let it drop. Not my business.

When I bring the fundraiser up a second time, his fingers tighten around his pen, and he lifts it from the elephant a fraction of an inch.

"I'm always up for meeting another artist," he says. "But I was more thinking that maybe you and I could get a drink."

I still.

Did he just ask me out?

My mouth drops open a little. Has that happened before? Have guys asked me out without me realizing it?

Do I want to go out with him?

As if this moment isn't confusing enough, a door down by the lecture well opens, and it's like a pot of boiling water is poured over the back of my neck.

It takes every bit of willpower I have not to focus my attention on Kepler as he strolls to a desk on the far side, a messenger bag hitting rhythmically against his thigh as he walks. And I'm suddenly staring at the outline of his wallet in his ass pocket as he turns his back to me.

Shit. I turn back to London, who's running his teeth over his bottom lip.

"I'm sorry." He shakes his head. "Did I read you wrong? The way you were looking at me, I thought..."

I swallow. "I, uh..."

And then, because I can't help myself, my eyes sail down to the well where Kepler's talking with someone.

It's the guy he was with last night. *The finger-toucher*. My pen rattles against my desk, my chest tightens. I still vaguely recognize the guy, but I can't place him.

Kepler nods in response to whatever the finger-toucher's saying, and then they take a seat—right next to each other—and scan through papers. Kepler reaches into the pocket of his tee and pulls out dark-framed glasses, then slips them on to read.

Jesus fucking Christ. Kepler Quinn in glasses isn't something I'm prepared for.

I rip my focus off him and back to London as the syllabus is passed back to us. His forehead is deeply lined, and I owe him an answer.

What should I do? "Uh, I'm—"

Professor Lacher knocks on the overhead. "Let's go," she says dryly.

And she means it. Full speed ahead, I don't think she takes a breath for the next hour. I'm not sure I do either. As much as I try to pay attention, my head's spinning.

I've got to answer London after lecture. He deserves an answer.

I mean, maybe this is exactly what I need? To go out with someone like London. He's attractive and smart. He knows a lot of interesting things about art. We also just had an easy conversation, and he seems like a cool guy. And I'm apparently attracted to guys.

So... why not?

The thought doubles down as Kepler leans closer to the finger-toucher in the middle of the lecture, his lips close to the guy's ear as he whispers something and then tips his legal pad toward him. The guy holds a laugh back behind his chubby lips at whatever he reads on Kepler's legal pad.

I shouldn't care.

And even if I did care, what am I supposed to do about it? Just fester away with this freaking *simkung* crashing against my chest?

I won't do that.

So I turn toward London when everyone's packing up, nerves spiking, and say, "Yeah, let's get a drink."

"Cool." London's smile is genuine, and we trade numbers before he ducks out the back doors.

I made the right choice.

I think?

I try not to second-guess myself as I take the steps down to the well, crossing right in front of Kepler and the finger-toucher as I dig the change request form out of my back pocket.

I stop by Lacher, my back to Kepler, as she gathers up her overhead slides. "Do you have time for a signature now?"

"Yes, thank you for waiting." She takes the request form and frowns. "What's the problem with my class?"

"Nothing." I shrug. "Just a scheduling conflict."

"Fine." She snags an overhead pen and scrawls out her signature. "You'll also need Professor Manford's signature."

"Yeah, no problem."

"And the signature of your TA for the lab portion." She

nods behind me. "Mr. Quinn can pull up the rosters in order to see whose signature you'll need."

I already know whose signature I need.

"Thanks." I drag a hand over my mouth, take the form back from her, and turn on my heel.

Kepler is standing now, six feet behind me, still talking with the finger-toucher. He's got on a pale-blue t-shirt today. And those glasses.

I take a step closer to him, clear my throat, and hold out the form. "Would you mind signing this?"

He pivots toward me, that smoky gaze plastering on me, his brow hitching up behind the top of his frames, and *fuck me.*

I swallow hard, my Adam's apple feeling about three sizes too big.

He pinches the form with his long fingers and slips it from me. "What professor are you changing to?"

"Manford."

He extends the form back to me. "Then I won't sign it."

I stare at the paper in his hand. What the *fuck*?

"Why not?" I demand.

"I don't think a change would be in your best interest."

"You've got to be fucking kidding me."

"Not at all." He keeps holding out the form, his thin lips in a line. I blink down at it and then back up at him before finally taking it. What else am I going to do here?

I glance over at Lacher and then back at Kepler. I need to get him alone. This isn't the place to start this argument.

Unless I can bypass this whole TA signature requirement? Why the hell do they need it anyway? Sounds like red tape to me.

I'm back in front of Lacher in two seconds, but she just

looks at me with cool eyes when I press the issue. "It's Mr. Quinn's decision. The request forms exist for a reason."

This woman is clearly a stickler for the rules.

"So, you can't do anything?" I press one last time. I don't want to be a dick. But I really don't want to be in this class either.

"I won't do anything." She nods behind me, toward where Kepler is climbing the steps, still chatting with the damn finger-toucher. The strap of his bag cuts a line between his shoulder blades. That outline of his wallet on his ass pocket flashes at me. "If you believe it's unfair, then take it up with Mr. Quinn. You've got a week to change his mind. After that, you'll have to withdraw if you can't continue the class."

A week.

It won't take that long.

4

FUCKING KEPLER QUINN.

I'm wound up by the time I arrive at my mom's house later that day. Doesn't help that I have to park across the street because an old blue truck is parked in the driveway. Mom has a visitor.

The house I grew up in is a small one-story with chipped green paint, a missing doorbell, and dead vines latched to the side. I don't remember when the vines died. A few years after my father, I guess. Now the front lawn is studded with prickly weeds and my mom's attempt at decor—a pair of faded pink flamingos.

And there's the lingering painful memories too. Can't forget that shit.

I inhale a deep breath at the front door. I never know what I'm walking into here.

I visit her every week—just to make sure she's still alive and remembered to take out the trash and pay the electricity bill. Shin used to visit too, but he hasn't been here in months now.

It's what he and I argue about. Every time we see each other. He thinks I'm enabling her.

I honestly don't know if he's wrong. All I know is that losing one parent was shitty enough. I can't handle losing another.

I pull the door open and step inside, wrinkling my nose at the too familiar smell of minty schnapps. The living room's dingy beige with one bookcase stacked full of Mom's collectible bird figurines. A few throw pillows from the couch are on the floor, but otherwise, nothing seems out of place.

I cross the living room and glance in the kitchen doorway, hoping to see her awake with a cup of coffee in her hands.

Instead I find a naked man. With his back to me and his hand in my mom's purse.

"Fucking seriously?" My voice bounces off sea blue walls.

The guy turns, pulling his hand out of Mom's purse. He tries to deposit a wad of bills into a shirt pocket but hits only skin and chest hair.

The guy's *big*. Not just tall, but broad and muscular. Tattoos run over his arms, long hair curls around his shoulders, a couple of scars mar his chest. He's probably mid-forties, doesn't seem to give a shit that he's naked, and generally looks like a guy you don't mess with.

Unfortunately, I don't have that option.

"Put the money back." I step into the kitchen.

He fists the wad of twenties. "Who are you?"

My jaw sets, anger sparking.

It scares the hell out of me that she lets strange guys like this one drive her home. That she stays alone with them in this house. She could get hurt someday. *Really* hurt.

Ever since my father died, I've wanted to protect her from assholes like this. And I fail. Every fucking time.

"Put the money back," I say again, keeping my voice deep and even.

His nostrils flare, one bare foot stepping forward, and my fists tighten.

"Jae." My mom comes out of nowhere, hand falling on my forearm. I don't take my attention off the guy, but I do notice that she smells like toothpaste and coffee.

She's sober. Or as close to sober as she gets.

"This asshole's stealing your money," I say.

She pales. "Oh, I'm sure he's not doing that. Jae, this is Fender."

"Fender?" I shake my head. "The money's in his hand."

She sets her mug on the counter. "I'm sure it's just a mistake, nugget."

The guy—Fender or whatever—flops the cash back beside her purse. It's a decent amount. Makes me wonder where she got it. If Shin actually stopped by, but I doubt that.

"See?" She shrugs. "All better."

"Yeah," I push out. "Perfect."

Fender's still glaring at me. "Who the fuck are you?"

Mom smiles. "My youngest son."

He swivels between us. I know what he's thinking. It's the same thing people always wonder when they glance between me and my lanky, blue-eyed mother. I got my height from her, but not much else.

"Hell, I'd be embarrassed," he says with an easy swagger.

Holy shit. Did he just say that?

I'm gonna punch him.

"*Kkeojyeo*," I curse at him in Korean. My voice is low, gritty. "Get the fuck out of here."

I'm done with this asshole. He's not just standing there disrespecting me. He's disrespecting my dad. My *halmeoni*—my grandmother—who lives just a few blocks away. Hell, he's insulting everyone on the freaking planet by being this kind of a jerk.

Fender's stare traces me up and down. "Leave us alone, kid." The words are low, almost eerily calm.

Tension laces across my shoulders and down into my fists. "Get. The. Fuck. Out."

"What if I don't want to?" He steps closer.

He's going to hit me.

I push Mom behind me. "You should go," I whisper to her, but I can't hear her answer over Fender's cursing.

"You're fuckin' crazy." He wipes at his mouth and then spits.

On the kitchen *floor*.

Just when I think things are going to get worse, he curses a few more times, and then stalks past us, grabbing his clothes from the bedroom before thudding to the front door.

I just stand there. Breathing. Keeping myself between him and Mom.

I hate this shit.

When the front door slams, Mom crosses to her purse, picks up the money, and tucks it inside. "You shouldn't have done that," she says.

"You shouldn't have him over again." I pull off a paper towel and use my foot to wipe it over the floor where Fender spit. An engine roars to life outside. Tires squeal before the noise quickly fades down the street.

She steps just out of the kitchen and stares toward the front door. "It's just a mix up, Jae."

"No, it's not." I toss the towel in the trash, frustration

blooming in my chest. "What about just taking a break, Mom?"

She flashes me a look. "A break from what?"

"Everything."

Drinking.

"All I ever do is take a break," she says quietly. And for a moment, she just looks at me, blue eyes clearer than typical.

It takes me back. She's funny when she's clearheaded. Full of silly jokes. I remember her, way back in my mind. Her blue eyes would light up, the lines around her mouth would deepen when she smiled. I can remember the person who Mom used to be.

I swallow hard, trying not to let any emotion show on my face. She doesn't need that. She doesn't need to know how much every visit here makes my heart fold more. Her knowing would just make shit worse.

I'm relieved when she shrugs and turns away, leaving me alone, and I concentrate on cleaning up the kitchen. Then take out the trash and rake the front yard.

All I know is that if I were a better son, I'd know how to help her.

I'd know how to help all of us.

5

THE REST of my week consists of me trying to track down Kepler, which is definitely a new thing for me. His office hours haven't started yet, his lab class doesn't begin until next week, and he skips the lectures.

Is he fucking with me?

But why would he do that?

Regardless, I don't have his phone number, and I don't know where he lives. I could ask Shin, but it's hard enough to talk with my brother right now, and on top of that, I'd have to explain to him why I don't want Kepler as a TA. And that's a truth I don't even want to approach at the moment. Shit's complicated enough between Shin and me already.

Instead, I send Kepler an email through his university account, but he doesn't respond. He might as well be a wisp of smoke that disappeared into the sky.

Then I find another freaking **KEPLER** Post-it on my door Thursday morning.

He's definitely fucking with me.

By Friday night, I'm so twisted up, I'm not sure what to do about it anymore.

I sigh and thunk down my water glass on the kitchen counter before leaning over to fix my crazy-ass hair in the reflection from the silver kettle.

Dex drops his pencil on the breakfast bar. "Who's this guy coming over?"

So... I haven't been honest with him about that yet.

Nerves spike in my stomach as I stand up.

"Uh, my date." I clear my throat and smooth a hand over my jaw to check my shave. "But he also might be interested in helping with the fundraiser."

Dex leans back on the stool, crossing his arms over his chest. "Your date?"

"Yeah."

Both his brows go up. "You're into men?"

I hesitate. He just keeps looking at me, completely open and easy. He's *Dex*. I can tell the guy anything.

"I'm thinking so," I finally say, leaning back against the counter.

He doesn't even flinch. "Cool."

Okay, I expected an easy response from him. But even that was more casual than I'd thought.

I study the way he's watching me.

It's like his green eyes are willing me to ask him something.

"Have you ever been with a guy?" I blurt.

He grins. "Yep. What do you think I'm doing when I crash over at Brady's? Drinking beer and playing *Call of Duty*? Well, I guess we do that too." His smile fades. "I've wanted to tell you."

"Did you think it would bother me? It doesn't."

"I knew you'd be cool with it." He rubs a hand over his chest. "I don't know why I didn't say anything. Guess I was looking for the right time."

"You don't need a 'right time' to tell me stuff."

"I know." He shrugs. "Honestly, I'm not really sure why I didn't."

Just like I haven't told him about how Kepler Quinn makes my heart pound like I'm about to skydive off a freaking cliff.

Maybe I should tell him?

I'm getting the feeling that I should tell *somebody*. And my somebody has always been Dex.

"So, do you consider yourself bi?" I ask him. With anyone else, I wouldn't press the question, but I know that Dex won't mind me asking. Besides, it's a question I've been asking myself a lot lately.

He shrugs. "Sure."

I laugh. "That doesn't sound so convincing. Do you prefer not having a label?"

"Nah." His face gets serious. "I guess I consider myself more pan. I just feel like it's a bit of an evolving thing for me. Like it's more fluid? So what I label myself as today, it might not be the same tomorrow." He tilts his head. "What about you, dude?"

I open my mouth, but a soft knock on the door turns my head. I smooth my fingers through my hair again. Shit, I'm *nervous*.

Dex gives me a wide smile. "Just have fun, man. Don't worry about anything else other than being you."

Me.

Yeah, okay. "I'll give that a try. And you know, Brady is welcome over here anytime you want. That goes without saying, but I figured I'd still say it."

He grins. "Thanks."

Just have fun turns out to be pretty good advice. London and I head over to this underground cocktail bar like an old-style speakeasy with black tables and dark-red walls. He orders up a lavender sour, I get a whiskey smash, and we share some small plates of food. A candle in a glass jar flickers on the table between us as we dig in, not saying all that much at first.

Truth is, I'm kinda nervous about being out in public with a guy as my date for the first time. Although a quick glance around the other tables tells me only one other couple even seems to notice, and London doesn't seem worried, so I just go with it.

As we get another round of drinks, I relax and focus on London as he pinches his straw and stirs the crushed ice in the bottom of his first glass.

"Did you grow up in Indigo Falls?" he asks.

"Yeah." I take a sip of my second whiskey concoction and steer the conversation away from myself.

London is a hell of a lot more interesting anyway.

He grew up in a military family that moved around a lot. We chat over shared plates, him telling me his parents were stationed in Germany, Mali, the Philippines. It sounds pretty freaking spectacular, like he got to dip into all these different worlds growing up, and I ask him a million questions.

After the plates are cleared, the corner of London's mouth pulls up. "You don't like talking about yourself, do you?"

I shrug, finishing up my drink. "There's not much to say."

"There's got to be something."

I rub a hand over my mouth, my leather wrist band cutting into my wrist. "Okay, well, I grew up across town from here. Went to school. Normal family. White picket fence and all that."

I haze right over the truth. There's no need to drag the evening down. I'd rather stick to the good stuff.

"I've got a brother," I offer. "Shin's a cop."

The piercing through his nose glints in the candlelight as he looks at me. "Here in town?"

"Yep. We're pretty much townies through and through."

So much that I've barely ever left Indigo Falls County. Other than a few drives down to Denver and the one time my father took Shin and me to Carlsbad Caverns, my life's been *here*. The only time I'd ever planned to leave was when I was nineteen and got accepted into the language institute at Yonsei University. But in the end, Korea was just too far—and the year there too long—to leave my mom.

Who knows what would have happened to her?

I push back from the table, suddenly feeling the lack of windows in the basement speakeasy, which hadn't bothered me up until now. "Are you ready to go?"

He blinks. "Cool."

I'm already moving. We jog the steps up to street level, and I draw in a deep breath of air at the top. The sun set while we were down there, and the streetlights have clicked on. The bars and restaurants within walking distance are filling up.

We linger on the sidewalk, my hand raking my hair back.

What now?

London drags his teeth over his bottom lip as he zips up his hoodie. "My roommate's having some people over to our place tonight. Want to go?"

"Sure." I swallow, a few nerves tingling against my chest.

Like a little pop of fizz when opening a soda bottle. A small echo of the *simkung* with Kepler. Maybe this is what I need.

Kepler Quinn's not the only hot and interesting guy on campus. Maybe I just need to open my eyes to the possibilities more.

London lives in an apartment on the far side of campus. It's one of those sleek apartment buildings that's empty during the summer but stuffed with kids from California or Hawaii or wherever during the year. A couple of the apartments have parties going on, balconies full, voices and laughter carrying over a parking lot packed with shiny new SUVs.

"More people than I thought here," London says as he opens his door, sounding almost like it's an apology. We step into a crowded living room, and London leads the way to the kitchen where we meet his roommate, Rhys, who's a stocky guy wearing heavy boots and a deep-green Henley. He welcomes me with a relaxed smile, and we chat for a bit before stepping back into the living room.

"Can I get you a drink?" London leans in to talk to me, his hand falling on my bicep. Splotches of ink dot his fingers —almost the same color as the black ink that covers my arms.

"No, thanks. My limit's two." I don't step back from him. "Do you have a soda or something?"

He nods, drops his hand, and winds his way through the crowd toward the kitchen. I watch him go, gaze sailing down to his ass as he cuts through the crowd.

"Are you here with him?" A voice rumbles close to my ear, and like smoke slipping around me, I can feel it on every part of my skin, simmering up the back of my neck and down my spine.

Christ.

I turn and just about lose my shit.

Kepler Quinn stands so close to me that I can see those flecks of brown in his eyes. How his bottom lip is slightly thinner than his top. His hair is smoothed back to reveal his high forehead and the sharp edge of his jaw and that goddamn mole.

Fuck that mole.

A soft gray tee stretches over his shoulders.

I'm suddenly aware of everything. The weight of the black button-down across my own shoulders. The press of my Chucks into the wood floor. The slight heft of my phone and wallet in my back pockets.

"Well, are you?" His eyes flick over my face, across my shoulders, down to my hands, and my entire body thumps in response. *Simkung.* My reaction to him is as vibrant and strong as ever, like it just swallows me right the fuck up.

And then my anger flares. "I've been looking for you."

His brows shoot up. "Have you?"

"You know I have." I reach for my back pocket only to realize that I'd actually left the form at home for the first time this week. I groan and shake my head. "I need you to sign the class change form."

His eyes narrow. "I don't think that's a good idea."

"Why not?"

He tips forward onto his toes, closer to my ear. "You don't want Manford. Trust me on this."

"I hear he's difficult," I say. "That doesn't scare me."

"He's not just difficult." This close, the warmth of his presence seeps into me. Omija tea and cloves, tickling over my neck and down across my chest. I release a shallow breath, my dick thickening against my zipper.

He's so damn close.

What would it be like to kiss him? Would he be the one

to back me up against the wall? I've never kissed anyone taller than me. Never kissed . . . well, a man.

I clear my thick throat. I should not be thinking these things while on a date with London.

London's been nothing but kind and respectful and nice to be around.

Focus on what you need from Kepler, J.

"What's the issue with Manford?" I ask.

"Unfairness," Kepler's breath tickles my ear. "I swear the guy throws all the exams down the stairs and whatever makes it to the bottom gets an A and the rest fail. He'd be canned for his failure rate if he wasn't tenured."

"Then I'll weight my paper so it lands at the bottom."

"You don't want to trust your graduation to a guy like that. He's a dick and he'll mess with your grade just because he can. His TAs are all just like him. No one with integrity would accept a job with him."

"I can handle it." I steel myself against the riot in my brain at Kepler's nearness. "Maybe you haven't noticed, but I can handle myself pretty well."

"I know you can." His fingers brush my elbow, a light touch, and my breath lodges in my lungs. The world narrows down to him standing next to me, his fingertips against my skin, our toes only inches from each other. "I'll be fair, Jin. I'll give you the grade you earn. No bullshit."

I puff out an uneasy laugh. "I just . . . can't do this class with you, Quinn."

He leans back, releasing my elbow. His eyes flick down to my lips, maybe waiting for whatever I'm gonna say. He's on the verge of saying something too when he pauses, his attention shifting to my right.

London's suddenly there, pressing a cold bottle of Coke into my palm.

"Hey, aren't you our physics TA?" he asks Kepler.

"Yes." Kepler straightens, that small mole on the upside of his left cheek shifting up, and it's like a window slams down.

He's all business. Distanced.

"I didn't know you knew each other," London says.

Kepler steps sharply back from both of us. "We were friends growing up."

"You were friends with Shin," I blurt.

"Is that all?" His eyes darken as he asks the question.

My brows pull together. "We were never friends."

"No, I suppose not."

Something just happened. I don't know what it was, but I can feel it. More than just him distancing himself because he's my TA. It's like something glacially cold passes through him.

What's he thinking?

He turns to London. "It's nice to meet you. I'm pretty sure you're in my lab section, so let me know if you need help with the concepts we're reviewing this week."

"And that signature?" I ask Kepler.

He stills, a slight twitch in his jaw. "Fine. I'll find you tomorrow."

He pivots and, without another word, cuts through the crowd to the front door.

6

Impulse
Noun
1. a change in momentum

I'M AN ASSHOLE.

I bailed on London. No explanation. He deserves more respect than that. Not only that, but I haven't called him or texted him.

I don't know what to tell him.

Or myself.

Instead, I meet with Vain to go over some of his syllabuses—the dude really does have a brutal schedule this semester—and then I shut myself into my room, drafting research papers that take me into another world. Lost in the details of an ancient Egyptian site near the apex of the Nile River delta. Then on to how social media has altered brain structure, and finally, the recent upswing in business fraud.

The research takes me out of my head and deposits me

somewhere else for a few hours. But every time I stop for even a second, my thoughts fixate on Kepler.

I groan and shove my iPad aside on the bed, my bare feet hitting the floor as I glance at the window.

Hell, it's *night*. I didn't even realize that. Dex knocked on my door a few hours ago to see if I wanted to grab a bite, but I didn't realize it was dinner time.

I stand up, stretch out my tight arms and shoulders, itch at my bare chest, and then pad over to open the window and drag in a deep breath of night air, studying the stars for a long minute. I wish I had that old telescope now. I wonder where it went.

SUVs and trucks pull in and out of the gas station across the street. The steady stream of movement never stops. I set my forehead against the cool glass.

I can't keep being so twisted up over Kepler.

I've never been twisted up over anyone like this. Girl or guy.

Something has to change. I just don't know how to make that change happen.

A man walks down the sidewalk toward our apartment building, the streetlight illuminating his hair and the messenger bag slung over his chest. He takes long, certain strides.

My heart beats out a hard, obnoxious, annoying thump.

Fuck me.

Even this far away—through glass and shadows and night—Kepler Quinn catches me.

I scrub a hand over my mouth, turning back to glance at the iPad on my bed.

Then I sigh, grab my phone and the form I need his signature on, and head to the front room. I run a hand through my hair, trying to tame it a touch, before swinging open the door.

Kepler's strolling down the hallway. His hands are deep in his pockets, the strap of the messenger bag cutting across his dark-gray hoodie. He's got on those well-loved jeans and a pair of black-and-white Vans. His hair is mussed like the wind's been playing through it.

When he stops before the door, I silently hold out the form. He takes it, bends over to settle it on his knee, and then signs with a pen he must have already had in his pocket.

He straightens up and extends the paper. "I don't think you should turn this in."

I take it. "Thanks for the advice."

He nods, eyes darting behind me. "You didn't go out tonight?"

"No." I fold the form and go to stuff it in my pocket when I realize I'm wearing an old pair of gray sweats. No pockets, and also no zipper, or boxer briefs to hide the half-wood I'm already sprouting. "Working on some essays."

He turns. "Then I'll leave you to it."

I rub a hand over my mouth. "Now who's making an escape in less than five minutes?"

Kepler stops, turning in a half circle so he's facing me again. He never looks at me over his shoulder, it's always full-on with him. "Maybe I'm just beating you to it."

Why am I drawing this moment out? Just like when I was a kid and coveting any time he gave me.

Except I'm not a kid anymore.

And neither is he.

He's really, really not.

I bailed on London because the truth became clear last night when I turned and saw Kepler standing behind me.

London is smart and kind and interesting and definitely hot. He's the kind of person I want to end up with someday.

But he doesn't give me the same thump that's obliterating my chest—and let's face it, my dick—right now.

Kepler's just *different*. He always has been. In a sky stacked with stars, he's the brightest one. The one I'm drawn to, again and again. Even though I can never tell what he's thinking. Even though he's Shin's best friend. Even though I'm not fully sure if I really *know* him because I've held him at such an arm's length. None of that matters because it's more than just some silly crush. That's why it beats so damn hard in my chest.

He's smart and stupidly hot too. Definitely interesting. And I don't know if I'd call him kind, but he's standing here, signing a form that he didn't want to sign, in the middle of the night when I'm sure he has better places to be.

What am I supposed to do about all that?

Because, apparently, I can't wish these thoughts away.

A wash of cold runs down my throat as I stare at him now, reality like a fist punch to the face. I *want* him. Not just my stupidly reacting body, but my brain too.

I'm not even fully sure what that means, but I feel the truth of it burning low in my gut and in the long, soft breath I let out that dries my bottom lip and in the realization that my sweats are hanging really low on my hips.

Also, we've been standing here staring at each other for almost a full minute.

What does that mean?

I ache to know every single thought in his head.

He slides his hands back into his pockets. "Feel like a walk?"

I blink at him. "Now?"

"Why not?" He upnods toward the open door behind

me. "Get whatever you need. I want to show you something."

I breathe out a laugh. "Always wanting to show me things."

"I was walking there anyway. You should bring your phone for a flashlight."

His seriousness freezes me to my spot. "And you want me to walk with you?"

He tilts head, brow furrowing. "Why wouldn't I?"

"I don't know." A quiver starts low in my gut. This is different than running into him at a college party. It's just him and me here.

He nods toward the stairs behind him. "Come on."

Come on. The same thing he said to get me to follow him onto the roof. Whenever those words pass his lips, I'm apparently rendered helpless.

I step back, pretending like all my cells aren't zinging awake. "Give me a minute."

I duck back into my room, tie on my Chucks, grab a hoodie because the nights are getting cooler, and then head out to find Kepler standing in the middle of the living room, staring at the pencil drawings that fill the back wall.

"Wow," he mumbles. "These are so detailed."

"That's all Dex. There used to be more, but some got damaged during that last rain. Our windows suck."

He nods, leaning closer to a drawing of me. I'm isolated on white with my head tilted back, face up to the sky.

"I remember him drawing before," he says. "But not like this. What's this one?"

"We were at a kite festival." Christ, I sound like a little kid. "Dex and I go every year. There are some artists who create these intricately beautiful kites. Also, there's a challenge where you make your own, and . . ." I realize that

I'm only making it worse. "That probably sounds silly to you."

He pivots to face me. "Why do you do that?"

I blink and focus on Dex's art. "Do what?"

"Assume that I'm not interested in the things you're interested in. You realize that kites are all about physics? Weight, lift, tension and drag. But even if it wasn't, it doesn't sound the least bit silly to me. In fact, I've heard about it and always wanted to go."

"Then maybe we should go sometime," I blurt. I dry my hands on my sweats, tugging the thick fabric across my dick in a way that makes me shiver. I really should have changed into jeans. Or at minimum, pulled on some boxer briefs.

"We should go next year." Kepler leans in to peer at another drawing. "Shit, that's you, me, and Shin."

I nod. The three of us are sitting just outside this old treehouse that we all built together. Shin is between us, but Kepler's looking across at me.

I don't remember this moment, but I have a ton of memories from that treehouse. I used to drag that telescope over there too.

He studies the image carefully. "Dex has some serious talent."

"Yeah, he does."

He inhales as he steps back. "You ready?"

"Sure." I close and lock the door behind us, and we head down the steps and to the right, toward the gas station, under the streetlight where I first saw him earlier. I keep my hands in my hoodie pockets, trying to quell the rattle in my fingers.

And trying to figure out what to say when he turns right a couple blocks past the gas station, down a dirt lane with no street sign.

I pause. "Do you know where we're going?"

He turns, walking backwards to look at me, expression unreadable in the dark. "Yes."

I shake my head. "Do you always know where you're going?"

I meant it as a throwaway comment, but he nods, still walking backwards.

"Usually." He holds up his hands. "Now whether I should be going to that place is often debatable."

He veers off to the left, pulling himself up over a metal gate that connects an old wooden farm fence, his messenger bag bumping his ass as he jumps over. There aren't any buildings or houses out here, just a stretch of grass as tall as our knees that runs until it's framed by trees on both sides.

I pull myself up over the gate and jog to catch up. We move from the grass and into the trees, twigs cracking under our shoes. A light breeze plays through the branches over our heads, the deep smells of evergreen and moss surrounding us.

It's cloudy tonight, only a few stars and a mostly full moon hang in the dark sky. We duck under the silvery leaves of a gnarled, old Russian Olive tree, its sweet smell filtering over the deeper scents.

"How do you know this place?" My voice feels loud in the quiet.

"I walk through here to campus sometimes."

"That's like three miles." We walk past the Russian Olive and jump across a small creek, using our phones to light the path.

"Where do you live?" I ask as soon as we cross over.

"In a house," he says with a shrug.

"That's a very detailed description," I deadpan. "Got anything else for me?"

He walks next to me, and I can just make out his features as some clouds part. "What do you want to know?"

I debate. The things I really know about Kepler can be counted on the fingers of one hand. But I feel like if I ask a big question, I'm just going to get a shrug off. "What color are your walls?

"Gray."

I laugh. "Why doesn't that surprise me?"

"Because you know me." He nods ahead. "There."

Ahead of us is the arching, shadowed form of a tremendous weeping willow. My lips part as I stare at the tree. It's not indigenous to Indigo Falls and pretty rare to see one growing up at this altitude. Especially as tremendous as this one is.

I stop just before the first fronds. "See, the thing is, I don't think I know you at all, Quinn. You're like the biggest fucking mystery I've ever met."

"That's not true at all."

"No, it's true. Trust me."

He frowns slightly, slipping through the dangling branches of the tree, which are so long the leaves almost brush the ground. I follow him under the canopy. The leaves waft around us with the low breeze. I can just make out how the dark trunk twists into branches above our heads, and the smells here are so deep and rich that they fill my nose and throat.

It's like stepping into another world. Just like getting lost in all those essays, except this is real. And Kepler stands next to me. Not two feet away.

I swallow, my throat thick, my sweats suddenly too hot. "Why did you bring me here?"

"Because I thought you'd like it." He steps to the side,

circling around the trunk as he talks. "And because we're not friends."

He finishes rounding the trunk and stops across from me, pulling the messenger bag strap over his head and then dropping it with a thunk. "You're right. Like in that photo, Shin was always between us. But we should be friends."

I blink at him. "You think we should be friends?"

"Absolutely." A breeze whispers through the willow's fronds, picking up the strands of his hair. "You should call me."

"Call you?" I gawk at him. "For what?"

"For no reason at all. Or you could text me." He tilts his head, humor edging in his tone. "Or send an exhilarating picture or two."

"An *exhilarating* picture?"

"Or a boring one. I'm not picky."

Now I'm smiling. "You want me to send you boring pictures?"

"Absolutely, I do." He takes another step closer, and tension rockets through me. Suddenly, I can smell more than earth and musk. I'm lost in omija berries and cotton and cloves.

My heart starts to race like it knows a secret, but the rest of me stills.

His eyes flick around my face—I can't see their color, just the whites—and I wish he could actually read my thoughts. That he could sift through them, sort them out, and categorize them into some kind of order. Because I sure as hell can't.

His lips part, and I fasten on them as he speaks. "I really want us to be friends."

I swallow, the ache to lean toward him roaring in my head. It's as concrete and physical as the breath in my lungs and the breeze against the back of my neck. So strong I can taste it on my tongue and feel it rippling down my stomach and fisting my already thick dick.

I want to touch him. I want to run my hand along the edge of his jaw and down the cords of his neck to that whisper-soft tee that sheathes his chest and abs. I want his mouth on mine, his weight against me, shoving me up against the trunk of the tree, his tongue fighting past my lips.

Or maybe I would be the one to shove him back against the tree. I don't know.

Simkung. A heartthrob so strong that it consumes every other thought in your head.

There's no freaking way he feels the same.

Right? Then why is he looking at me like that?

What if I kissed him? Would he kiss me back?

And then what?

Kepler doesn't move. Both of us just stand there. Something holding us apart.

Shin.

Christ. I tear my eyes away and stare at the wafting branches of the willow tree.

"What did you and my brother do the other night?" I ask.

Did I seriously just ask that question? It feels like I just dumped a bucket of cold water over my head.

Which is what you should be doing, J.

"Nothing," he says quietly, stepping back slowly. "We just had a couple beers."

"I haven't seen him in weeks," I admit. "And I know he hasn't been by the house in forever."

"Have you been to see your mom?"

"Uh, yeah. Last week. There's this new guy she's seeing."

"Is he a problem?" He steps into my line of sight. "I'll go with you next time."

"No. It's fine." I scoff out a laugh at my own words.

It's not fine. It hasn't been in a long time.

Kepler waits for me to speak.

"It just sucks," I finally say. "She was sober when I saw her, but I don't have a good feeling about this asshole."

"Have you talked to Shin?" His hand comes up to cup the back of his neck.

He does that when he's nervous.

"Why?" I ask.

He shakes his head. "Nothing, I just . . ."

"What is it, Quinn?"

His hand drops from his neck, and it's a long moment before he talks. I can see the decision happening, and I wait.

"She was picked up for being drunk and disorderly," he finally says. "Last week."

I digest this, a sick, twisted knot growing in my stomach. "Shin told you this?"

"Yes."

"He didn't tell me." I rake a hand through my hair, turn away from Kepler, and then turn back again. "Why isn't shit ever simple?"

"I don't know," he says quietly. "Maybe because truly caring about someone is never uncomplicated."

7

WHEN I GET HOME, after I pretty much torpedoed the moment—if it even was a moment—I pull out my phone to text my brother. I stare at the screen for a long minute, fingers still jittery from being so close to Kepler. I'm not sure what to say to Shin.

Things weren't always so complex between my brother and me, and I miss when we were younger. I miss being *brothers* with him. And I can't believe he didn't tell me about our mother getting picked up.

He should have freaking told me.

But it's not something I want to deal with over text, so I finally shoot off a lame—*S'up.*

He responds an hour later, and I push aside my iPad to focus on the message.

You awake? We need to talk.

I frown. *I could say the same thing.*

His response is quick. *Meet me out front in five.*

I grab a hoodie and take the stairs down, stopping under a streetlight and shoving my hands in my hoodie pockets.

There's still a couple of cars at the gas station, but it's

quieter now. Kepler walked past here after leaving my apartment. That was thirty minutes ago. I'm sure he's home now. In his gray-walled abode.

Wherever that is.

Twenty-five minutes later, Shin's black-and-white SUV turns the corner and stops in front of me.

I tug the passenger door open and slide in. "You said five minutes."

My brother taps the steering wheel with his thumb. "I had to stop and check something out."

There are lines around his mouth and dark patches under his eyes. I don't know half the shit he has to deal with as one of Indigo Fall's finest, but it looks like it's weighing on him tonight, so I just say: "I'm glad you're okay."

It's the truth, no matter what else is going on between us. No matter how awkward it feels in the SUV right now.

He stays silent as I extend my fingers through the divider bars that partition off the backseat so that Kima, his Malinois K-9, can give me a sniff. Even though I've met the dog countless times, she still studies me warily, cautious brown eyes darting to Shin as if asking him a question.

"*Goyohan*," he says. She responds to the Korean word for *calm* and settles, sitting back on her haunches and letting her tongue loll out for just a moment before she snaps it back and closes her mouth.

"Where are we going?" I click on my seat belt.

Shin sets his wrist on the wheel as he pulls away from the curb, scanning the road with his square jaw set. My brother doesn't look that much like me. His dark hair is shorn and his navy cop uniform stretches tight across his broad shoulders. Seems like there's always a slight frown on his face, too. Although maybe that's just for me.

"I want to swing by East Lake," he says. "But before that,

we need to take a quick drive by some apartments on Belvent."

"First of the year parties?" My knee is bouncing, and Shin notices it before focusing back on driving.

I can practically chew on the tension in the SUV. The last time I saw him, we got in an argument so intense that both of us had to walk away, and I'm worried that's going to happen as soon as I bring up the drunk and disorderly.

"Yep, first of the year parties." He shrugs, not looking at me. "Got a noise complaint for The Six Pack. There's no need to stop, we'll just make our presence known."

"Ah. Scare them a little?" The Six Pack is a group of six apartment buildings that are known for renting primarily to underage kids and having almost nightly keggers. It's where they go when they want to drink a shit ton of cheap beer and do stupid stuff.

I've done stupid stuff there plenty of times.

"Yep," he says.

There's another long pause as we drive through town, getting closer to the taller university buildings.

"What'd you want to talk to me about?" I finally ask. I'd rather get whatever's on his head out of the way before talking about what's on mine.

"Later," he says gruffly. "I'll show you."

"Okay." I tug at my seatbelt, relieved when we get to the apartments along Belvent just because there's finally something to talk about.

Also, it turns out it doesn't take much to scare a bunch of underage kids. They're out on the stretch of grass between apartment buildings, and as soon as we roll up, Shin blaring the siren for less than ten seconds, there's a frenzied movement of cups dropping and people heading back inside.

My brother spotlights the grassy area with his megawatt flashlight, and everyone exits, except for a dude who freezes. He's got one foot in the air, eyes like saucers, arms out. It's like he thinks he's invisible if he doesn't move.

"Well, he can't be that drunk." Shin keeps the light fixed on him. "Standing on one foot is half of the sobriety test."

He drops the flashlight, and the guy takes one step before Shin pins him again. And, of course, he refreezes. It's like a game of Red Light, Green Light all the way up to the apartment doors, and we're both laughing by the time he makes it inside.

Shit, it feels good to laugh with my brother. It reminds me of years ago, when Dad was still alive, and things were simpler.

I get this swell of *missing* my brother. So much that it pains me to think of asking him about the drunk and disorderly since we're probably going to argue about it.

His laugh fades. "Do you think it's worth it?"

I blink at him. "What's worth it?"

He shrugs a uniformed shoulder. "I drive over here all the time and break up parties because that's my job. But do you think it really matters?" Shin scans his spotlight over the balconies, and curtains fly shut. "What good does it really do?"

"Not sure," I admit. "But you know better than I do what happens when these parties get out of control."

I've never heard my brother question his job before. For all I've thought, Shin's a cop deep to his bones. He's never wanted to do anything else. But looking across at him now, the line down his forehead and tension in his lips . . . maybe there's more to the story than he's told me.

"I guess." Shin does another once over of the building

and then nods. "Regardless, that'll be good for now. There's really only a handful of kids. Although I wouldn't be surprised if I'm back here later for another noise complaint."

Before I can say anything else, he's on the radio to dispatch, and then he pulls back onto Belvent, pointing the SUV toward East Lake after we make a quick stop at a park for Kima to do her business.

East Lake is a decidedly different part of town. Indigo Falls has always been this way—there's the campus and then there's everywhere else with a stark line dividing the two. We head out past some fast-food places and then take the turn up.

Before long, we pull into a neighborhood with small, ranch style houses. Most are pretty run down, with the occasional one tidy and neat.

Shin flicks off his headlights as he pulls over to the side of the main road and comes to a stop.

Three or four houses down, there's a cluster of people. In some ways, it's not that different from the party back by campus. Music thumps from a crowded house, people gather outside, their voices carrying down to us, and vehicles crowd the curb and driveway.

I stretch out my legs, cramped against the dash. "Why are we here?"

Shin leans back in his seat, scanning the house. "Took me a while to track that new boyfriend down." He itches over the top edge of his bulletproof vest. "Fender," he continues. "Real name is Leonard Courtney. He's got a rap sheet a mile long. Assault, burglary, a ton of shit."

I shake my head. "Where does Mom find these guys?"

"Everywhere." He shrugs. "They really are everywhere, Jae. You've got no idea."

"No, I suppose I don't."

"It's not just that though."

My stomach knots. "What else?"

"He was arrested for cooking up meth last year. He got off because he convinced a jury that it was someone else's, but looking over the file, I don't know." He pivots the dash-mounted computer toward me and pulls up a query for Leonard Courtney, address where we are now on Bauder Drive. Brown hair, blue eyes, 6'3", 275 pounds, and the list of encounters with the Indigo Falls police takes up more than one screen. A DUI is listed too.

I drag in a tight breath. "We can't let that shit happen around Mom."

"She's a grown woman." Shin taps a button and the screen goes black. "I'll haul his ass in if there's even a chance he's cooking or carrying, but she makes her own decisions. I just wanted *you* to know who you're dealing with."

"Well, now that we both know, we can't just let her get sucked into a guy like this."

"We're not *letting* her do anything," he says. "You can't assume control of her addiction."

"It's our mother. Doesn't that mean something?"

"Yeah, it means I feel like shit about it." His voice rises, and Kima stands at attention in the backseat. Shin exhales slowly, glancing in the rearview mirror at her and rolling his shoulders to calm himself down.

And here we are, right back in the same old argument.

His jaw still works as he puts the SUV in drive and flips on the headlights. We drive in silence past the house. Unlike the party at The Six Pack, there's no quick exit, even though all eyes are on the SUV as we drive past.

Shit. "That's him." I nod toward the asshole standing in the middle of the yard with a beer in his hand. He's wearing clothes this time, thankfully. His blue glare fixes on the SUV, and I get a chill down my back. The SUV windows are darkly tinted, so I doubt he can see inside, but his glare still unnerves me.

Then Shin pulls off down the street and turns the first corner. He drives around the block to get back on the main road out of East Lake.

My fingers tap against the armrest. "Why didn't you tell me that Mom got picked up for a drunk and disorderly last week?"

He grumbles. "Because you don't need to know."

"The hell I don't." I tug on my seatbelt, which feels like it's slowly trying to choke me. Every day, I fail her more and more. "She needs to get back into rehab."

He guns the SUV at the green light. "Do you really think it would do any good?"

"Maybe." But even as I say the word, my mouth dries.

No. It won't help. It didn't help the first three times, either.

We both know the fucked-up truth.

We struggle with what to do because there's nothing we *can* do. Even as a cop, Shin doesn't have the answers. There are none. Not unless she finally wants to get help.

That's the cold, hard reality of having a parent who's an alcoholic. And the guy who could have helped us through it —our dad—well, he's not here anymore.

I scrub a hand over my face, the SUV feeling really damn small.

"I wish you'd told me, *hyeong*." I toss on the Korean for *brother*, figuring that it'll cool down the rapidly rising tension in the SUV.

After that we drive in silence for a bit. Shin focuses on the road, although the lines around his mouth remain tight.

Kima whines from the backseat, eyeing me like I'm going to do something shifty.

We cross through town, and I fight for something to say that won't cause an argument between us. "Hey, do you remember that telescope I had?"

His laugh is tight, but at least it makes the frown vanish for a moment. "How could I forget?"

"Do you know where it went?"

"I think it's at *Halmeoni*'s. She had it out on her back porch at one point."

"Yeah? Maybe I'll borrow it. I need to go see her anyway." The anniversary of our dad's death was three months ago, and that's the last time I was over to see our grandmother. As she pointed out rather bluntly in a text two days ago.

My phone dings, and before I even think about it, I dig it out and blink at Kepler's name on the screen.

Waiting for my first boring pic.

Shin stretches his neck to look at the screen. *Shit.* I flip the phone over.

Not fast enough.

He frowns as we pull up to my apartment, confusion flashing through his eyes. Which is admittedly better than the anger that was there a few minutes ago. But this is a whole ball of confusion that I'm not ready to let roll around yet.

"You're texting with Kepler?" he asks.

"It's nothing." I scrub a hand over my face and then reach for the door handle. "I just needed his signature to get out of a class."

"What class?"

"Physics. He's my TA."

Shin's jaw hardens. "You sure that's all?"

My hand falls from the handle. "Why wouldn't that be all?"

"Nothing," Shin says flatly.

What the fuck?

Once again, my brother's not telling me something.

But then, I'm not talking either.

"It's just weird." His thumb taps against the steering wheel. I nod, not sure what else to say, and push out of the SUV.

"Jae," he says, stopping me as I'm about to close the door. "Wait. I've got to say, uh . . ."

I blink at him. "What?"

"You need to live your life."

I huff out a laugh. "Who else's life would I be living?"

"Mom's."

I still, hand clutched around the doorframe. "That's not what I'm doing."

"You sure?"

"She's sick, bro. Addiction isn't a choice, it's a disease. And you know that as well as anyone else."

"I do." He leans partway over the passenger seat to get a good look at me. "But there comes a point when both of us have to admit that there's not going to be a happy ending here. Maybe she's never going to want to get better."

"I can't believe that." I just *can't*. "Someday she'll—"

Hit bottom.

Except she never does.

Shit. I grip the doorframe, heat rising behind my eyes. "I won't just give up on her."

"Then at some point, it *will* be just you and her."

That hurts. Right down to my core. I swallow and slam the door shut.

I can't see him through the tinted glass, but a little part

of me hopes that he's going to get out, that he's going to ask me if I want to head upstairs and play some *Call of Duty* or grab a beer or *anything*, but instead he revs the engine and then he's gone, taillights disappearing around the corner of the gas station.

I pound up the stairs, shoulders tense, stomach tight. I'm not living her life. And I'm not giving up on her. And I really don't want to think about this shit anymore.

Our apartment's dark—no lights. No Dex tonight. I'd welcome his talkative distraction, but I guess he's at Brady's again.

I shove off my shoes, grab a glass, and fill it with water. I drink it all back and then down another.

My phone sits on the counter. I snatch it, and before I can think too much, I load up the camera app. I glance around and then snap a picture of the most boring thing I can find: my empty glass sitting on the counter.

Then I pull up Kepler's text and reply with the picture.

Christ. What am I doing?

I wait. He's probably asleep. Or if he's not, he's staring at a picture of my empty glass and wondering, *What the fuck?*

Twenty seconds later my phone dings and downloads a picture.

A pair of black-and-white Vans on dirt.

He's outside. One of his shoelaces is frayed at the end, and there's a scuff mark across the white tip of his shoe. For some reason, that makes me smile, and it's like this huge weight lifts off my chest and slithers away.

I head to my room, snap a picture of an empty paper bag on my desk, and then the chair by the window that I never sit in. I send them before I can debate myself.

He sends photos back. A balcony railing with his hand

resting on the top. A legal pad with equations scribbled all over it.

And more.

We send each other pictures for the next two hours.

And the most boring pictures of Kepler's life?

I don't find them boring at all.

8

I GET another text from Kepler first thing in the morning. He couldn't have slept more than a few hours.

Although, I didn't either.

This one is a photo of a narrow dirt road through a front windshield, one of his hands on top of a black steering wheel. The road's one car length wide with lodgepole pine trees shooting up on each side.

He's going somewhere. Probably campus. Physics lecture begins in two hours.

I snap a picture of my iPad and tea and send it back.

I can faintly hear Dex singing. He does that in the shower—out of tune and with complete abandon.

I should be heading to campus too. Today's the day to turn in the request form to switch out of physics.

Now, really. I should be moving now.

Not sitting here. Drinking tea and waiting for Kepler to text.

Fifteen minutes later, he finally responds. This photo is of the math building on the very edge of the liberal arts quad. It's close to where I'll be soon.

Christ. My knee bounces, my foot almost slipping off the rung of the breakfast bar stool. My throat constricts so hard that I'm not sure I can drink the rest of my tea. Even just the thought of being within a half-mile radius from him apparently sends my body into overdrive.

I force myself to calm as Dex steps into the kitchen.

"Hey, man." He pulls open a cabinet. "How was your date? I haven't really seen you since then."

"Uh, good." I'd pretty much forgotten about the date.

Although not about London. I'll talk to him today. Tell him . . . something. Probably not a good idea to tell him I've got the hots for a physics TA.

"Cool." Dex grabs a granola bar and eats it in two solid bites before dropping the wrapper in the trash.

I lean back on the stool. "Have you heard anything about Professor Manford? He teaches physics."

"Just a few rumors about him and his TAs." Dex frowns. "Although I think Paulie had him. Remember that dick who almost failed him? Paulie questioned him in class, and the next thing he knew, his grade plummeted. He nudged out a pass, but he lost his scholarship."

"Christ," I mumble. Paulie is whip-smart. He's also a chemistry major, so he knows his way around science labs. And Dex brings up a good point about scholarships. The essay job gets me by, but it's not like I've got a trust fund sitting around that could absorb the tuition cost for next semester if I lost any of my scholarships.

I stare down at my phone.

Kepler said he'd be fair.

"Are you heading to campus soon?" Dex asks. "I've got to get to a study group early."

"Yeah, sure. I can drive." I stand and stuff my phone in

my back pocket next to the class change request form. "So, you're still seeing Brady? You were late last night."

"We're just fucking." Dex grabs a second granola bar and stuffs it in his backpack. "Neither one of us are looking for anything."

"Just fucking," I repeat. He makes it sound so easy. "Hey, have you ever heard anyone call us the 'hotty-pants twins?'"

He responds with a full-on belly laugh, just like I knew he would.

"Totally the truth, dude." He cuts the laugh to bounce his pecs, striding to the kitchen door with a shit-eating grin. "And you know it."

I shake my head but find myself grinning as I follow him.

It's cooler outside today, so I zip up my hoodie before sliding in the car. We should get the first snow soon.

I wait for Dex to get in and glance down the street before pulling out.

There's a couple of guys on bikes at the gas station. One at the gas pump, but the other parked at the curb. He's straddling his bike, thick thighs on either side. His blue eyes focus on me.

Fender.

A knot twists in my gut. Is this a coincidence? I mean, it's a gas station. People are going in and out all day long.

We fix on each other as Dex plugs in his phone to find some music.

"Hey," Dex says, knocking his elbow against mine. "Are we going?"

"Yeah." I take a breath and pull out. I upnod Fender as we drive by, and his lips curl into a sneer.

Fuck. He's a scary dude.

I'm still contemplating the situation twenty minutes later, after circling a few times to find a parking spot. Dex jumps out of the car as soon as we're parked, late to his study group. I dig out the class change form and head toward my advisor's office. He's with another student—door closed—so I jot down my name and a message for him to text me when he's available and head next door to the library to study a bit and then pull up those past exams for Vain.

I've always liked the library. I rarely come here, doing most of my research online, but my shoulders relax as soon as I step inside the arched entryway. There's something about this place that calls to me. All that knowledge. Each book is like a doorway into another world.

Worlds far, far away from Indigo Falls.

A peaked ceiling with skylights runs down the main room. Long tables stretch down to the far end. There are a few hushed conversations, but it's empty this early in the semester, so the buzz of my phone is loud and garners me a few turned heads.

Somehow, before I even dig my phone out of my back pocket, I already know it's Kepler, and I can't help the smile that stretches across my face as I pull up his text.

The photo takes a second to download in the heavy steel building. As it comes up, I blink down at it.

It's *me*.

Standing right where I'm standing now.

I swallow, spinning to find him.

Kepler sits at a table on the far side of the room, closest to the deep, dark rows of the stacks. A few thick textbooks, a yellow legal pad, and a stack of Post-its sit in front of him. A pale-green tee stretches across his chest. Not a gray tee.

I don't know why that catches me.

But I'm standing in the middle of the damn library

thinking about the color of his tee like it's some relevant life or death detail. I drop my bag on the table next to me and slide down into a seat.

Across the room, Kepler taps a pencil against his legal pad, the sound echoing lightly. He's holding his phone in his other hand, and he tilts his head as he watches me through his black-framed glasses. His attention drops to his phone as his thumb moves over it.

My phone buzzes a second later.

Sit with me.

I turn off my sound before answering.

Are you sure you're allowed to sit with one of your students?

Then you decided not to drop the class?

I've got the form in my back pocket. Just waiting for my advisor to text me when he's got time to see me.

You're making a bad choice.

You've already made your opinion clear. I snag my iPad out of my backpack and click it into a keyboard. My phone lights up with another text.

The bad choice was referring to your choice of seats. The sunlight's about to come through the skylights, and it heats that spot. You'll be sweating in a few minutes.

I don't plan to be here that long. Advisor, remember?

Ah, yes. Besides, I'm here, so you won't stay longer than five minutes.

My smile falls. *We made it past five minutes the other night.*

Was it so awful?

I glance up. His eyes are so light right now that they almost look silver.

He looks playful. It's not only in his gaze, but also in the ease of that sharp jaw. In the way he clutches his pencil between long fingers, slowly tapping it against his legal pad.

Shit, that playful ease looks so damn good on him. I can't remember the last time I saw him like that.

My thumb lingers over my phone, debating what to type. Then I hold it up and snap a picture of him. I don't know why. Maybe I just want to see him looking like this again. I'm pulling the picture up when I get another text from him.

You're smiling.

I just stare at the words for a long moment.

He's right, as usual. I'm sitting here, phone in hand, with a stupid-ass grin on my face.

What the hell am I doing? Keeping pictures of him on my phone? I swallow, my smile fading as I exit out of the photo. I set down my phone, turn to my iPad, and pull up the research I'd been working on about nuclear power. Not my favorite topic, but I try to focus on the work.

And not think about Kepler Quinn.

And not wonder about what the fuck is going on between us.

Nothing's going on. Just two dudes sending each other copious amounts of pictures. That's normal, right?

And because I can't help myself, and I'm a glutton for punishment, I pick up my phone again.

What are you working on? I text him.

Dissertation.

Topic?

The evaluation of data related to geomagnetic storms.

Space storms? That sounds pretty cool.

It is. I'll tell you about it later.

I swallow and stare down at the message, not sure how to respond. I finally just type okay and turn to my iPad. I scroll through some websites to get a basic outline established, and the sun starts to shift. Sure enough, it slides from the skylight over my table, inch by inch, first highlighting my keyboard, then my forearms.

I unzip my hoodie and tug it off, but that doesn't help much. I feel Kepler's attention on me as I gather up my iPad and slip it into my backpack. I still need to look up those exams for Vain, so I stand to pass by Kepler and walk down the first row of the stacks toward the section in the back.

Kepler watches me, his pencil pressed against his bottom lip, notes scrawled across the legal pad in front of him.

As I pass, he stands, dropping his pencil with a little clunk on the table.

My throat tightens, my pulse picking up as I head deeper into the stacks where the light dims and the air is thick with the dense smell of old books.

Two more turns and I'm at the back corner. It's quiet, isolated. One shaft of sunlight darts down behind me, dust floating through it, and all I can smell is old books and a faint whiff of lemon cleaner.

Kepler steps around the corner and stops a couple feet away. Tall bookshelves frame us on both sides.

My hand tightens around the strap of my backpack. "What are we doing, Quinn?"

"You tell me." His voice is soft, and it simmers over me, just like always. But then his eyes narrow. He's thinking. He slips off his glasses and tucks them in the front pocket of his tee.

I'm not used to feeling this lost with people. It's like he's always pushing me off balance. Making my brain work overtime just to figure him out.

I drag a hand over my mouth. The full truth lingers just on my tongue. How he wakes me up. Head to fucking toe. But once said, it can't ever be taken back. It'll be out there.

And who am I to him? Shin's little brother? Or was there actually something happening under that willow tree?

Whatever this thing is, there's no way that it's the same for him. There's not even a remote possibility that I light him up in the same way he lights me.

Christ. I hate how he's considering me with all those damn thoughts in his eyes.

He tilts his head. "Are you good?"

I frown. "Uh, sure? I'm just studying at the library, man."

"I saw that." His gray eyes are so damn steady on me. "I also know you saw Shin last night. And I know you don't want me to get into things between you and your brother, but learning about Lilah getting arrested had to be hard."

It's weird that he calls my mom by her first name. Although, what else would he call her?

I loosen my shoulders, keeping my voice low in the quiet library.

"I'm . . . worried," I admit. "But I guess I'm always worried."

He nods. "You'll tell me if there's something I can do?"

"That's just it. No one can really do anything." My throat tightens. "I can't imagine what you must think of us. Ten years later, and we're still running around the same endless maze."

"I think that you and Shin both love your mom." He pauses. "And I think that you all miss Yeong-Su."

My dad. It's weird to hear his name spoken aloud too.

"I guess that's the crux of it." I scrub a hand over my face and drag in a breath. "Talking about this with you drags me back ten years. You must think I'm such a kid still."

Kepler flinches. "I haven't thought of you as a kid since the first time I saw you on campus."

"When was that?"

"You were on the other side of the Quad with Dex, the ink peeking out just at the neckline of your tee." He pauses, lips pressing. "He was showing you something on his phone."

I frown, my hand going to the back of my neck, cupping over the ink that I know is there. "I don't remember that."

Although Dex is pretty much always showing me something on his phone.

"Why would you?" Kepler shrugs. "Regardless, there's only three years between us. You act like it's a decade."

"It feels like a decade."

"Not to me." He shakes his head slowly. "Not at all. I would have asked, had I guessed."

"Asked what?" I'm left with that feeling I always have of not knowing what's going on in his head.

His eyes fix on mine. "I would have asked you to go on a walk with me. A long time ago."

I drag in a slow breath. "Why did you follow me here, Quinn?"

His tongue crests that slightly thinner bottom lip. "Multiple reasons."

I groan. "You're frustratingly opaque."

His eyes narrow. "What does that mean?"

"It means you're a puzzle, Kepler. A mystery. A serpentine thing I can't fucking figure out."

Shit, that's way too close to the truth. But there's relief that comes with saying it too. Just setting it out there, and as I admit the shit I shouldn't admit, I realize just how frustrated I've become. I need to figure out what's going on between us. Maybe it's nothing. But it doesn't feel like nothing.

"You're serious?" His jaw tightens and I can't tell if he's frustrated or angry or annoyed or all of the above.

"Yeah, I am." I blunder on, keeping my voice soft enough not to carry over the stacks. "You show up on my doorstep at midnight and walk me to that damn willow tree, saying you want to be friends. And then we text all night. And then you follow me back here to ask if I'm okay. And don't even get me started on the freaking Post-it Notes."

"What's confusing about all that?"

I pause. "I don't know. You're Shin's best friend. And I guess we can be friends too, but—"

I fucking want you. And it feels like maybe—just maybe, possibly—it's mutual.

I'm two seconds away from saying it, but I pin my lips because once that gets out, there's no taking it back. But how are we going to figure out what's going on if neither of us *talk*?

"To me," he says quietly, "it feels like I'm the most obvious person in the world. I leave you Post-its because I selfishly want you to think about me."

I freeze. Well, on the outside. On the inside, a shit ton is happening. Stomach tightening, chest pinching, heart thumping up into my throat.

Kepler's lips part slowly. "And I text you because every one of those pictures you send feels like it breathes life into me. I walked with you to the willow because I want every second I can get with you. Even if it fucks up my head a bit, even if I *know* that it's crossing a line." His pupils flare, the gray darkening. "I followed you back here because I wanted to see how you are since I know you had a difficult night. And also, selfishly again, because I imagined shoving you up against the bookshelf and kissing the fuck out of you, even if I'm pretty sure that won't ever happen. Even if I've imagined doing just that ever since that first time I saw you on the Quad."

I'm still frozen. Shock is too weak of a word to describe the heat that races through my body, head to toe. Adrenaline is pumping *everywhere*. My throat dries, my knuckles ache from clutching the strap of my backpack, my pulse skitters. The world blurs, hazy books on vague shelves with a nebulous background.

But Kepler is in sharp detail. Dark blond hair across his high forehead, pale-green tee stretched across his shoulders, that small mole on his cheek.

I need to say something, but I don't have words in my head.

A shot of panic bolts through his eyes. "I'm sorry. I shouldn't have said that."

He takes a step back.

Shit, he's going to walk away.

Say something, J.

I unstick my tongue from the roof of my mouth. "Then do it."

He stops. "Do what?"

"Kiss me."

"*Kiss* you?" His brows go up.

"Yeah." My voice is hoarse, my throat dry.

Another pause, and then he takes half a step forward.

I just about jump out of my skin as he closes the distance. Two feet, down to one foot, down to just a couple of inches. His eyes flick around my face, thin lips parting slowly like he's going to say something.

He's going to ask if I'm sure.

And I have no clue how to answer that question.

No, I'm not sure.

But I want him to kiss me anyway.

"Don't say anything," I mumble. "Just do it."

One breath.

Two.

Are we going to do this?

He tips closer, and then slowly, so fucking slowly that it feels like I'm counting each and every millisecond, his lips meet mine. It's light, barely a kiss, just a brush and a breath.

It's not enough. I let out a soft moan, and when he goes to pull away, I fist the front of his shirt.

"Fucking *kiss me*, Quinn." I close the distance, my lips flattening against his, and it's like something between us snaps. His mouth crushes against mine, and the kiss is *instant*—no pretense, no second-guessing, no questioning—like this kiss has been lingering there between us, just waiting to happen. His lips are warm, and his tongue slides lightly against mine.

And with that one tiny slip of his tongue, I'm a livewire. A vibration resonates so deep inside that it feels like it's coming from the freaking DNA in my cells.

My backpack thunks to the carpet, and I barrel headfirst into our kiss, meeting him full-on, mouth on his, my hand releasing his tee to cup the nape of his neck, the tendons there tight. My fingers dig into the short, thick hair at the base of his skull. My other hand clasps his bicep, and this sexy-as-fuck low rumble winds through him and vibrates my chest.

His taste, his smell, it's *masculine*, and it curls right down to my hardening stomach and the tightening of my jeans as he shoves me back with his chest, the sharp edge of his glasses cutting into my pec.

I grasp at him, balling the bottom edge of his shirt in my fist. I want it off of him. I yank up on it, making his breath hitch, and then I smooth my palm across his stomach and the ridges of his abs. The rough waistband of his jeans scrapes against the heel of my hand, his skin warm on my fingertips.

Fuck me, fuck me, *fuck me*.

I can't stop touching him. And it's like he can't stop either. His hands rove over my biceps and then down, one hand brushing lightly over my inked forearm while the other slides around and cups my ass, *hard*. With a firmness that drives straight to my dick.

We're grasping at each other, right in the middle of the library stacks. The long, lean height of him solid against me, tongue delving deeper with the perfect amount of force, his hand palming my ass hard as he backs me up against a bookshelf, the spines pressing into my shoulders, and all on its own, my pelvis grinds forward, looking for contact, and—

Holy fuck. A needy moan crests my lips as my dick grinds against his. He's solid behind his jeans, and I pitch forward again, scraping myself almost painfully against my zipper, my thoughts shattering as his tongue delves into my mouth.

Is this real? Am I fantasizing right now?

Something thumps behind me. First one thump on the ground, then another and another. Books push through the shelf and fall somewhere behind my back, but I don't even care right now. I fit my hand between our stomachs and yank up on his tee again, then tug down at the top hem of his jeans, my fingertips just scraping at the elastic of his boxers.

More thumps.

We're both groaning, both ripping at each other.

My shoulders press back, and the bookshelf behind me shifts.

Fuck.

"Quinn." I tear away just enough to say his name, and it jerks both of us out of the haze.

The bookshelf behind us sways, and I picture a kid's cartoon where the bookshelves all collapse, one after the other like dominoes, book pages flying up, everyone in the library turning to stare at us with open mouths.

I breathe out in relief when we step back and the shelf wobbles but stays standing. There's just a gaping hole where books plummeted into the aisle behind.

"Christ," I mumble. Kepler's standing to my right, breathing hard, an expression on his face like he doesn't know what just happened.

And I'm probably wearing that expression too.

My backpack's on the ground two feet away. The bottom of his tee is wrinkled and stretched from where I'd clutched it in my sweaty palm.

"That was—" He stops when we both register movement to the left.

A librarian steps into the aisle, her focus zeroing in on the gaping space where the books had been. "What happened?"

"A couple of books just slipped through to the other side." Kepler's voice is rough, his lips reddened as he licks them, his dick tenting his jeans.

It's got to be desperately obvious what we were just doing.

She grumbles something under her breath about college students and then stalks back down the aisle, appearing on the other side of the shelf.

"We'll help you," I say, reaching down to grab my backpack and throw it over my shoulder. My phone buzzes in my pocket. Probably my advisor.

"No." She bends to pick up a book and dusts it gently with her hand. "They need to be put back in the right order." She eyes me through the open space. "You two can go now."

In other words: stop groping each other in the back of the library.

I glance over at Kepler, who's seemed to regain some composure as he shifts one brow upwards. But as cool and collected as the motion is, uneven breaths still expand his chest.

We *kissed*.

That's about the only thought in my head as we head back down the long aisle, Kepler in front of me. My attention drops to the way his jeans hang on his ass as we walk past the study carousels and back into the larger area of the library.

He stops just at the end of the bookshelves. His books and legal pad still sit on his table, but there's a guy in a beige button-down reclined in Kepler's chair.

The freaking finger-toucher.

Kepler's shoulders stiffen. "What the fuck is he doing here?"

Christ. Kepler's still my TA. The form's still in my back pocket.

There's no way we're supposed to be kissing in the back of the library.

The finger-toucher scans through whatever Kepler had been writing on his legal pad. He hasn't noticed us.

I hook a thumb back down the aisle and keep my voice quiet. "I'll head out the other way."

Kepler turns to face me, brow lined, his hand coming up to smooth over the back of his neck and then sliding down, over his chest and where those ridged abs are hiding, to adjust his dick.

I *stare*. Even as his hand leaves his dick and sinks into his pocket, his forearm rolling, stretching his jeans across narrow hips.

We *kissed*.

We kissed.

We motherfucking *kissed*.

"Jin." He takes half a step toward me, his voice sinking to a soft whisper. "It shouldn't have ended like that."

I blink at him.

Am I dreaming? Is this a fantasy? Am I about to open my eyes and find that I've jizzed all over the bed? I can't think of a more inelegant ending to this moment than waking up and realizing this is a teenage wet dream.

No, this is real.

He's here in front of me. Chest rising with his inhale. Angled jaw. Hot-as-fuck mole.

Jonna jalsaenggyeotta. Although *handsome* doesn't begin to describe it.

I clear my throat. "Uh, how should it have ended?"

"I can think of a variety of ways. I just"—he nods over his shoulder toward the finger-toucher—"can't talk here. See me tonight? Damn, wait." He grinds his teeth, jaw clenching. "I've got something. It would have to be late. Will you be up?"

"Are you sure that's a good idea? With . . ." I nod toward his occupied table. *And Shin.*

"No." He blows out a breath. "But I don't care."

My lips part. "You should."

We both should.

"Probably." His tongue slides along that thinner bottom lip. "The selfish asshole in me suddenly wants you to turn in that class request form."

"I'd planned on it."

"No." His head dips closer, fingers coming up to tap the

side of my phone, and the hard knock of his fingertips echoes quietly in the silent library. "It's not the best choice for your education. Trust me, and I'll see you in lecture. In an hour."

He turns to go and then stops, twisting back, gray eyes sparking.

"Were you thinking?" he asks.

I blink. "When we kissed?"

He nods, studying me with a tilted head.

"Uhhh . . ." I clear my throat, my mind darting back to the *taste* of him. Omija and spice. That low rumbling sound he made. The heat of his abs against my fingertips. *Fuck me.* "I was thinking about a whole hell of a lot."

"Good." He turns and walks out of the aisle, toward the finger-toucher, and I'm not gonna lie, I know I should duck out, that I should wake up and remember exactly who Kepler is—Shin's best friend and my freaking TA. Instead, I stare at his ass the entire freaking time he walks away.

I MAKE A STUPID CHOICE.

I don't do it because it's what Kepler told me to do.

I don't do it because everyone tells me Manford is a dickhole who messes with GPAs.

I don't do it because my advisor is pressing me to keep my current schedule.

Nope.

I do it for a stupid reason. I do it because I want to see Kepler.

When I'm sitting in my advisor's office, I realize that I just can't seem to pass that form over, no matter how much I know that I should. Logic goes out the window.

We *kissed*.

I don't know what that kiss meant for Kepler. There's no way it's actually the start of something, he's my brother's best friend, and I shouldn't even be thinking about it.

Kimchigukbuteo masiji malla is a phrase I heard a lot growing up. *Don't get ahead of yourself.* Or, more literally, don't drink the kimchi soup first.

But all that aside, that kiss wasn't a subtle shift for me. It was an avalanche tumbling all of my rational thoughts down. It was the hottest kiss of my life, and now I can't wait to be in the same place as him, no matter the consequences.

An hour later, I take the steps up to the physics building, tossing back the energy drink I bought on the way. I lick my lips. I can still taste him. I can still feel the trail of hair that runs down into his jeans, how his tongue carved so perfectly into my mouth, his body aligned with mine, the throb of my pulse—in my throat, in my chest, in my dick.

All of it.

I open the door at the back of the lecture hall and pause, my heart just about thudding to the floor like those books did. Kepler sits in the first row, back to me, pale-green tee pasted to his shoulders, head tilted as he talks to the finger-toucher.

The guy laughs and Kepler shrugs, then he leans down and pulls his legal pad out of his messenger bag. But his shoulders stay tense for the entire exchange.

I dry my clammy hands on my jeans and walk down the first steps. I want him to turn and look at me.

He can't.

I mean, he really, *really* can't. He's officially my TA for the semester now. I don't care if he had that moment of not caring, because that's not the Kepler I actually know. He cares. He's always cared about his education. You don't get to be valedictorian or a physics doctoral student if you don't care.

I take a breath and quell my disappointment. When I turn toward the back row, London glances up from his notebook, black pen in his hand, already sketching.

"Hey." I pass into his row and take the seat one down from him. "I'm sorry I didn't call you. I'm a dick."

His pen pauses as he shakes his head. "You're not a dick."

I scrub a hand over my mouth. "Well, I'm definitely dickish. It's just that you're too nice a guy to call me on it. And I had a good time. I really did."

His brows go up, the light catching on his piercings. "But?"

I need to tell him the truth.

Or the closest thing I can say to the truth, which eats at me, because I really do like London.

"There's someone else," I say. "I'm sorry, man."

A half-truth I'd blurted out to Michela.

It's more honest than I've ever realized. There's always been someone else. Even if I haven't been able to admit it. I don't know when it began for me with Kepler, but it's always been there like my own heartbeat, my own breath, the stars above—ever present. And always drawing my attention in the same way that my eyes want to draw down to the lecture well right now.

We kissed.

That fills me with awe. With pulse-pumping wonder.

I'm never gonna get over it.

So . . . how am I going to concentrate on the lecture?

Focus on London, J. He deserves an explanation.

A smile spreads across his face. "That's a relief."

I emit a laugh. "Is it?"

He drops his pen. "Well, if you didn't notice, I didn't call you either. I mean, it *seems* like we'd be a perfect match. And you're funny and charismatic and really freaking good looking. But it just wasn't . . ." He shrugs a shoulder. "So, friends?"

"Fuck yeah." I nod eagerly, a huge-ass weight lifting off my shoulders.

He grins, but it fades quickly. "And I kinda have someone else too. I hoped our date would get my mind off him but, well . . . it didn't work."

I watch him for a long moment, not sure what to make of his admission and the unease that overtakes him. He crosses his legs tightly, shifting in his seat before picking up his pen. It lingers an inch over his sketch of an . . . octopus?

"Do you want to talk about it?" I ask.

He wrinkles his nose. "He doesn't even know I exist. Not at all. And I'd really rather not talk about it."

Okay, then.

I rush to fill the uneasy silence. "It's his loss."

"I don't know about that. But thanks for saying it." He sets pen to paper, and it glides smoothly along one of the tentacles. "I'm still interested in that fundraiser. I, um, don't know many people in Indigo Falls yet. My roommate has a lot of parties, but I'm not into them that much."

"Yeah, that's been me lately too. Dex is having some of the other student teachers over to chat about the fundraiser later. You should come."

"Thanks, man."

"Of course." I dig out my notepad and flop it on my side desk. "Dex would love the help. We both would. This is good."

And I really fucking mean that.

Our professor clears her throat. I glance down toward the lecture well and freeze.

Kepler's twisted in his seat, pale-green tee stretching, and his smoky gaze fixes on me. My breath cages in my chest.

He shouldn't be looking at me. There are a million, billion reasons he shouldn't be looking at me.

But he is.

9

Mom's house is eerily silent. There are a couple of burnt down candles on the coffee table. And a flashlight.

Shit. It's too quiet. No hum of the refrigerator.

I reach out to flick on the light.

Nothing.

I scrub a hand over my mouth as I step into the kitchen and tug open the refrigerator door. It's dark and only partly cool.

How long has the power been off? I was here two days ago, and it was fine. She didn't say anything about an overdue bill.

"Mom," I call. Silence greets me.

I walk through the house, the floor creaking under my feet. I head to her bedroom and peek in. Empty.

Bathroom door is open too. It's also empty.

There's only one closed door, and I stop before it, swallowing before I turn the handle. Inside is the room Shin and I shared growing up. I open the scratched-up door to the green-walled room. Our old bunk beds are pushed into a corner to make room for the boxes that fill every other spot.

I step inside, coughing from the dust.

Everything my father had is in here. Clothes, books, his old baseball collectibles, his challenge coins from his military service. None of the boxes are labeled, because they're never going anywhere. She's kept all of it. Down to the change he had in his pocket the day of his heart attack.

A steadfast reminder of the man we lost.

Part of me will always exist in this room. Except Shin and I both moved out. He whipped through college in three years—taking classes summer and nights—before applying to the academy. I've meandered a bit more, but I still moved out of this house as soon as I could at eighteen.

It would have made more sense to stay, but I just couldn't be here night after night. Day after day.

But our mother's been here, in this house, surrounded by the past. Other than those three-day stints at Sunshine Crossing, she's endured so many hours alone here.

I should have done more for her.

What, J? What could I have done?

Voices filter through the house from the living room. My mom's laugh and then a low voice following it.

Shit. They're at the far end of the hallway. Fender follows behind my mom. She pauses as soon as she sees the open bedroom door, then pales as she looks at me. Fender curses when he bumps into her and tells her to be more careful.

What a fucking prick.

A thick layer of scruff covers his jaw, and he half-snarls when he looks up to see why she's stopped.

"What are you doing here?" he demands.

It's like he thinks he's the man of the house or something. Which is stupidly outdated, but regardless, he'll *never* be that.

My mom says something in a whisper. He shakes his head and stalks back down the hallway.

At least he listens to her.

Mom approaches me and stops in the doorframe, the toes of her baby blue sneakers an inch outside the room. "What *are* you doing in here?"

"I don't know," I answer truthfully. "What are you doing with him?" I nod toward the sound of the front door slamming.

She doesn't respond, just keeps standing there, an inch outside the door, her eyes parsing over all the boxes and memories that surround me. They stop on the open closet. Dad's shirts all hang neatly in a row.

"I should do his laundry," she says.

"Dad's laundry?" It seems like such a bizarre thing to say. "He still has dirty laundry?"

She wrinkles her nose, her fingers picking at the ends of her hair. "Of course not. But I do all his laundry. At least once a month. He wouldn't want it to get musty."

"*All* his laundry?" I didn't know this. "You wash all his shirts? Pants? Everything?"

"I wash everything." She worries her bottom lip.

"You can't do laundry, mom. The power's out." I finally step over and slide the closet door shut. "Maybe it's time to see if someone else could use them."

She shakes her head. "No, I—"

"He would have wanted that." I struggle with what to say that won't hurt her. "He wouldn't have wanted you to still be washing his shirts years later."

Her breath starts to come hard, pupils widening. "No, Jae. You can't. It's too soon. It's—"

"It's been nine years." I pause. "Maybe it's time to look at selling the house? We could get you an apartment." Somewhere she isn't smacked with memories every time she turns a corner.

She shakes her head again, panic flaring in her eyes. "No, I can't, Jae. I can't leave."

"Okay, Mom." A sick feeling settles in my stomach. I just wish I knew how to help her. I wish I had the first fucking clue.

She's white as a sheet, and I cross toward her, not stopping until my arms loop around her, and I just . . . hug my mom. I *squeeze* her, feeling how bony she is, how her thin arms wrap around my biceps, how she hiccups a little against my shoulder, how strange this feels, and how I should hug her more often.

When I step back, her hand darts up to her hair again, fiddling.

"Mom?" I frown, studying her. Earlier I thought her pupils were wide, but this close . . . they're dilated.

She's jumpy, and when I hugged her, she felt warm.

She doesn't smell like liquor.

Fuck.

"What are you on?" I ask.

She shrugs. "Nothing really. Just . . . I don't know."

"You don't *know*?"

She steps back from the door. "You always get so intense about it. It's just that I was thinking about a lot this morning, and so I took some Xanax. Or that's what I thought they were, but I don't know, I've been feeling a bit more jittery instead."

"Did you get it from Fender?"

"Sure." She shrugs one shoulder and heads back down the hallway.

I follow her to the sea blue kitchen. "Do you still have the pills?"

"Um, maybe?" She grabs her bag off the counter and digs around, then pulls out a blue prescription bottle with the label peeled off.

I hold out a hand. "Let me have them."

She looks between my hand and the bottle. "You don't have to take them."

"Yeah, Mom. I kinda really do."

She sighs and extends them, then pauses. I wait. And wait. She finally drops them in my hand.

I pocket them. "You shouldn't take shit if you don't know what it is."

She fills a glass with water. "It's seriously no big deal, nugget. Don't you have class?"

Yeah, I do. I sneak a peek at my phone and inwardly sigh. My first lab section of physics starts in seven minutes. With TA Kepler Quinn. I'd just planned a quick stop by here.

I shake my head. "I've got a few minutes. Just"—I back out of the kitchen—"stay here for a bit."

I head into the living room before firing off a quick text to Shin.

You working? Mom's on something and I'm not sure what.

There's no sign of Fender out the front window. His truck is gone too. At least I won't have to deal with that asshole right now.

My phone dings with Shin's response. *Shift begins in an hour. Shouldn't you be in class?*

Yeah, I type, *that's my problem actually.*

I'll come get her.

I blink at the message. I don't know what I expected, but it wasn't that response.

Thanks, I type out. *I know you don't think we should be babysitting her.*

I'm not doing it for her. Now get your ass to class. I'll be there in five.

I pocket my phone. An empty schnapps bottle sits on its side in front of the couch. I pick it up, feeling the weight of the cool glass in my hand, and walk into the kitchen to drop it in the trash.

"How long has the power been out?" I ask.

She shrugs. "Not sure. It's no big deal."

No big deal.

Just like that.

"Where'd the money go?" I ask. "You had some set aside for the bills."

"I, um . . ." She fills her glass with water again and takes a sip. "I'm not really sure? I had it. I know I did."

I itch at my jaw. "Did Fender take it?"

She shakes her head. "No."

I don't believe that for one second. Maybe I need to deal with the bills more directly. Just . . . take care of it for her.

Shit. That's not right either. Taking care of *more* for her isn't the solution.

My phone dings. I grab it out of my pocket and see a text from Kepler.

Everything ok?

I frown at his message. Class began one minute ago. He should be going over the syllabus, getting shit started. Not texting me.

Yeah, I type back. *I'm taking care of some stuff. I'll be there in 20.*

Sorry, I tag on.

Don't be sorry. I'll catch you up later.

Thanks.

I pocket the phone. "Shin is coming by, Mom."

She perks up. "Really?"

"Yep." I nod toward the door. "I've got to run. Stay here until he shows up?"

She nods and starts opening cabinets. "I'm sure he'll be hungry."

That makes me laugh a little. "Yeah, I'm sure he is."

I head out, glancing at the time and groaning. It'll take me ten minutes to get to campus, another ten to find a parking spot, then even longer to get into class. If I'm lucky, I'll make it to the second hour.

I slide into the car and crank the ignition.

The engine starts. And then promptly dies.

I frown, turn the ignition again. Same thing. It starts and then immediately snuffs out.

Fuck. I exhale and get out, pop the hood, and stare down at shit I don't understand. Nothing *seems* out of place. Not that I know much about cars. Most of my knowledge is limited to subjects that come up in college research papers.

I groan and pull out my phone.

I debate before texting Kepler, but I have a feeling he'll be texting me again in twenty minutes when I don't show up.

Actually, I'm gonna have to miss lab entirely. Car died.

My phone rings immediately.

"Where are you?" His voice is just above a whisper, and I picture him stepping out in the hallway, glasses on, class behind him through the open door. "I'll come get you."

"Aren't you *teaching*?"

"Just doing a pre-assessment. Smith can take over. We sub each other's sections all the time."

"No way, Quinn. Besides, my brother is on his way over. I'll get him to drop me off at campus."

"Then text me when you get here."

"You want me to text? No boring pictures this time?"

"Hmmm." The hum of his voice just about makes my heart clatter out of my ribcage. "I'll take both."

"That's a bit selfish."

"Absolutely."

I glance up to see Shin's black-and-white SUV pull up to the curb, and my smile falls.

"Shin's here," I say.

"Don't forget to text me."

How could I forget? It's like he has no clue what he does to me. How much he's in my head.

"I won't." I hang up because Shin is already strolling up to the driver's side door, and I shove my phone in my back pocket.

"Who was that?" Shin always seems bigger in his uniform, blue shirt puffed out from his bulletproof vest. He props sunglasses on his head as he evaluates me.

I shrug. "No one."

It's such a lie that I'm surprised that some celestial being doesn't smite me with a lightning bolt right here.

"What are you still doing here?" Shin asks, eyeing my open hood. "Car trouble? Let me look."

He does, asking me to start it as he hovers over the engine. After a few minutes he slams down the hood. "Not sure what the issue is. We'll get it towed. Has it been giving you trouble?"

"No more than usual."

He speaks into his radio, asking for a tow as he strolls back to his SUV and opens the back door. Kima jumps out and waits for her orders. When he points to the scraggly grass, she runs and squats.

"Tow truck will be here within an hour," he says when he gets the call back. "How is she?"

"She seems fine, but I've got no clue what she took." I dig out the pill bottle and hand it to him.

He twists off the cap and peers in, rattling the pills. "Looks a bit like the Molly that's been going around lately."

"Crap."

"Yeah."

"This new guy . . ." I suck in a breath. "Shit seems like it's about to get bad."

"*About* to get bad?" He pockets the pill bottle and crosses his arms over his chest. "I think we're there, brother. We've been there for a long time."

"THE FUEL LINE WAS KINKED." Two hours later, the mechanic leans heavy forearms on the desk between us. "Hard kink."

I almost laugh at *hard kink* but manage to pretend I'm an adult. "What does that mean?"

He shrugs a meaty shoulder. "Not sure. But if it were my car, I'd wonder who's been under it."

I freeze. "You mean someone *did* this?"

Another shrug. "You coulda hit something, I guess. But it was a weird kink."

A weird kink.

That's not much better than *hard kink*, but my mind is going in other directions now. The image of Fender snarling at me before he walked down the hallway flits through my head.

Although what kind of man would resort to disabling a car? That's something a pissed off teenager would do. Not a fully grown man with a fist nearly as big as my face.

Unless he's just trying to fuck with me?

I sigh. Figuring out why he'd do this shit doesn't solve the problem in front of me right now. "How much to fix it?"

"About four hundred, but I can't get the part here until tomorrow. You'll have to leave it."

I finish dealing with the mechanic and step out of the shop, glancing toward the sun that sits midday in the sky. My phone's filled with texts. Shin saying that Mom took a nap and there's nothing we can really do for her now, Dex asking if I'm coming to the fundraiser meeting later, and Kepler with a photo.

It's of his legal pad sitting on a birch wood table. Complex equations fill the yellow paper, and I assume they're related to his dissertation. A green table lamp sits on the far side of the frame. He's at the library.

Site of mind-blowing revelations and first kisses. And also a reminder that I still didn't get those professor exams for Vain.

I was completely and thoroughly sidetracked.

I smooth the pad of my thumb over the photo, like I can somehow touch him over the phone. There's a text attached too.

Call me if I can do anything to help.

10

"Christ." I'm standing outside the mechanic's shop, staring at the Jeep that just pulled up next to me.

A gunmetal-gray Jeep. But not the dinged up, dirty one that Kepler used to drive when we were younger.

This one is new. A four-door Wrangler with a lift kit, orange neoprene seats, and bar doors.

This Jeep has to cost as much as my education. Not just a semester. My *entire* five years of tuition.

And Kepler's sitting calmly in the driver's seat.

His brows go up when I don't move. My hands are stuffed deep in my pockets, backpack hanging limply over one shoulder.

"Still want that ride?" He reaches a long arm over and unlatches the bar door.

"Yeah." I keep standing there, tongue heavy in my mouth, my stomach tightening around a hard knot. "This is yours?"

He nods slowly. "Yes."

I glance around. I'm not even sure what I'm looking for or what I'm thinking. Some hint that this is an alternate reality? But all that's there is the oil spotted parking lot, wrenches clanking somewhere behind me, and my old crappy car with its faded bumper stickers parked in the open garage.

I swallow and tug the door the rest of the way open and pull myself up into the seat. I stuff my backpack at my feet, that spicy warm scent of his hitting me full force. My one-track dick responds. Heat vibrates down my spine and pools low. But for once, my mind is somewhere else.

"Is something wrong?" he asks quietly. He doesn't pull away, just sits there, right in front of the garage, not checking his mirrors or focusing on anything else. He's fixated on me, like there's nothing else in the world.

I don't even know what the fuck to say.

That complete attention from him mesmerizes me in a way that nothing else can.

"Nothing's wrong." I reach for the seatbelt and click it closed.

He rests one wrist on the steering wheel, shifting slightly so that he's facing me. Legs a few inches open, eyes a misty gray. "Then why do you look like you just ate a razor blade?"

He's right. My jaw is tense as fuck.

"I don't know," I admit, but I'm not sure that's really true. It's not that I don't know. It's more that I don't know how to put it into words.

For as long as I've known him, I'm still so lost when it comes to certain things about Kepler Quinn. It's not just the mystifying thoughts in his head. It's the basic facts: where he lives, who he lives with, what he eats in the morning, and what he does at night. And all this Jeep does is present more questions.

"How's your car?" he asks.

"Getting fixed. Can we just drive?" I nod toward the road.

"I need to get caught up on all the shit I missed this afternoon."

"Understood." But he studies me for a moment longer before finally pulling out of the parking lot.

We drive in silence. Wind filters through the open sides, the faint sound of rock music echoes through the speakers, and there's a feeling in my chest like something is about to collapse. It's only when we get to campus and he parks that I finally turn to him.

"Thanks," I say, my voice rough. There are worry lines across his forehead, but otherwise he's still. His wrist is propped on the steering wheel again, and the tie of that leather bracelet sticks straight up. His lips part, and I'm suddenly staring at that mole that turns me on for some unfathomable reason.

Fuck me. Those thin lips.

On me.

No. Stop thinking about it.

I grab my backpack, unlatch my seatbelt, and slide out.

"Jin," he says. There's a hint of urgency to my name, something that I rarely hear from him. It stops me cold.

I pull my backpack over both shoulders, grasping hard onto one strap.

He upnods me. "I'll give you a ride home later."

"Dex can get me." I shift my weight from one side to the other.

"I'm sure he can." He grabs his messenger bag from the backseat. "My offer still stands. Stop by my office hours later." He's wearing a light-blue shirt today, and a yellow Post-it sticks partway out of the pocket. Numbers are scribbled all over it in pencil.

There's always something in his tee pocket. A pencil. Glasses. A Post-it.

He follows my gaze down to it and then tugs it out, flips it over, clasping it between two long fingers.

"I was working on this when you called." His right brow hitches. "It's the secret to the future of our universe."

I huff out a laugh, despite myself. "You wrote the secret to the future of our universe on a Post-it?"

"Can you think of a better place?"

"Not really." I tip my chin toward it. "What is it?"

He tilts his head. "It's just a couple of Euler-Lagrange equations."

I frown. "I know that. The shortest distance between two points is a line."

His eyes light. "And that's a prediction, right? Every equation in physics is an attempt at predicting the future. It gets pretty abstract, but if you take this equation and expand it, it lets you predict how the systems of our universe evolve over time." He drags in a breath. "Not that it works. Complex systems are too difficult to predict. But sometimes the exercise of exploring what *could* happen brings us to a new place." He pauses. "Like you showing up at the end of my office hours so I can give you a ride home."

"That's a prediction?"

"No." He shakes his head slowly. "Just an exploration of what I hope for."

I PACE down the quiet hallway of the physics building. Worn white tile lines the hallway and a bleachy-granular scent lingers. It's almost dark, campus mostly empty, and far past Kepler's office hours. I don't know if I expect him to still be here, but he didn't text to say that he's leaving, and I don't know what to text him, so I climb the stairs up to the TA offices.

My thoughts are not smoothing out. Not through my time catching up with classes and getting started on a few essays in the library. Not as I googled "living with an addict" and stared blankly at all the shit that came up, my throat closing up until I exited the browser. I can't deal with the internet. I already know more than half of the stories will end with a funeral. I just can't handle that right now.

And my thoughts about that fucking Jeep are definitely not clarifying as I approach the door at the far end of the hall.

So why am I here? Why didn't I just text Dex?

You know the answer to that, J.

My stomach clamps tighter and harder with every step, like a star collapsing in on itself, gravity crushing down, heat blistering.

I'm torn down the middle when I knock on the door and hear his low voice tell me to enter. I step into a small, mostly bare office to find Kepler sitting behind an oak desk, one leg bent so that his heel rests on the seat, his shin pressing into edge of the desk. A legal pad rests on his thigh and he looks up at me, pencil in hand, black-framed glasses on.

"You came." A light flashes through his eyes, but it darkens as I slam the door closed behind me.

"Why didn't you tell me?" Heat burns in my chest, and my voice is loud in the tiny room that's mostly all wood with one old window held open by a physics textbook kicked up on its end.

"You're talking about the Jeep." He tosses his legal pad on the desk.

I set my feet. "Yes."

"Why? It's just a Jeep."

"No, it's not." I grind out the words. The breath in my lungs seems to press so hard against my chest that it feels clogged.

"Okay," he says thickly. He pushes back his chair and drops his foot to the floor before he stands. He takes slow steps around the desk. His arms cross over his chest as he leans back on the front edge, facing me.

I'm three feet away from him, hand clutched around my backpack strap, feet shoulder width apart, fingers trembling so hard I'm sure he can see it. But for once, I don't fucking care.

"Then what is it?" he asks softly. "If it's not a Jeep?"

"It's proof. Proof that I don't know you. *At all.*" I try to steady my breathing. "How do you have the money for that, Kepler?"

His teeth graze over his bottom lip. "Money is the issue?"

"No," I snap. I shake my head, drop my backpack onto the chair next to me, then scrub a hand over my face and blow out a frustrated breath. "It's not just money. It's that . . ." I shake my head again, trying to focus on the words that have been twisting around my brain ever since he pulled up in that Jeep. "I don't fucking *know*. You've been to my house. You know what it was like with my mom. What it's still like. You've been to my apartment and seen my shitter car. And I don't know a single thing about you. So, no, it's not about money. It's about you not letting me into anything that's about you. That Jeep today? It was a motherfucking surprise, and after fifteen years, it shouldn't have been."

He nods, but there's not a scrap of emotion on his face.

And that messes with my head even more.

Is he angry? Annoyed? Bored?

And *why* was that Jeep a surprise? It really shouldn't

have been. I mean, I noticed years ago that Kepler always seemed to have whatever he needed when he needed it. So maybe I wasn't paying attention? But it feels more like he came over to our house and hid the rest of his life away. Like he didn't want anyone else to see him.

But now I'm really fucking looking. Straight at him.

"I let you into things," he says quietly, but firmly. "I've texted you fifty-six photos. I also took you to the willow."

I draw in a breath. "Was the tree that important to you?"

"I've never brought anyone there before." He leans back farther, crossing his ankles, his legs long and lean. And my stupid dick twitches against my stupid zipper, shooting little sparks up to my stupid stomach.

There's too damn much going on in my head. Frustration. Desire. It all twists together into a funnel cloud of confusion.

"Why didn't you tell me the willow was that important to you?" I dig my hands into my hair, tightness binding in my chest, pulse thumping.

"That was before we even kissed," he says evenly. "I didn't know if you would even care that it was important to me."

"Of course I fucking care," I shoot at him. "I've cared for fifteen years, Kepler. And after all that time, I don't even know where you live. I've got no clue about your parents or where you live or *anything*. It's like you're conjured out of starlight."

His eyes darken to molten gray. "Why does it matter what the walls around me look like? What kind of vehicle I drive? All of that is material. Just packaging that doesn't—"

"*Because I need this to mean something.*" I say back, hotly, the words echoing in the small room.

And, *fuck.*

What if it doesn't to him?

What if it's just a stupid, regrettable kiss with his friend's little brother?

What if I'm a complete fucking fool?

And that's the real truth. Right there. It's not that I don't know where he lives—although I do want to know that too—or that I give a shit about what he drives. And I *see* that he's trying. That he's texting me. He told me he wanted to kiss me in the library, for fuck's sake. But I can't even start to guess what's really happening between us, and that scares the life out of me.

What if this means more to me than it does to him?

Heat rises behind my eyes, and it pisses me off that he's seeing it. That he's witnessing the whole glut of human emotion ravaging through me when he's standing there, silent and composed, as if none of this touches him.

Maybe it doesn't.

Maybe this was a huge fucking mistake.

"Just . . . let me know if you think this could mean something." I grab for the strap on my backpack, yanking it off the chair and almost upsetting it.

I turn toward the door, but I'm pulled back.

When I look over my shoulder, Kepler's clutching the other strap. I stop, staring down at his hand there, the backpack strap is a tether between us. My breath is coming in hard fits, my throat closing up.

He takes a step closer to me, still seemingly so composed. "I don't show you everything in my life because most of it isn't something I'm proud of."

"What wouldn't you be proud of?" I'm at a complete loss. He's a doctoral student with a TA position. He's ridiculously intelligent, sexy as hell, gets my brain going every time I see him, and he has a level of control that I could never hope to possess. "If anyone has a life they shouldn't be proud of, it's me."

His jaw clenches. "No. You've spent your life trying to keep your family together." A flicker of emotion darts through his eyes. Just this tiny little hint, but I'm starting to realize how much lives in those tiny flickers. How much depth he carries in every little tense of his jaw or slight parting of his lips. "You're surrounded by so much. People are drawn to you because you have so much life. I don't have that. Things are . . . empty. *I'm* empty. And I don't want you to see that."

Empty? My mouth drops open. "I've never thought of you as empty, Kepler. Never in my life have I even had a glimmer of that thought."

He shakes his head, emitting a breathy laugh with way too much sarcasm tucked in it. "You also don't think I'm off-putting, which I know for a fact is true. Maybe you're not the best judge when it comes to me."

"Maybe not, Quinn. But I gotta tell you, I like everything I see."

His shoulders stiffen. "Everything?"

"Everything." I just set the truth out there, good idea or not. "And it's *full*, not empty. There's nothing you could show me that would make me think less of you."

He clearly has no clue how much I think of him.

He runs his tongue over that thinner bottom lip. "I'm trying to let you in. Sending those pictures . . . it's new for me."

"You seem so calm about it."

"I'm not." He leans forward, a palm pressing to his chest. "I'm not calm at all. Not even a little fucking bit. And I promise you, *this means something to me*."

Standing there across from me, he comes into sharp

relief just like he always does. The office around us fades into opaque oblivion, and my eyes plaster on his bottom lip, slightly shiny from his tongue.

"Kiss me," I mumble. The words slip out, just like they did in the library, but I can't even bring myself to second-guess them as he steps closer to me, measured, controlled, and then he dips his head, his lips finding mine. Our mouths open slowly, and he reaches up, cups the back of my head, and yanks me against him, into a kiss that's almost painful in its severity. My backpack thunks on the ground as I grab for that tee, my fingers twisting in it, both of us pitching against each other.

Maybe I still struggle to read Kepler's thoughts on his face, but as soon as his tongue brushes mine, I *feel* them. Washing over me, his want, his need, the cup of his hand on the nape of my neck. It's the *way* he kisses me. With that same intensity he has when he studies me. One-hundred-fucking-percent.

Like he's thinking about a hell of a lot. How I taste. The softness of our lips. The sounds I make. The warmth of our skin.

We stumble. The chair rasps across the wood floor as my ass bumps into it. His chest is unyielding against mine. It's firm, muscular. A hard press that makes me sputter into a groan.

He's so masculine, and it's sexy as fuck. The rough edge of his jaw scrapes against my palm, and the sheer force of him shoves me back. His tongue demands entrance past my lips.

All of me pulls toward him, from lips to hands to hips to knees. They all urge forward, my pelvis moving with the remembrance of having his dick pressed against mine.

We shouldn't be doing this here.

The thought echoes in my mind even as I emit a half-moan, half-grunt against his lips. We're gasping for breath, the kiss shifting to desperate, my fingers clutching his shirt. He groans when I yank hard on the hem of his tee, kicking his pelvis forward.

"*Yes.*" *That.* I moan needy words into his mouth, releasing his shirt so I can angle my dick closer to his.

"Fuck," he mumbles, biting my bottom lip lightly and shifting back just enough to palm me over my jeans. I beg out a curse for more and he yanks at my button, tugging it open as he kisses over my chin and the slope of my jaw, his tongue liquid against the tendons of my neck. I gasp as my zipper is yanked down, and his warm palm covers my boxer briefs.

"Christ," I bite out as he cups me with a firmness that makes my eyes roll back in my head. I'm listing backwards, hardly able to stand, knees buckling, thoughts spinning.

Is this real? Is it a fantasy?

I really fucking hope it's real.

"Put your hands on the desk." The certainty in his voice drives straight down to my balls.

This has got to be a fantasy. It's too damn good to be anything else. I'm sure of it as he takes my hands and sets them behind him—on either side of his thighs—flat down on the top of the desk.

I'm hunched over to reach around him, awkward with my jeans unzipped around my hips. My dick is achingly hard and tenting my white boxer briefs.

Here in his TA office. We shouldn't be here, but right now, I don't give one single fuck.

Because it's Kepler Quinn. And that trumps everything.

He cups my dick again, and it's all I can do to stifle my groan as he slides his palm in a torturously slow stroke down the full length of me, rasping the fabric of my boxer briefs against my shaft and making my head spin. Then he lowers—breathless and unhurried—down to his knees.

He looks up at me, heat filling his smoky grays as he tugs the elastic over my dick, and I spring out almost comically between us, but I'm not laughing as he fists me.

"Perfection," he says quietly. He's still, not stroking, not moving. His breath warms the head of my cock, his angled jaw pulls tight as he stares up at me. He's unmoving except for the slow expansion of his cotton-covered chest and the almost imperceptible tightening of his fist around my dick.

Real or fantasy?

Maybe it's both.

I'm so damned turned on that my fingers are trembling against the desk, my knees wavering, my abs tightening to hard ridges as I stare down, completely mesmerized by his every movement as he rolls his thumb over my crown, already shiny with precum.

His eyes trace over me, his thumb massaging my slit. "You look even sexier when I'm on my knees."

"Christ, Quinn," I hiss out, my hips pitching forward. My wrists are turning white from my weight pressing down on the desk to keep myself standing. There's something so sexy about the way he's at ease with my dick. No one's ever thumbed my slit.

"Please . . ." I trail off, not knowing how to finish.

His brow lifts, a hint of a tease in the slight rise of his lip. "Please what?"

"I don't know," I groan. My dick twitches so hard that it hurts. "Whatever you want."

"Can you keep quiet?" His voice is close to a whisper and much, much quieter than the groan I'd let out.

"I don't know." My nostrils flare as he tips forward, his lips closing around both his thumb and the tip of my dick.

My mouth drops open, and it's all I can do just to mumble, "*No.*"

He jerks away, eyes flashing open, a flicker of surprise in them.

I shake my head. Trying to form complete sentences is more challenging by the second. "I mean, *no*, I can't keep quiet. But, *yes*, do that again. Right now. *Please.*"

One corner of his lips rise even more, and his laugh feathers over my impatient boner.

"Kepler, please just—"

In one smooth movement, he envelops me, and I let loose a string of hushed *fucks*, only stopping myself with a hard bite on my tongue. A coppery taste fills my mouth, and my muscles spasm as I fight to stop from burying myself so deep in his mouth that neither of us can breathe. I shove my palms hard against the desk and breathe through clenched teeth.

"Tell me this is real," I bite out as his cheeks hollow, pulling me deeper. He does it slowly. As deliberately as when he kneeled, as controlled as he always is, drawing it out, lingering and prolonged, and when I pitch my pelvis forward, he pulls me in even more.

Fuck me.

I have some hazy thought about never having done this with a man before, but it vanishes completely when his throat contracts around the crown of my cock, and I *shout*. It crests my lips before I can stop myself, half cut off when I realize what I've done.

We freeze. My dick's throbbing in Kepler's mouth, my breath's caged.

A door opens down the hallway. Footsteps echo. Shoes

click on the tile, like women's dress heels, getting louder as they approach.

Kepler pulls back, and cool air sends a shiver up my shaft and into my abs.

"Don't move," he mouths.

The shoes approach the door. They're *loud*. And they're not even half as loud as my shout was.

My heart launches up into my throat. The footsteps stop. A low rap echoes from the door.

Fuck, fuck, *fuck*. We're motionless, staring wide-eyed at the door. *Is it locked?*

Another pause and then the footsteps echo back down the hallway. A far-off door closes.

"Shit," I mumble, finally letting out a breath.

Kepler stands sharply and reaches around me, forearm rolling as he clicks the lock.

My eyes about bug out.

"Fuck, man," I hiss as I shove my dick in my jeans, grimacing since I'm so painfully hard. And I'm wet from his mouth and snagging on my boxer briefs. *I want to be in his mouth again.* I groan. This is so messed up. "You didn't think about locking the door *before* you swallowed me?"

"I didn't think we'd go that far," he says evenly. "What are you doing?"

"Uh . . ." I'm so swollen that I can barely get the zipper started. "Putting my dick away?"

"What if you don't?" Kepler reaches back and pinches a stack of Post-its off the desk. "Open your mouth."

I blink at him, jeans halfway zipped, dick twitching with unconcealed excitement. It doesn't give a shit that we were almost caught. "What are you talking about?"

"Open your mouth."

Holy shit. Are we still doing this?

"The door's locked," he says. "No one's coming in."

"You're a bad influence." I stand there a moment longer. This is a bad decision.

Then why doesn't it feel like a bad decision?

Because it's a fantasy. And if I don't do it, then I'm going to regret it.

I drag in a breath, and I open my mouth.

He rests the Post-it stack on my bottom lip. "Now close."

My stomach vibrates with tension. The paper dries my tongue when I clamp my lips around it.

"Don't drop it," he orders.

Fuck, that's hot. His steady confidence is like a bolt of lightning zapping right down my spine.

I nod, lips clamped on the Post-its, as he reaches out and slowly drags my zipper all the way back down, and before I can even fully register what he's doing, he fists me and takes two strokes with that measured, deliberate perfection, and then he's on his knees. He sucks on the head of my cock and then pauses, letting me be the one to push into his mouth this time, burying my dick so deep that my eyes roll back in my head.

I groan around the Post-its, keeping the sound soft, relishing the way his tongue circles my crown as he sucks me. My pelvis pitches forward eagerly, trying to fuck harder, and I'm so lost I don't know what sounds I'm making—until his fingertips graze my balls, and I'm mumbling curses. Then his warm palm cups my sack, and all hell breaks loose.

Never has someone done that before. His hand *galvanizes* me, creating a sensitivity that multiplies his mouth on my dick by a thousand, and I shove so deep that I'm pretty sure I might choke him.

He pulls back, thin lips swollen, not seeming to be

surprised by my urgent push to the back of his throat. "You like that."

I can't speak with the Post-its in my mouth. All I can do is nod and stare down at him as he cups me, rolling my balls in his fingers, roughening his movements a touch. Seeming to test me—pushing to see my limits.

I have no clue where my limits are.

Considering that I'm gripping onto a desk, a stack of Post-its in my mouth, first time with a dude, and getting sucked off in my TA's office while he fondles my balls, I'm not sure I have any limits.

At least none that are going to come roaring to the surface right now as he takes me so fast that *I* almost gag. Everything reels as his fingers shift under my balls, and then I'm clenching my teeth down on paper as he's shoving my jeans even lower so that he can smooth a finger along my taint.

I *light*, my hips jackknifing. He presses his fingers more firmly under my balls, sensations humming down into my thighs and up to my navel.

Everything disappears. The office. The need to stay quiet. Everything except for him.

I spit out the Post-it stack and it thunks on the desk.

"*Kepler.*" I can't keep his name off my lips. Or my lips off his. I rip a hand off the desk to curl it in his hair and yank his head back, then my lips find his in a messy, upside-down kiss. His mouth is warm and wet from my dick, mine dry from clamping down on that Post-it stack, and I slide my tongue roughly against his. My grip tightens on his short hair, and a deep noise filters out of his mouth, vibrating against my tongue.

He doesn't get up from his knees, and as soon as I break the kiss, he pulls my dick into his mouth again, seeming to know exactly what I want. And I don't think that's just because he's a dude. There's something else at play here—some kind of connection that goes beyond just an office bj.

Something that goes beyond fantasy.

My other hand comes off the desk, and my fingers thread through his hair as he sucks me down, my hips shifting forward and dick sliding so deep that my vision flashes white, my mouth opening, abs tightening, every part of me focused on the man below me as he takes me apart, setting a rhythm that drives me faster and threatens to shatter me with every bottomless thrust.

My release builds, heightened by his fingers along my taint, cupping my balls, and that gray gaze on me when I look down.

His eyes are *reverent*. He's the sexiest thing I've ever seen. His angled jaw is wide open to take me. His gaze simmers with a kind of warmth that's indescribable.

"Fuck," I grate as his throat muscles contract around the head of my cock.

I shallow my strokes as I pick up the pace, heat racing from his palm on my balls down to my thighs and up to my ass where a shock of nerves suddenly comes alive.

He's touching me. Fingers pressing against my hole. I only have a blink to register it before I lose myself. Fucking his mouth so fast and hard that there's no holding back.

"*I'm close.*" Before I even get the words out, I'm coming in deep, ball-trembling strokes so hard that my knees buckle, and I tip forward. His hands whip up to hold me above him, planted against my sternum as I let out ragged breaths.

Before I even get a solid footing, he's kissing me again. I groan at not just the taste of myself, but the slickness of my cum as it slides into my mouth.

Christ. He didn't swallow all of me yet. It feels so fucking dirty, and it sets me *ablaze*. He must feel it because he deepens the kiss, and I'm pawing at the bottom hem of his shirt as he rises, backing me against the door—the one we really shouldn't back up against. My jeans are down around my knees, and the full weight of him shoves me against the wood. My fingers clutch in his hair as he kisses the life out of me.

I don't know how long we kiss for. Until our lips are raw, until we have to breathe, until it's even darker outside the window, the tall streetlights clicking on and cutting through the pane. Until I believe that this is really happening. That it isn't all in my head. That there *is* something different here. The realization comes in a split second—when we're lip-locked and his hand finds mine, our fingers lacing effortlessly. *Kepler Quinn is holding my hand.*

That's when I know it's truly beyond fantasy.

It's really fucking *real*.

At least for me.

11

CAMPUS IS dark by the time we leave Kepler's office. We walk side by side down the wide sidewalk that runs along the Quad. There's a safe three feet between us, our hands in our pockets, and I'm trying my damnedest not to let my eyes linger on him.

Act cool, J.
And not like you just came in your TA's mouth.

Luckily, because I'm pretty sure I'm shit at pretending to be normal, there's almost no one around. The few people who rush past on bikes or hurry between buildings seem more caught up in their own thoughts than anything else.

Kepler nods toward the STEM faculty parking lot. "I'll give you a ride home."

Of course, he has a spot in the faculty lot.

I chew on my bottom lip as we step into the permitted lot. Even the parking spaces are bigger here.

His Jeep sits alone on the far side, deeply shadowed along a line of blue spruce.

"Do you want to drive?" Kepler pulls his messenger bag off his shoulder.

"You're kidding, right?" I scoff at him, but he shakes his head.

"No. Drive." He digs out a key fob, pushes a button that makes the Jeep unlock, and the engine starts when we're still a few paces away. He heads toward the passenger side.

I can't hold back my smile as I pull open the bar door and step up into the driver's seat. "You're all about giving me new experiences tonight, aren't you?"

His brows rise as he slides in next to me. "Am I?"

"Uh, yeah." I drag in a breath, looking across as his legs shift open slightly, and our gazes flash up and down each other, apparently both of us alerted to our nearness.

My dick still feels warm from his mouth.

Christ, this man makes me have dirty thoughts.

And I know that it's been long enough for my dick to return to normal temperature, but I still simmer in the thought, remember his throat contracting around my—

"Jin?"

"Yeah? Oh right." *He doesn't want to hear about your dick-warmth. Focus, J.* "You're the first guy I've, uh, kissed."

He looks at me steadily, no outward emotion other than a slight tightening of his jaw. "I am?"

"It wasn't completely obvious?"

"Not at all." His teeth run over his bottom lip. A hesitation. I might have missed it before, but I'm slowly figuring out those tiny facial tics of his.

I frown. "That's a problem?"

"No."

"I don't believe you, Quinn. You look like you've got a thousand thoughts in your head."

"I always have a thousand thoughts in my head." He twists fully toward me. "But I promise you, it's not a problem for *me*."

"So, you think it's a problem for me?"

"I don't know." His chest expands with a breath. "Is it?"

"Nah." I click on the seatbelt and adjust the rearview mirror, trying to focus on what I'm physically doing because the thought of Kepler going down on me again is creating a full brain spasm. "I think I'm definitely bi. It's just that, back there, when you went down on me, and I didn't, uh, return the favor—"

"It wasn't a favor." He leans closer, breath warm against my cheek. "And it's not any kind of exchange. Honestly, I didn't even think about it. I was pretty much just dialed into how perfect it was to have your dick in my mouth."

Fuuuuck. That was sexy. I want to hear him talk about my dick again.

I swallow hard. "You had to notice that I didn't go down on you."

"Yes, I noticed. But I didn't *think* about it." His fingers lightly feather against my knee as my foot settles on the gas pedal. He tracks up my thigh and stops an inch from my crotch, leaving a quake of goosebumps behind. "Whatever you're comfortable with."

I huff out a laugh. "We probably shouldn't be comfortable with any of it, considering that faculty sticker on your windshield."

And Shin.

My stomach hardens, and I glance out the back window before reversing out of the spot, hotly aware of his focus on me as I maneuver onto the narrow, one-way road that leads out of campus. A few snowflakes land on the windshield, and he flips the heater on high.

"What are you doing this weekend?" he asks.

"Uh, I've got a couple of essays to write, and then probably getting some drinks with Dex. And I promised to visit *Halmeoni*."

The orange glow of the dash lights the side of his face. "Ah, *Halmeoni*. The woman who made me not afraid to eat tofu. And who taught me to crush garlic with a hammer."

I laugh and focus back on the road. "Don't forget cleaning the vacuum in the dishwasher."

He nods. "There's not another woman on the planet like her."

I lick my lips and concentrate on the road. Kepler's Jeep drives stupidly smooth compared to my shitter car. But then, I'm pretty sure he's smoother than me in every single way. I turn onto College Avenue. The traffic here is heavier than around campus. "I'd ask you to go, if things were different."

"And I'd go," he says quietly. "Can I see you after?"

"Are you sure that's a good idea?"

"Yes."

A laugh shoots past my lips. "Are you always so certain about things?"

"Usually." He stretches out his legs as far as he can, his knees touching the glovebox. "I tend to know what I want."

I clutch the steering wheel. "Maybe we should wait, Quinn. One semester isn't an eternity, and then we . . ." I side-glance him. Would he want to wait?

Kepler taps his long fingers against my thigh. "As an answer to that question, I'd like to tell you something that no one else knows."

That gets my full attention. Fuck traffic. "Not even Shin?"

"No, not Shin," he says quietly. "It's about Virginia."

"Virginia?" I blink, trying to zero in on the road when all I want to do is turn and try to get a read on him. "The state or a person?"

"The state."

"What's in Virginia?"

"Langley Research Center."

The air sucks out of my lungs. "NASA?"

"I applied for a postdoctoral position. Evaluating data related to geomagnetic storms."

"Shit, that's what your dissertation is about."

His brows go up. "You remember?"

"Of course, I remember." A smile spreads across my face. "Christ. You're serious?"

"I haven't heard back yet." His forehead lines. "I made it through the first round of interviews, and I have an in-person interview next month. Although Smith does too—we're both up for the job. I don't know how likely it is that I'd get the position, but Lacher's my advisor, and she seems to think I've got a shot."

"That's freaking incredible. That's what you want to do after you graduate?"

"Yes." His fingertips tap a rhythm on my thigh, shooting sparks straight up into my dick. Do I always have to be hard around him? He's got no clue what he does to me. "I'd have to leave after this semester, finish up my dissertation while I'm there, and then fly back here to defend it."

"How soon after the semester?"

"Immediately."

Too soon. I struggle to process what he just told me—he's leaving Indigo Falls. Fuck it. I flip on the turn signal and pull over, parking in front of a dark optometrist's office.

Kepler keeps focused on me, not seeming to even notice that we stopped. "I don't want to wait. I can't wait. It'll be too late."

My hands fall off the steering wheel as I turn to face him, my brain in overdrive. "And we risk your potential position at NASA? That's a stupid choice, Quinn."

"No, it's not." He leans forward, only an inch because apparently I've already closed most of the distance. His lips brush softly against mine. It's not like the kiss from earlier. Or the one from the library. It's warm, and it's lingering, and it's as much a caress as a kiss, and it doesn't shift to desperate or needy or anything else. It's just a kiss.

A kiss like this is going to change things.

I want it to change things.

But I break it, leaning back only an inch, but far enough to catch my breath. "You're risking too much."

"I don't see it that way." He drags his tongue over his bottom lip. "We keep it between us. At the very least, we'll remember to lock the door."

"It's so much to risk."

"I hear what you're saying. Every word. And you're right." He dips closer. "But I'm incapable of walking away from this right now. The real question is . . . can you?"

Can I?

I open my mouth.

I think about saying *no*.

What it would feel like.

What it would sound like.

There's no fucking way I could walk away from this.

I won't.

"What about Shin?" I ask.

Kepler's lips tighten as he leans back in his seat. "I don't want to lie to him."

"Good." He shouldn't want to lie to him. But then, the thought of telling my brother makes my stomach twist up in ways that inspire nausea.

He drags in a breath. "But giving this a chance is worth it to me. I can't express how much."

I stare at him for a long minute. Is that really how he

feels? He's opaque as always. But I don't think he's ever lied to me. What if there's really something here, for both of us?

"What if we set a time?" I suggest. "Two weeks? We don't tell anyone for two weeks. And then only Shin."

Although, will Shin also keep this secret? We still have to worry about the fact that Kepler's my TA.

I scrub a hand over my face. I just don't know.

But any longer than that, and it'll feel like we're hiding shit from my brother.

Kepler drags in a breath. "Two weeks."

I hit an issue with "two weeks" as soon as I step into my kitchen to find Dex hunkered over a binder, forehead lined, pen tapping against the countertop.

I can't lie to him.

The feeling grows when he looks up, eyes pinning on me. Not in a good way.

"You better have an excuse." His words are hard, the planes of his face even harder.

What did I forget? Shit, the fundraising meeting.

"Dude, I'm sorry." I drop my backpack at the door and cross over to him. "There's no excuse. I should have been there."

Instead I was so freaking lost in Kepler that everything else went out the window.

"Yeah," he says, rapping the pen against the edge of the binder. "You said you'd be there, so you should have been there. Or called or texted or something."

"You're right." I feel like shit. He looks like he hasn't slept in a week, and his usual grin is completely missing. I've been so focused on my own stuff that I hadn't noticed. "I'll be at the next one. I promise. Give me a task before then. I'll do anything, man."

He sighs and drops his pen on the counter. "There might not even be a next meeting. Not unless we can find a venue."

I sit on the stool next to him, tugging down the zipper of my hoodie. "Still haven't found one?"

"No." He swivels to face me, leaning back in his seat, legs spread wide. "Everything big enough is booked up for weddings and shit. And I can't plan anything without a location and a date. I'm starting to think it's not gonna come together."

"It's just the venue that's holding you up?" I lean over to glance at the top page of his binder, which displays a messy list. Half the items are crossed out, and "Venue" is circled in Sharpie enough times to almost rip the paper.

He crosses his arms over his chest. "That's the sticking point. I've got donations for sixteen artists. That Eli guy really came through. Hell, I've even got donations for catered food and a band. And I've got so many people helping, and some of the kids found out, and they're beyond excited." He closes his eyes. "I'm gonna let them all down."

"No, we're not."

His eyes flash open. "This isn't something that can be solved with determination. If there's not a location, there's not a location. It's as simple as that."

"No, it's not as simple as that." I reach out for his binder, spin it toward me, and flip to the section labeled "Venues." I scan over the list. Shit, he has called a lot of places. Often more than once.

I glance up. "We'll solve this, Dex. Remember the treehouse."

The treehouse is what we always bring up when something seems insurmountable. It was the summer before fifth grade, and Dex and I decided we were gonna build a treehouse in his backyard. We convinced my dad to buy the wood and then we set out, having not a single freaking clue what we were doing, but we started with the steps up, and then the floor, and then the walls, and somehow, we just powered through.

With the help of my brother. And Kepler.

Just *thinking* his name makes my abs tighten and balls quiver.

"The treehouse." Dex smiles, dimples popping out, green eyes lighting. "Man, I haven't thought about that in a while. It's still there, you know. Roof collapsed a bit, and the ladder's missing a couple rungs."

"Maybe we should fix it?"

"You, me, Shin and Kepler." He shakes his head. "We spent so many damn nights in that place."

We did. Lying in our sleeping bags, talking about random shit, staring out the open skylight up at the stars.

Kepler was there, laughing and chatting along with us. My stomach tightens again as I think about it, going back all those years. Things were so different. Kepler used to smile. And Dad used to come out and bring us popcorn and Milkis, which is a soda he'd buy at the Korean market that Dex loved.

Sometimes it was all four of us in that treehouse. Sometimes just me and Dex.

I scrub a hand through my hair. "Did Shin and Kepler ever sleep up there? Just by themselves."

"Yeah." He nods. "All the time. Especially after."

He's talking about after my dad died. Although Shin and Kepler were seventeen then. A little old for sleepovers in the treehouse, but then, our dad had just died. Maybe it was how Shin needed to deal.

And Kepler saw him through it.

Kepler saw us all through it. Thinking back now, he actually took care of a lot of shit around the funeral, and he notified my dad's job and our family back in Korea.

"I was with Kepler." I clear my throat, not sure if the expansion in my chest right now is a sign of relief, or guilt, or just confusion. "That's why I missed the meeting."

Dex's forehead lines. "Why? Something happen?" He sits up, worry darkening his face. "Is Shin fine?"

"Shin's okay," I reassure him. "Kepler and I, well, we hooked up."

Hooked up. What a lame-ass term for what happened back there.

Dex's mouth drops open. "You're *fucking* him?"

I freeze. For so long that Dex says my name. Twice.

It probably looks like I forgot how to talk.

Fucking Kepler Quinn?

I mean, yeah, I guess we were going somewhere when he tugged down my zipper and got on his knees. But . . . *fucking*?

What would that be like? His lips on mine, his jaw tightening as he pushes into me.

Or would I fuck him?

Christ.

"No," I mumble when I realize Dex is still waiting for an answer. "I can barely get past the thought of kissing him without my brain going on lockdown."

"That's either a very good sign or a very bad one." Dex shakes his head. "Does Shin know?"

"Just you."

He breathes out. "I don't know what to say. I guess . . . it makes some kind of odd sense. Except I always thought he and Shin had a thing."

A wash of cold runs down my back. "That's not possible."

Dex flips his binder closed. "Okay."

"That's not possible," I repeat, as if that'll make him believe me. "They're friends. And Shin has never dated a guy."

"As far as you know." Dex shrugs. "But Shin never really dates anyone."

"That's true." I just keep shaking my head. "He's always said he doesn't have the time, and I've wondered if he even has the interest, but him and Kepler, that's not . . ."

I push off my seat and walk around the counter. Grab a glass and fill it with water.

"Shit, now I feel like a dick," Dex says. "I didn't mean to freak you out. I don't know anything. It was just an offhanded comment. I shouldn't have said it."

I chug down the water. "No, man, you can say anything. I'm just kinda messed in the head right now about all of it."

"Yeah, I bet." He sets his elbows on the counter. "Good thing you switched out of his class."

"Uh-huh."

His eyes widen. "You didn't?"

"Nope."

He plants both feet on the floor. "Remember that Darin guy? He got expelled."

I stiffen. "That was a professor he was fucking. Not a TA. And like I said, Kepler and I aren't—"

I can't say it. Even that sends my brain into a tittering frenzy and muddles all the words on my tongue.

"Do you think it really matters? Does he handle your grades?" Dex shakes his head, lips tightening, brow furrowing. "I've bitched at you about the essay job before, and I'm gonna do it again now. You can't take this shit lightly. You might not care about graduating, but—"

"I care about graduating."

"Do you? Like really? Because you pretty much risk it at every turn."

I chew on my bottom lip. "You've got a point. Especially about the essays. But it's . . . *Kepler*."

I let it all spill out. All the thoughts that I've had about him over the years. How confusing it's been. From standing on the roof with him, to my date with London, to trying to make sense of it all, to boring pictures, to *simkung*. All of it, just dumped on Dex's lap, and afterwards, he stares at me like I've sprouted a second head.

"Shit, I didn't know," he says. "You'd think I would have noticed. And he feels the same?"

"No." I shake my head. "There's no freaking way. It's not possible."

He frowns, rolling his pen between his thumb and index finger. "You sure about that?"

"Yeah." I nod to his venue list. "Now let's get to work."

12

I'm fit to be tied by the time London and I step into lab the next day. Heart pumping in my throat, it's an effort not to look like I'm about to jump out of my skin as we walk through the door.

I haven't seen Kepler since the Jeep ride home. We've been sending those photos. Sometimes twenty a day now, back and forth, and I smile every time I get one. We talk too—late at night, his voice low in my ear.

But I haven't *seen* him, and you wouldn't believe how hard *simkung* hits when I take him in, standing by a small desk in the far corner of the lab room. I'm pretty sure my knees are gonna buckle.

He's sorting through a stack of papers, black-framed glasses on, and that soft gray t-shirt stretched across his shoulders.

I plow right into the back of London as he stops and nods toward two empty seats close to Kepler's desk. "Sit over there?"

"Nah," I say. "Farther back?"

"Sure."

We take seats at the long, black table that cuts down the middle of the room. There's only twelve of us.

And Kepler.

Be cool, J.

It's impossible. When he glances up from the folder that he's flipping through, smoky eyes flicking from London and pinning onto me, a vibration simmers low in my gut.

I get a flash of his lips around my dick, his palm cupping my balls, then of me sucking my own release off his tongue. And then in the Jeep, him telling me about NASA before that perfect kiss.

Images pulse through my head, like a faucet suddenly turning on.

Is he thinking about it?

London says my name, and Kepler coolly shifts his attention off me.

There's a little crunch in my chest at the way Kepler just goes right back to reading that folder.

I shouldn't feel that way. He shouldn't be looking at me.

But damn if my neck doesn't heat as we pull out our notebooks, and I take steady breaths, trying to calm the pulse in my throat.

London pushes his notebook toward me. "You can copy the notes from last time."

"Thanks, man. I appreciate it." I grab his art-covered notebook and flip it open when I *feel* Kepler behind me. I'm not even sure how I know it's him, I just do. Maybe that slight scent of omija and spice and cotton. Maybe the pacing of his footsteps or the cadence of his breath.

Maybe I'm just so attuned to him that it's instinctual.

Kepler sets a lab syllabus down next to me, his fingers not three inches from my forearm. "You missed this from last class."

His breath brushes my cheek, and my body responds: my balls and abs tighten, my palms become clammy, and my wrist band cuts into my skin as I make a fist to keep my fingers from reaching out toward him.

How am I going to do this? Lab is *two hours* long. And it hasn't even started yet.

I clear my throat. "Thanks," I tell him, trying to make it sound off-handed and like I'm not thinking about the way his tongue carved around mine.

"Let me know if you need any help." His words are so smooth, but he swallows sharply before he steps away.

He feels it too.

He sidesteps away from me, and I'm so freaking aware of the distance between us as he hands a piece of paper to the girl next to me. Then he passes behind me and strolls back up to the front of the class, that outline of his wallet in his ass pocket taunting me.

Lab begins and he goes over the work we're expected to do.

People ask questions.

He answers them.

I have no clue what's going on. I'm so damn hard that I'm about to rip through my jeans, my Adam's apple feels so big that I don't know if I could actually talk around it, my pulse pounds, the pen in my hand is slippery from my damp palms.

To make it even more awkward, we're jammed at this table, my elbow four inches from bumping into a pink-sweatered girl.

We've got to be at least halfway through class. Right? Maybe an hour more and then I can cover this hard-on with my notebook, like a damn middle school kid, and get out of here.

I tug out my phone to glance at the time and can't help the frustrated groan that comes out.

It's been fifteen minutes.

Fifteen minutes.

How the fuck am I going to make it through two hours?

It gets easier when we start a lab on the specific heat of a metal. At least I've got something to focus on as I slowly heat a beaker of water on the heating pad, and London drops the lead shot we're measuring into a test tube.

I'm supposed to grab the test tube with clamps and submerge it in the boiling water, but the tremble in my fingers is making it difficult.

"Here." London takes pity on me and grabs the clamps.

"Sorry," I mumble. "I'm just nervous, I guess."

His low laugh is warm, and he wrinkles his nose, the hoop in it moving as he does. "Boiling water makes you nervous?"

"It's a debilitating problem." I smile. "You should see me try to make spaghetti."

"Then you're going to make for an interesting lab partner."

I pull the lab report toward me. "I'll take the notes." I scan over the rest of the lab. "And do all the calculations? I'm pretty decent at math."

His smile widens. "Deal. We're going to make a good—"

"Crap," the girl hisses as something thunks against the table just behind me.

Glass shatters, the sound unmistakable as I turn, and something sharp digs into my neck.

"Crap, crap, crap," she's saying.

Water runs over the table, shards of glass littered everywhere. I reach up and feel the back of my neck and come away with blood.

Everyone is backing up, stool legs screeching against the floor, voices rising.

Before I can blink, Kepler is there, guiding the girl away when she tries to pick up the glass with her bare fingers.

"Don't touch it." He palms her shoulder, voice calm and firm. "We'll clean it in a second. Let's get everyone out of the way and fixed up first."

He's in complete control of the situation. Which doesn't surprise me at all.

Once he's got her and her partner back from the table, he scans the room, his face paling when he gets to me.

"You're bleeding." He points toward the sink along the far wall. "Get to the sink. I've got some Band-Aids."

"Oh God," the girl mouths, her eyes saucers. "Are you hurt?"

I shake my head. "It's nothing."

"Get to the sink," Kepler repeats, stronger this time. Pupils flaring slightly, lips curving down.

I'm surprised how easy it is for me to read those tiny facial tics of his. But I see it clearly: he's worried.

I don't think he needs to be. It's hardly more than a scratch.

But I slip off my stool, careful to step around the glass, as Kepler instructs London to oversee the cleanup. Kepler gives specific instructions, then he follows me to the sink and pulls open a cabinet before grabbing some paper towels.

"It really is nothing." My voice is throaty and full of gravel as he wets a towel. He reaches out and presses it lightly to the side of my neck.

"I need to make sure." The damp paper towel is cool, his smoky eyes simmering over me, along my neck and arms, then down, a beat of a look at where I'm obviously rock-hard under my zipper.

The pitch of his chest is unmistakable, but his attention flicks back to my neck. He pulls away the paper towel, his fingers still lingering an inch away, his lips parting softly, that bottom thinner one slightly damp.

He must have run his tongue over it.

Kiss me.

Christ.

Wrong place.

My back is to the rest of the room, but I hear movement behind me. The clinking sound of glass, which they must be cleaning up.

Kepler grabs a clean paper towel and presses it to my neck.

"Go out with me," he whispers. "On a date. This weekend."

Did I hear him right?

I swallow. "We shouldn't talk about this here."

His almost-smile is faint, that mole drawing my attention. "If you want me to stop talking about it, all you have to do is say yes."

"Kepler," I hiss.

He dots the towel against my neck again. "Say yes."

Who am I kidding? Is there even a slim chance I'm going to say *no*?

So, I just do it. I look across at my physics TA and say, "Yes."

"Perfect." He pulls the paper towel away, his thumb brushing just under my chin. "The cut isn't deep. Thank fuck, that scared me."

"Told you I'm fine."

"You're more than fine," he whispers. "I'd say breath-catchingly sexy."

Holy shit. Did he just really say that? I'm at a loss for words.

He lets his hand fall. "You can go back over to your station. I'll help clean up after I wash up."

"Yeah, okay." I swallow hard, and it takes every bit of effort to drag myself back a step.

He drops the paper towel in the hazardous bin and turns to the sink. I cross back over to London, that strip of skin along my neck cool and tingling.

"Everything cool?" London asks, his lips pursing slightly.

"Yep, good." I pull back my stool so it's out of the water dripping off the table.

The lab pair next to us works to mop up, and the girl whose beaker broke asks repeatedly if I'm okay. I reassure her until we finally sit back down and return to the lab.

We're getting the water heated up again when London leans closer to me. "You need to be more careful."

I blink. "With the lab?"

"No. With the lab instructor."

Fuck. "You saw?"

"It's painfully obvious." He turns our burner up. "If you want to hide it, then you need to do better."

London's right.

Dex is right.

I don't always do the right thing in any given situation, but it seems like I'm on a downward roll lately.

Still, there's no way I'd say no to this date with Kepler. I'm a glutton for punishment.

I stir my watercress soup, not hungry, which is a rare event. I've been hunkered over my iPad for the last couple of hours, finishing up some proofreading jobs and dropboxing them back to their owners all fixed up and pretty.

It's boring work, so when the deadbolt flips, I perk up.

Dex strolls into the kitchen. "We're going out."

I look over at him. "Do I have a choice?"

"Nope." He drops his bag on the counter.

"Cool. Let me take a quick shower."

I get up to dump out my soup, but Dex points to it. "You gonna eat that?"

I slide it across to him. "What's the occasion?"

"Brady and I aren't fucking anymore." He hunkers down over the bowl as I grab him a fresh spoon. "This smells good."

I frown, leaning back against the counter. "Wanna talk about it?"

"Nope." He slurps a spoonful. "I want to get laid."

"Alright," I say, nodding in agreement even though there's not a shred of conviction in his voice. "Then let's go out."

An hour later, shots in hand at a packed bar, it's pretty obvious that Dex is bummed about the situation with Brady. Not broken, but definitely bummed.

We'd picked up London and swung by Taverns, which is the closest thing to a gay bar in Indigo Falls. It's more like an "anything goes" bar with a packed dance floor, a million dark corners, and this feeling like everyone's been shaken up and suddenly let out of a box. Dex and I have been here a handful of times. London too, apparently, since he knows the bartender. It's always an interesting time.

Dex sways a touch as he lifts his shot and yells over the music. "To hot guys with hotter dicks." He pauses, eyeing his shot. "But not to the jerks. To the ones you can fucking *trust*."

He smiles when we cheers, but it doesn't quite reach his eyes. He also hasn't talked to a single person outside of London and me tonight, so the getting laid thing isn't gonna work out for him. Which is probably good because he'll likely need someone to look after him tonight.

You'd think that would bother me considering everything with my mom, but it's entirely different with Dex. I'm not saying it's healthy to drown your problems in shots, but he's never *needed* it like my mom does. Tomorrow he'll wake up, curse his headache and dry mouth, and then do the shit that he needs to do and get on with his life. Nights like this are rare.

I throw my shot back, grimacing along with him and London.

Theirs are tequila with a lime chaser. Mine is straight lemon juice. All the kick, none of the liquor. I've already had two tequila shots, so I'm at my two-drink limit.

Dex slams his empty shot on the bar and then turns to palm my shoulder, leaning close enough that the smell of tequila swamps me. "You get me, J. You're the best fuckin' friend a guy could ask for."

I shake my head. "I don't know about that."

"No." He slips off his stool and catches himself with a foot planted awkwardly on the floor. "You're the best. I luv ya, man." He twists toward London, clasping his other hand on London's shoulder. "I luv *both* of you. You came out with me tonight. I don't know what I woulda done at home alone. Besides stare at my dick wishing that it had a friend." Dex sways, tugging on both of us. "Maybe a hot jock. I could do a hot jock." He grins at us. "Man, I luv you guys. I've got the best fucking friends."

"We love you too, dude." I laugh. It's about time to get him home.

Dex has always been a love-everyone kinda drunk, which is who he is at his very core. But he's also an oversharer.

London's laughing too. "You're a good man, Dex."

"I am?" Dex beams like the sun just came out. "Hey, there's Shin!"

No freaking way.

My head whips around, eyes fixing on my brother. And then, because I can't help myself, I immediately zero in on the man standing next to him.

My breath shallows, my stomach knots. That reaction taking me full force. Except it's worse than usual, because my dick seems to remember that good things can happen when Kepler Quinn is around, and it's had two tequila shots, so it jumps to attention, thickening so fast against my zipper that I let out a grunt.

Dex lets go of our shoulders and crosses the room with fairly direct steps toward where Shin and Kepler lean against the bar, chatting with the bartender.

Shin notices Dex first, his lips parting in a smile as he takes in my grinning and obviously liquored up best friend. Dex pulls my brother into a hug, slapping him on the shoulder and saying something loudly in his ear.

Probably that he loves him.

Then he reaches over and fist bumps Kepler.

Who isn't looking at Dex at all.

Kepler stands, one hand flat on the bartop, the other held out a little too long for Dex's fist bump, thin lips parting as he says something, but his smoky gaze is fixed on me. His fist falls and releases, his palm brushing the thigh of his jeans.

I need to go over and talk to my brother, but I can't seem to unstick myself. I'm in another freaking world. One that's all Kepler Quinn. His hair is slicked back to reveal that high forehead, and he's wearing this zippered leather jacket with a gray knitted hood that shows off the tall, lithe lines of his body. He's sexy as fuck.

Sexier than fuck. Because of all those thoughts flashing through his eyes and the bold confidence that oozes from him.

I suddenly feel a bit lacking, which isn't a common thing for me. Except Kepler's not looking at me like I'm lacking. *At all.* Smoky eyes pin on me, tongue just wetting his bottom lip, that hand leaving his thigh to subtly adjust himself.

Fuck me.

London steps in front of me. "Is that your brother?"

"Hungh, what? *No.*" I blink, then realize London's tipping his head toward Shin. "Oh, yeah. Shin. My brother, yeah. Shin and Kepler are best friends, but Shin doesn't know about Kepler and me."

London shakes his head, emitting a low scoff. "I'm starting to pity you."

"Yeah, me too."

"Here's the plan." He raps his knuckles against my chest. "We'll say hello to your brother, and then we'll make the excuse that we need to get Dex out of here. Which is the truth. He's looking a little unstable now, and I don't fancy trying to carry him."

I nod and suck in a deep breath. Which only seems to supply blood and oxygen to my dick because nowhere else is getting it. "Sounds good. Thanks."

"Don't mention it." He turns and strides over to them. I'm right on his heels, forcing the easiest smile I can muster. He holds out a hand for Kepler to shake.

"Hey, bro." I stop next to Shin, keeping my attention on him. "Didn't know you came here."

He stiffens, broad shoulders widening. "Surprised to see you here too."

"Well, yeah, uh . . ." I nod toward Dex. "We needed to get out."

"Fuck, yeah, we did." Dex is grinning, seeming genuinely happy for the first time tonight.

I steel myself and turn, because it would be weird if I didn't, to greet Kepler.

"Quinn." I upnod him, that vibration humming at the base of my spine.

"Jin," he says, voice low, elongating my name like he always does, and a full-on volcano bursts low in my gut. I'm rock hard, struggling to breathe, and standing right next to my brother.

Kepler tugs down the zipper of his jacket, revealing a plain white tee stretched tight across his chest and abs. I rip my eyes away and focus on my brother.

"You're not working tonight," I say to Shin.

"No." He frowns, glancing around the packed bar. "We played some *Call of Duty* and then decided to get a beer. I've never been here before. It's . . ."

He trails off, and I turn to follow his line of sight to where two guys are going at it on the dance floor, hands all over each other, open-mouthed kissing with full-on tongues.

Shit, that's hot.

"Good," he finishes as he turns back at me.

I look harder at Shin, trying my best to focus around the lava pulsing in my veins. I can't really parse out what my brother's saying. There's a thick belt of tension between us, but I don't know if that's just the usual tension or if it's edged with something more.

He seems uncomfortable. Is it because of me? Because of this bar?

"It's a laid-back place," I say, trying to keep the conversation easy. "No judgments. People come to blow off some steam."

"Is that why you come here?" Shin's brow lowers as he gives me a serious, cop-like once-over. My muscles stiffen, unease flickering through me.

Something's up with him.

And Kepler and I are lying to him.

Guilt bores through my veins, like a thick sludge weighing me down. I don't want to lie to Shin. Things are uneasy enough between us, but there's no way that telling him the truth would make things easier.

It takes every ounce of my willpower not to glance over at Kepler.

Pretend he's not there. Pretend that I'm not thinking about how we could be stepping onto that dance floor, Kepler's tongue delving into my mouth like the dudes who don't seem to give a fuck, his dick grinding against my zipper as we move to the music, his palm splayed on my ass, the spice of omija berries on my tongue and in my nose. Right here in public, out in the open for anyone to see.

Christ. *Focus.*

"Sometimes," I answer Shin's question vaguely, not fully remembering what he asked. I jump when London's hand settles on my shoulder.

"Probably time to get out of here." London gives me a pointed look.

"Yeah." I clear my thick throat, leaning over to punch Dex on the bicep. "You ready, man?"

Relax. Be cool.

"In a sec," Dex says, and then starts telling a story about the last time we were here and how I hooked up with a girl in the back alley. *Shit.* He better not start talking about me and Kepler. Luckily, London cuts him off, and my brother's voice echoes somewhere over my shoulder as the three of them break into a small circle a couple of feet away. I have no idea if they're still talking about me, but I trust London to direct the conversation to something safe.

London's becoming a damn good friend.

I swallow when I realize it's just Kepler and me by the bar now. We're two feet away from each other, the space between us thick with silence. He doesn't seem to give a shit about whatever story they're telling. His hand is flat on the bartop, that leather bracelet tied around his wrist, just above the cuff of his jacket. The knot had brushed against my thigh when he was down on his knees in his office.

I *want* him. On his knees again, right fucking now.

Or me on my knees?

He leans closer to me, omija filling my nose and tickling down my throat as his breath feathers my ear, and I bite back a groan.

"Are we still on for this weekend?" he whispers, voice tight, and I know what he's really asking.

Did this just change things?

The reality of what we're doing just slapped both of us across the face. Guilt like a Mack truck.

This isn't a fucking game.

And Shin's going to be . . . I have no idea what he's going to be, but the thought of him finding out curls my stomach.

Shit's already tense with my brother. What if this makes things worse?

But I'm an asshole—because Shin being bothered by it

doesn't change my answer. I have never, in my life, responded to anyone the way I respond to Kepler Quinn. It's beyond fantasy, beyond logic. He was right in the Jeep, I *can't* turn away from this.

I'll regret it for the rest of my life if I do.

"Yeah," I say. "We're still on. And, uh, I gotta tell you something."

I hesitate, nerves flicking hard. We said we weren't going to tell anyone, and then I went and told Dex. Is that gonna piss Kepler off?

His brows rise at my hesitation.

"I, uh, kinda told Dex," I say. "I couldn't not. But I'm sorr—"

"It's fine," he cuts in.

I blink. "You sure? Because we agreed and then I just went and told him anyway."

He tilts his head. "You needed to tell him. I'm glad you did."

I don't know what to say. I'm not well versed in relationships considering that I've never had all that much interest in one before Kepler. But don't they usually come with more arguing when one half of them goes rogue on an agreement?

"It's that easy?" I ask.

"Yes." He sounds so *certain*, and it makes me want to step closer to him and kiss him like we did in the Jeep. Soft and open, sensual—a caress.

But I can't do that. I glance over my shoulder at where Dex is talking loudly, telling a story to London and Shin with big hand gestures.

And then I back away from Kepler because one more millisecond of standing this close to him and I won't be able to resist. I'll drag him down by the nape of his neck, bruising those thin lips with a hard kiss, shoving him back against the bar, and grinding our pelvises together. I won't care who's watching.

Somehow, I make my feet move. My dick's so hard it aches with every step. I say goodbye to my brother, not fully registering whatever we say, and then Dex is chatting about something on the way to the door.

I step outside, the cool air prickling goosebumps over the back of my neck, and I twist back, a quick glance over my shoulder, as the door swings shut.

Shin's taking a seat next to Kepler at the bar. Both pivot on their stools to face each other, and Kepler's long fingers reach out to grasp a dark bottle of beer off the bartop. My brother laughs at something Kepler says. It's an easy laugh, a big laugh. One that I rarely see.

Their friendship is palpable. I can feel it from all the way out here on the street. There's a tether between them. Something they've both relied on over the years. Something they value.

The same way I value Dex. Because a friendship like that —like theirs, like Dex and mine—should *never* be taken lightly.

Then the door swings shut, and because there's nothing else I can do, I jog to catch up with London and Dex.

13

Gravity
Noun
1. a force caused when the mass of physical bodies attract each other

I AVOID Kepler on campus for the rest of the week.

There's a difference between taking a risk and being stupid. I'm not sure which side of the line we're on—probably the stupid side—but I do care about my education, even if I don't know what I'm going to do with it. And Kepler cares about his. He didn't get to be valedictorian or a PhD candidate without a pretty intense level of care.

And we both care about Shin.

The days until we tell him are counting down.

Kepler shows up at my door on Saturday just after five, which is two hours earlier than I expected him, so I'm still in my sweats and stuffing half an orange into my mouth when I answer the door.

"Shit," I choke out around the orange, not very elegantly. I glance down at the other half in my left hand and then back up at him. "What are you doing here?"

He steps one foot back, his hand going up to the back of his neck. "I should have texted."

"No." I scrub my free hand over my bare chest, grazing over my nipple piercing awkwardly, and swallow the rest of the orange, which hurts like hell going down. "I mean, yeah. Texting is fine. But showing up is good too. I didn't mean to curse at you. I'm just . . ." I gesture down to myself. "Kinda sweaty."

"I noticed." His eyes sail over my pecs, lingering on the piercing, and then down to my stomach, all my abs, to my dick, then carving back up over the ink along my obliques. It's the most blatantly sexual once-over I've ever experienced.

It's *hot*. 'Cause it makes me feel pretty hot.

I shake my head, a smile spanning my face. "*Dude.* You trying to memorize me?"

But I'm doing the same thing because Kepler Quinn is standing in my doorway, hair damp from a shower and slicked back, freshly shaven, wearing a pale-blue button-down that brings out his eyes, and dark wash jeans. A faint waft of minty aftershave and omija makes my mouth water.

He dressed up for our date.

That tiny fact hits me hard. There's only one more week before we tell Shin, and this date feels like the biggest test of all. If this thing between us really matters. If we're actually *doing* this.

Three feet and a doorframe stand between us, and I can feel every molecule in the air right now. Charging, bonding, colliding.

I clear my throat and step back. "Come in, man. It's getting weird now."

More like I'm approaching the stupid line again, and I'm ready to plaster myself against him in the hallway where anyone could walk by. There aren't a ton of college students in our building, but all the ones who live here are townies and know us both.

He nods and takes a firm stride inside. He tips toward me after he closes the door and gives me a soft kiss like it's the most natural thing in the world.

His hands don't reach for me, just the brush of his lips before pulling back. "I came to ask you a question."

"Shoot."

"You've got two options. One is that I made reservations at a tapas place over in Rustic. Candlelit, back corner table, highly unlikely that we'd see anyone we know there."

Romantic.

I like that.

"Okay," I press when he pauses. "The other option?"

"Second is . . ." He hesitates, tongue sliding over his bottom lip as he seems to think about it. "Well, I got a call an hour ago. My uncle runs classes at an observatory, and he can't make it in tonight, so he needs a substitute. It's a drive, and—"

"An observatory? Like an actual observatory?"

"Yes."

I'm staring at him in complete disbelief. "Option two, man. All the way."

That almost-smile flits to his face before fading just as quickly. "It's volunteering for a session with kids."

"I love kids."

"It's a ninety-minute drive. We'd have to leave right away."

"Just let me take a quick shower."

"And we'd have to pack up at the end, so we'd be pretty late getting back."

I pause. "Are you trying to talk me out of it?"

"No." His brows go up. "Not at all. I want to take you. I'd hoped to take you." His hands sink into his pockets. "My grandfather helped build the observatory, and I thought you'd like to see it but figured we'd wait until later, seeing as I usually just crash there."

"In the observatory?"

"No." He shakes his head. "With my aunt and uncle. They aren't actually my blood relatives, but I've thought of them like that. They were my grandfather's partners when he was younger."

"His romantic partners?"

"Yes."

"Holy shit, Quinn, you have never told me so much about your life as you just did in the last ten seconds."

His eyes narrow on me. "I thought that's what you wanted."

"It is. But next time, warn a dude first." I cup the other half of the orange in my palm, forgetting for a moment that I'm a sweaty mess just back from the gym. "Saturn is at opposition tonight." Meaning it's at the most visible.

"Yes, it is." That almost-smile returns. "Do you want to crash there?"

"Uh..."

Yes.

Fuck yes.

Absolutely fucking *yes*.

I itch at my chest. "I don't want to intrude."

"No intrusion."

"You mean, with your aunt and uncle?"

"Yes." He nods, that mole shifting up. Why do I like that mole so much? "Although we wouldn't be in their house. It's slightly more private than that."

"What do you mean?"

He shrugs a shoulder. "It's better as a surprise. Are you in?"

"You bet. Just let me shower. And I, uh, got something for you." I point at a brown paper bag that's on the arm of the couch, and then feeling awkward as hell, walk over to pick it up and cross back to him, holding it out. "I guess I should have wrapped it or something."

"You didn't have to." He takes it from me carefully.

"Just open it."

He uncrinkles the top of the bag and peers inside, he's still for a moment, and then he reaches in and pulls out a keychain.

I suddenly feel really fucking stupid. "I know you've got a fob for your Jeep, and you probably don't need a keychain, I just..."

He holds it up. A little ball dangles on the end of a silver chain: a tiny likeness of the sun, a solar flare shooting off it. It's bright orange, like the seats to his Jeep. And the orange in my hand, I guess.

"You got me a solar flare," he says quietly, eyes fixed on it.

"Yeah, I did."

He keeps staring at it, hand raised, and keychain swinging like a pendulum. That almost-smile graces his lips, and then it expands, spreading across his face as he glances up.

Kepler Quinn is smiling at me with a kind of delight I haven't seen on him in years.

My damn heart grows in my chest, filling it up, closing my throat.

There's nothing that prepares me for what he looks like when he smiles. It's so *genuine*.

I swallow hard. "It's just a little thing. Like I said, you probably don't need a keychain for your Jeep—"

"I'll put my observatory keys on it." He flips it over, tucking the ball part in his palm, still smiling. "Thank you."

"You're welcome." I hook a thumb over my shoulder. "Gonna go shower."

NINETY MINUTES with Kepler in his Jeep is one of the best parts of my week.

I'm not joking. It ranks up there with that bj in his office. Okay, maybe slightly below. But, still, we get to talk for the entire drive.

And even though his thumb rolls up my thigh more than once, and I'm pretty sure he's teasing me, *and* I'm half hard for the entire trip and wondering if we could pull over for just a few minutes, we end up talking for the full ninety minutes. He tells me about his dissertation, and I can't pretend I understand half of it, but his intelligence lights me up, so much that I actually mumble a "that's hot" in the middle of his explanation about nanokelvin temperatures.

He hitches a brow. "Actually, it's pretty damn cold," he deadpans, and I'm grinning.

The Kepler Quinn I had in my head for all these years is different from the reality. I'd held him at a distance, *simkung* beating so hard I wasn't able to notice the rest of him. The *real* parts.

Like how he tells me that he was raised by his grandfather, who was an inventor that focused on green energy. That he died when Kepler was sixteen, a year before my dad, which explains why Kepler knew how to help with my dad's funeral. I also learned that he's an only child, and he lives alone, and I get a peek into what he meant by "empty" that evening in his office.

Not him, but it feels like his world has a lot of vast space in it.

That genuine smile crosses his face again when he talks about heading to see his aunt and uncle, Flora and Adelard, after we're done at the observatory, and he gives them a quick call to let them know we've made it to town safely.

We pass the elevation sign for Rustic and Kepler slows down, taking a smaller highway off the main one. This one winds up a steep incline, cutting between lodgepole pines that only give way intermittently.

We're at a higher elevation, across a valley from Indigo Falls, where there's very little population and low light pollution for the observatory. There's only the Jeep's headlights as we bump along the path, when the trees suddenly give way to a hill rolling up. At the top is a domed white building on a cement block base.

I suck in a breath, excitement zipping through me. "You weren't kidding."

Kepler laughs as he parks around the back. "Did you think I was?"

"I had some doubt, Quinn," I tease him. "I thought you might lure me out here for dubious activities."

"Well, that's still a possibility." He winks at me before he slides out of his seat, and damn, that gets my brain churning as we walk around the side of the building, gravel crunching under our feet, and pause at the door while Kepler digs keys out of his pocket, new keychain attached.

I tighten the leather band around my wrist, my eyes trailing over his ass in those dark jeans and the way his shoulders expand under the fabric of his shirt.

Christ, I'm attracted to him. A balls-deep, nerves-spiking kind of attraction, which is not new information to me, but next time, *I* need to act on it. In his office, it was all him going down on me. But if we're gonna do this, really do this, then it can't always be that way.

I don't want it to be that way. I want to be all in.

"Stay here for a second," Kepler says as he opens the door.

Inside is pitch-black, and I can't see shit as Kepler relocks the door behind us. He moves around, and then the lights flick on.

My mouth drops open at what's in the center of the room.

"Christ," I croak out.

A small smile crests his lips as he clicks on the last of the lights and motions me toward the telescope that takes up the bulk of the room. "It's got a 94-inch fused silica mirror. Weighs more than 140 tons."

The tube must be at least eight feet tall.

"It's a beast," I say, taking a step toward it, my head tilted back because the telescope sits on a platform.

Kepler grins. "His name's Clyde."

I laugh, feeling lighter than I have in a long time. "Sexy."

He raises a brow, leaning down for one of those quick kisses. "It is."

And he's right. Although not about the telescope.

"Wait until you see this." Kepler crosses the room, grabs something that looks like a drone remote off a computer desk, and then flicks a switch on it. The dome above us seems to rotate before a crack appears, steadily growing wider, until a third of the dome is open to the night sky.

So many damn stars up there. So many other places.

I'm so taken with the view, staring up with my head tilted back, that I don't notice him approaching until his hands slide over my shoulders from behind. And that's all it takes, I'm turning to kiss him, hands coming up to position his face exactly where I want it. He pulls in a surprised breath, right in the middle of our kiss, and that only gets me going more. I'm grabbing at him, palms grazing down his back to the rougher fabric of his jeans, and then around, cupping over his zipper, and he lets out a murmured curse.

"Jin," he breathes out. His forehead drops against my shoulder as I rake my palm up and down the front of his jeans. He's hard.

I do that to him. That's a mind-fuck.

"We have ten minutes at the most," he says quietly.

Christ, this is it. Right here, right now. I didn't plan for this to happen when we only have ten minutes.

Before I think too much, I tug open the top button of his jeans. "Then you better come fast."

"*Fuck*." He grits out the word as I pinch his zipper pull. "What are we doing exactly?"

"I'm taking control."

"Are you?" He looks up, that sexy-as-fuck smile tipping up the corner of his lips. I'll never get tired of that smile.

I drag in a deep breath, fingers squeezing the little metal pull so hard it'll leave an impression. "Yeah."

His pupils flare. "Then get on with it."

Okay, so . . . I'm nervous. Flutters light in my stomach, my breath shallowing. I focus on the physical. Step one: pulling down on his zipper. I use two hands for step two: tugging down his jeans. He watches me, eyes pinned to my face, tongue running over his bottom lip. I drop my gaze to my fingers, heart thumping hard.

Step three: I slide one hand over the front of his boxer briefs. He's hard as fuck, thick against my palm. *Christ, that's hot.* My balls tighten. Saliva pools in my mouth.

Go all in, J.

I take a breath and then trail my thumb across to the waistband of his boxer briefs. I tug them down. *Holy fuck.* His dick's beautiful. Smooth and long, thick with blood and bending out toward me. A shot of electricity jolts up my spine, my eyes about bugging out. I close a fist around him.

His lips part. "That feels good."

"Yeah, I bet it does," I say. I bite on my bottom lip thinking that sounded really freaking stupid. And I'm not even stroking him, just standing there, his dick in my sweaty palm.

His laugh is soft, making his abs clench and his cock vibrate. "We don't have to do anything more than this."

He's so at ease, and that helps me relax a bit.

I clear my throat. "Didn't I just tell you that *I'm* taking control?"

"You did."

"So then let me do it."

"Go on then."

"Okay." I flash a smile, more saliva pooling in my mouth as I stare down at his dick fisted in my hand. *This is it.* I slowly stroke up, mesmerized by the way his dick looks in my hand, by the way he twitches, his head swelling.

He stands there, not touching me, but his breath hitches as my thumb brushes against the smooth rounded head of his cock.

"So, I'm gonna suck your dick now." Shit, I don't know

why I said that. This is probably the least sexy bj he's ever had.

Tension ricochets across the top of my shoulders. Am I messing this up?

I look up. His tongue wets his bottom lip, his gaze fixed on me as he nods slowly. It's all heat and electricity between us.

He's into this.

Even if I am making it awkward.

I drop to my knees and blow out a breath. The puff of air must brush him because he shivers.

Here goes. All in.

I lean forward and lick over his crown.

Holy fucking fuck.

The taste of him explodes in my mouth. Salty and slick, warm flesh, and so damn potent that it takes over my senses. I dip my head and lick again, a deep eagerness simmering through me. I pull back to stare at the bead of precum that wells out, like I've never seen a dick before.

But it feels like I haven't. Not really.

Fuck me. He's hot. Really, really fuckin' hot.

"Jin," he groans softly. His jaw tightens as I touch the tip of my tongue to that bead.

Fuuuck. I want more. In one desperate move, I swallow his dick deep into my mouth, the weight and girth of him thick against my tongue, his taste simmering all the way to the back of my throat. He utters a string of fucks, thighs tightening so hard it pulls the waistband of his boxer briefs tight across his balls.

I grip the base of his shaft, stroking as I suck him, trying to do a good job at it, but my thoughts are stuttering. All I can think is *this is so freaking hot.* And I'm *into* it. I'm a dumbass for this being my first time going down on a guy.

Not just any guy.

I startle when his fingers tangle in my hair, a ragged breath coming out of him as he tugs lightly on my head, making me take him deeper. My mouth thickens with saliva, and my tongue slides up and down the bottom of his shaft even as he pushes in deeper.

It's messy. Spit is everywhere. My hand's not always finding the same rhythm as my mouth. And in the back of my head, I'm positive this is the most inelegant bj he's ever had, but then when I look up, our eyes snag on each other, and all the worries rush away.

He's tall and lean above me, and his pupils flare as I suck him to the back of my tongue, his abs and thighs so tight that he's trembling. At the sight of him, I groan around his dick, creating a vibration that makes his fingers curl into my scalp. And then he's fucking me, carefully, with controlled strokes. Our eyes never leave each other as he drives steadily into me, finding our rhythm together, his dick seeming to get even thicker and heavier in my mouth with every thrust.

It turns into pure need, buzzing all around us, snapping like electricity and shooting in rivulets down to my dick and everywhere in—

"*Fuck.*" Kepler freezes, the tenor of his tone making me do the same. That wasn't a turned on "fuck."

Faintly, I hear tires on gravel.

I pull off him, my lips feeling stretched, my tongue thick. "Christ, we have bad timing."

He nods, jaw working. "I can't—"

"The door's locked." I watched him do it this time. "Finish or stop. Up to you."

He groans, gaze falling to my lips, which are probably red and slick with saliva.

"Stop," he mumbles. He steps back, one hand tugging up

his boxer briefs, the other swiping at his face. "I can't. They're kids."

He's right.

"Shit, I'm sorry." I get up to unsteady knees. "I probably shouldn't have started."

I expect him to hurry and get himself zipped up, but he drags me in for a kiss, his tongue warm in my mouth, his weight sinking against me. His jeans are still unzipped, the rough fabric scraping against the back of my hand and calling for me to fist him again.

When he pulls away, we're both breathing hard, and there's this quivering new thing between us. We're on equal footing now. Maybe it was just a bj on the outside, but it was an earthquake inside my thoughts.

I'm ready for this. For whatever comes. And I'm in. Fully.

"Don't be sorry. *Never* be sorry." His hand slides down to cup the outside of my jeans and he squeezes me, making my dick throb. "Later?"

"Fuck, man, I hope so."

He releases me. "I don't know how I'm going to concentrate."

I laugh. "You can. Hell, I find a way in every physics lecture and lab." I run the back of my hand over my mouth as he steps back and tucks himself back in his jeans, buttoning himself and then tugging up on his zipper with a grunt.

"You're not the only one struggling to concentrate." He nods to the telescope. "I still need to get set up. It'll take about five minutes."

"So, then we really didn't have ten minutes?"

Someone knocks on the door.

He laughs softly. "No, we really didn't."

I'M NOT LYING when I say I like kids. I always have. There's something really genuine about them, and it takes me back to all those years before my dad died. When things were still good and we'd be up in that treehouse or riding our bikes out past Crander Hill.

And these kids are even better than normal kids because they're into the same thing as me, so when I dump out random astronomy facts—like the sun's core releases the energy equivalent of 100 billion nuclear bombs per *second* (mind boggling), or Saturn is the only planet in our solar system that would float on water—I get a "whoa, cool!" from the girl who'd been the first one to knock on the door.

Eight kids signed up for the class and most of them have been coming out to the observatory for as long as they can remember. They ask about "Mr. Adelard" and I'm not fully sure what to say, but when Kepler comes around from behind the telescope, they all cheer—calling him Mr. Kepler—and cluster around him, seeming to forget.

Kepler smiles at them. One of those rare, genuine smiles.

He's a good teacher. I picked that up from our lab class, of course, but it's even more vibrant here. There's a constant press of excitement in the room. As the kids take turns at the telescope, Kepler fills the moments in between with stories, and his smile widens when I share a few of my own. After adjusting the telescope for the next kiddo, he glances over their heads toward me, meeting my gaze, a deeper thought flashing through his eyes.

What's he thinking?

One of the kids asks a question and he's back with them. From that point on, we're busy until their parents come back to pick them up, and it's like this sudden whirlwind of kids and movement that crashes to an end.

"Shit, that was fun," I say when the door closes behind the last one, leaving us in sudden silence. There was something about it that reminded me of helping out Vain too.

"It is fun." Kepler takes two long strides toward me. At first I think he's going to kiss me, but he takes my hand instead, looping his fingers around mine.

"Come on." He tugs me toward the telescope. "You didn't get to look."

He leads me up a couple of steps to the platform and then uses his foot to push away the stool that was there for the kids. He grabs the remote and rotates the dome, the stars outside shifting as the platform we're on slowly moves with it. My smile grows as we center on a patch of sky opposite to the new moon. I pick out the constellation Ophiuchus and immediately know what he's focusing on as he bends over the eyepiece.

He leans back and gestures to the telescope.

"Saturn?" I ask.

"There's no surprising you, is there?"

"I wouldn't say that." I lean in to look. "But I know it's a good night to see it and . . ." My words fade as I stare through the eyepiece, sucking in a deep breath. Saturn. Like I've never seen her before. I get a thrum of excitement in my chest, a kind of yearning. "It's incredible."

"It is." Kepler's voice is quiet next to my ear, his breath on my neck. Goosebumps shoot across me, but I can't tear myself away from the eyepiece.

His fingers slide just into the top hem of my jeans, lightly tickling me right over my hip. "Why didn't you major in astronomy?"

"Me?"

"You're obviously interested in it. And you very clearly have the brain for it."

I lean back, straightening as I look across at him. "I don't know that I could have handled the math."

His eyes narrow on me. "I call bullshit. You do all the calculations for lab. I recognize your writing on the write-ups. Besides, there's no way you couldn't learn what you don't know. You're a fucking smarty-pants, Jin."

"Smarty-pants?" I'm grinning. "That's a better compliment than hotty-pants, I suppose."

He laughs. "Yes, I've heard that one about you too."

"Seriously? Even you?"

"*Even* me. And you are pretty hot, if you didn't already know." He hitches a brow. "But give me the real truth. Why didn't you major in astronomy?"

"Not sure, really. I guess . . ." I shrug a shoulder. "What would I do with a degree like that in Indigo Falls?"

"That matters?"

I glance up at the splay of stars. "Yeah, man. It does."

"Maybe you shouldn't let it." He frowns. "Your life could be wherever you want it to be."

No. It can't be.

But it's clear from watching him over the last hour that *his* life can be.

14

"Why does this feel suspiciously like meeting your parents?" I shift in the passenger seat, not finding a way to sit comfortably. Or maybe that's just the growing bundle of nerves in my stomach as we turn onto a narrow gravel road only a few miles away from the observatory.

Kepler drives smoothly, one hand on the wheel, and apparently not so uneasy. "I was thinking the same thing."

We come around the bend and an old log house comes into view, modern solar panels stacked across the roof. I stare—not even knowing what to think—at the bright purple door with matching shutters. Lit up glass flowers decorate the walk and the yard, in an array of yellows and pinks and oranges, brilliant in the dark. It's a field of glass and color and light.

The house feels like a mix of new and old. Perfectly represented by the old rusted truck parked out front next to a sleek electric SUV.

"Where are they?" I ask, still taking in the scene as Kepler parks behind the SUV.

"Who?" Kepler twists to face me. "Flora and Adelard?"

"No, your parents. You never mention them."

"No, I don't." He unclicks his seatbelt but then leans back against the headrest, one long arm extended in front of him with his wrist propped casually on the steering wheel. "There's nothing to mention. My mom got pregnant when she was sixteen. She took off right after I was born, and my grandfather raised me." He takes his wrist off the wheel and itches at his brow. "I'm not sure where she is now. I haven't seen her in twenty years."

"So, your grandfather raised you?"

"He did. Along with Adelard and Flora." He nods to the house. "I spent a lot of weekends here. A month or two during the summer too."

"So, it really is like meeting your parents." I drag a hand through my hair. *Nerves.* They're non-stop tonight. "And they're going to be cool with me being a tatted up Korean guy?"

"They'll love you." Kepler's hand settles on my thigh, roaming over my jeans, and it's all I can do not to let out a low groan as he leans closer to me, breath brushing against my neck. "Flora already does just from what I've told her."

"What you've told her," I repeat. Kepler talking about me is a mind fuck. What I wouldn't give to be a fly on the wall for that conversation. "Have you ever brought anyone else here?"

"Yes."

A sharpness cuts into my chest. Of course, it's unreasonable to expect that he's never brought anyone else here, but that doesn't stop the pinch I get when I think about it.

And then I catch the way he's staring at me. Like there's something just on the tip of his tongue. Or like he expects me to put two and two together.

"Someone recently?" I ask, my throat drying. The finger-toucher? With his chubby lips and cleft chin? I don't like the thought of that at all.

Kepler shakes his head. "No, a long time ago. Shin's been here."

I freeze. "Shin was here?"

"Yes."

"The observatory too?"

"Yes."

I swallow hard, scrubbing a hand over my face. And then I *am* connecting the dots. In a way that I never have before. In a way I never even thought to question. The things Dex said resonate in my head.

It can't be true.

"Were you and my brother ever together?"

He blows out a breath, puffing his cheeks. "Jin. I can't answer that."

Holy fucking shit.

I push out of the Jeep, not even a first clue where I'm going, just feet on the cement, away from the house, to the dirt road. I stop there, heart pounding, throat dry.

"Jin." He's right behind me, hand reaching out for my elbow, but I yank it away from him.

"What the fuck?" My hands dig in my hair. "Are you serious?"

"It's not like what you're thinking."

"How do you know what I'm thinking?"

"You're right, I don't." His hand comes up to the back of his neck, fingers digging hard along his nape.

"Tell me," I say.

He sighs. "We never dated. We just got each other off a few times after a couple of beers. But we were never together. We never kissed. Never did anything more than hand jobs between *Call of Duty* rounds."

"Christ," I mumble. I don't want to know this.

"Shin and I are friends." Kepler continues, "There wasn't anything else there. There never was. And if we're being completely honest . . ." He sighs, glancing toward the house when a porch light flicks on. Unease rolls off him in waves.

"Be honest." My jaw ticks.

His eyes meet mine, gray and intent. "When his hand was around my dick, it wasn't him I was thinking about. It was you. And that's why I stopped it."

"But his hand was on your dick?" I'm tightening up like a bow, muscles popping.

He sighs. "Yes."

"*Fuck.*" I let the word roar out of me, willing myself not to dip into the image that steamrolls into my brain. I spin away from him, digging my hands into my hair, too many new bits of information flying through my head. I pace to the far side of the road.

One at a time, J. Just take it one at a time.

I cross back and stop in front of him.

My limbs feel numb, my feet unsteady, my voice cutting hard. "When was the last time?"

"College. Maybe sophomore year. At least five years ago." Kepler squeezes the back of his neck. "It wasn't like we had a thing. It was only a couple of times, and we never even talked about it afterwards."

"And bringing him here?"

"As friends." He steps closer. "I've never brought anyone here the way I'm bringing you."

"How are you bringing me here?"

"As my date." He doesn't pause, doesn't hesitate. "As the man I want to see if I have a future with." The force of his conviction strikes me hard, like a punch to the gut, and the jaw, and the balls.

He means that.

"Does this change things?" His voice is quiet, but there's a strain in it I've never heard before, like something is rattling just underneath his words. I *feel* the rattle. It's shaking in me too.

"You should have told me this before."

"I couldn't." His hand drops from his neck. "I don't even know if I should be now, but I couldn't lie to you either."

I let out a breath, my chest releasing a fraction. "Because you just outed my brother to me."

He nods, lips pressing together. "I know it doesn't change how you feel about him, but it's still not my place to speak for him."

"No, it's not." I shake my head. Is my brother interested in men? I think back to the way he was staring at those two guys making out at Taverns. As usual, I'd been so focused on Kepler that I'd missed something else. Something important. I close my eyes, trying to still this rattling in my bones, breathing in the deep scent of the evergreens.

And Kepler Quinn.

Standing across from me, I hear his feet scruff on the dirt, the shift of his jeans, and the dart of electricity down my spine tells me he's moving closer to me.

I react to him. Every single time.

Now isn't any different.

But I open my eyes and step back. "I don't know, Kepler. I need time to think."

His jaw tightens, a muscle fluttering just under that mole. "Do you want to go back to Indigo Falls?"

"*No.*" There is nothing on this entire planet that could make me want to go back. "This isn't me walking away. I'm just taking a moment."

He nods once, thin lips pressed together, eyes an inky gray. "Then I'll wait."

"Just like that?"

"*Exactly* like that."

Flora and Adelard's house is the kind of place that pretty much begs you to relax. I feel it the moment I step up on the porch. Yellowy light from the windows casts over a little wooden bench sitting just outside the front door. There are coffee rings on one of the arms like someone sits there often, watching the morning sun crest the peak.

It's welcoming, and I feel like a freaking intruder with the confusion still in my head. Shoulders tight as a bow, throat closed.

Shit. Maybe we shouldn't be here right now.

But it's too late because Kepler's already holding the front door open for me, and a woman sweeps toward us from the kitchen as we step inside.

"Kepler," she calls as she crosses to us before reaching out to grasp my hand in more of a hand-hug than a handshake.

"I'm Flora." Same height as me with green eyes, she's thin, wearing a bright yellow, sunflower-patterned dress and sandals. Her hair is a wild mass of black curls streaked with silver. She nods toward the kitchen, dropping the hand-hug. "I'm making mojitos. You want one?"

"Uh, sure." I smile at the way she somehow strips off my first layer of unease. "Thanks."

"Perfect!" Flora is already moving, waving us in at the same time. "Come in, sweeties. Dinner will be up in a few."

It's an open concept house, and I'm flooded with color

just inside the door. Paintings hang on every available wall space—as brightly colored as the glass flowers out front. And the smell . . . I inhale deeply. Despite my grumpy-ass mood, it smells *incredible*. Like freshly toasted bread, lemon, and mint. My stomach grumbles as Kepler closes the door behind us.

"Come meet Adelard." Kepler reaches out to grab my hand, long fingers extended.

I pause.

I actually *pause*, staring at that hand.

"Fuck," he mumbles and then lets his hand drop to his side, pressing it against his jeans as he turns. He takes long strides toward a man sitting by the fireplace on the far side of the room.

I follow him, feeling like a dick.

I should have taken his hand, I just . . .

I don't even *know*.

I sigh, pull myself out of my own head, and focus on the man sitting by the dark fireplace. He doesn't get up, but he watches us as we walk over. Short dark hair, scruff on his jaw, and a flannel shirt, he's got a New York Times crossword folded neatly to the puzzle on his legs.

"How are you feeling?" Kepler asks.

"Like shit, thank you," the man says gruffly, then eyes me. "This him?"

"Yes." Kepler says, an almost-smile flitting across his lips before it fades.

I clear my throat and turn to Adelard. "So, how long did it take you to build that telescope?"

Adelard frowns and then tips his chin toward the empty chair next to him. "Sit your ass down, and I'll tell you."

Kepler's eyes flash up and down me. "I'll go help Flora in the kitchen."

I nod, stomach tightening as he turns, his shoulders just as tight as mine. I sit in the overstuffed leather chair next to Adelard, who picks up the crossword.

"Something uncomfortable is going on between the two of you," he says gruffly.

I huff out an uneasy laugh, surprised by his directness. "Is it that obvious?"

Kepler steps into the kitchen, and Flora starts talking immediately, setting him to work on a cutting board at the counter that runs between there and the main room. Kepler's long fingers move deftly as he halves a lime, saying something in a low voice to her that I can't hear.

I want to hear it.

I want to hear every single thing he says. I never get tired of listening to Kepler Quinn.

"Well, if it helps, you should know he talks about you," Adelard says. "All the damn time. Won't shut up about you. Flora has been on him to invite you here for years."

I scrub a hand over my face and turn back to him, confusion flitting through me. "Years? What does he say?"

"He talks about when he sees you out somewhere. Or once you wrote an essay or something for a friend of his, and he asked to read it. It was on . . . oh . . ." His forehead lines as he thinks for a moment. "Corporate responsibility in developing countries," he concludes.

I laugh, shaking my head. "I didn't think Kepler was particularly interested in that."

"He's not." He *harrumphs* and studies the crossword. "He's interested in you."

Across the room, Kepler squeezes the lime into glasses as Flora drops in mint leaves.

After the last glass, Kepler looks up, his smoky grays pinning on me from across the room. When he finds me watching, he upnods, and I return the gesture, my heart thumping hard in my chest.

I can't stop this. Don't want to stop this.

This is more than a crush. More than me exploring this sexual awakening situation. More than friendship.

What if I could fall in love with Kepler Quinn?

What if I'm a bit in love with him already?

What if I have been for years?

Adelard grunts. "Do you know a noted Hungarian-born conductor? Begins with *S*."

"Yeah." I don't take my eyes off Kepler, even as he spoons sugar into the glasses, a small smile growing on his face. *He feels me looking at him.* "Uh, Solti."

Adelard pencils in the answer. "Goddamn, kid, that fits."

I nod. "Georg Solti. He was director of the Chicago Symphony Orchestra."

Adelard harrumphs again. "What about this one: bread whose name derives from Sanskrit for the same?"

"Roti."

He snorts. "You got a lot of info in that head."

"I write a lot of college essays." I shrug. "And I've just always been interested in stuff."

"Stuff, eh?" He picks up the crossword. "How about: it's calculated relative to the speed of sound?"

"Umm," I pause, unsure. "Any hints?"

"Four letters, C on the third."

"Mach?"

He grins. "I knew that one. I was testing you."

I'm smiling too. "Give me another."

We're still going back and forth, almost done with the Sunday crossword, when Flora calls us over to the table to a spread of food the likes of which I haven't seen since my dad was alive.

"Hope you like vegetarian Cuban," she says as she sets down a bowl of what looks like roasted chickpeas. "And mojitos."

"It's incredible," I say—not just the smell, but the colors. The food matches the flowers, the paintings.

Flora pats me lightly on the arm before heading back to the kitchen.

"Are you the artist?" I call after her.

"No," she answers. "My sister is. But I do the glass flowers out front."

"No shit?" I kick myself internally for cursing, but no one seems uneasy about it. "Those are incredible."

"Damn right they are," Adelard cuts in, taking a seat across from me. "You should see them in the sunlight."

"You should." Kepler slides in next to me, his fingers brushing the side of my thigh, and this time, I look over at him, and my heart damn near oragamis in my chest. "In case you were wondering, that's an invitation."

I nod, sliding my hand over and lacing my fingers with his at the table, squeezing as Flora comes back, telling me about her flowers and the art of glass blowing. I ask about a hundred questions, and then that gets into Dex's fundraiser, and then it's Flora asking me a hundred questions.

"You still haven't found a venue?" Kepler asks after I go into our troubles.

"Not yet."

He frowns. "Have you checked at the IFU?"

"Booked."

Flora leans across the table. "What about over at the Archway?"

I blink at her. "Archway?"

"It's a new coffee shop. Just opened last week." She spreads her arms out, some gold bangles clinking on her wrists. "Huge, open space with art on all the walls." She tips her chin toward Kepler. "Kep knows the manager from way back. Gina was my sponsor."

I still, glancing at her half full mojito. "For sobriety?"

I wince. That was a fucked-up question. Me and my stupid tendency to blurt shit out.

But Flora just gives me a soft smile. "No. Gender transition. Gina helped me through the first steps of my transition. I mean . . ." Her smile widens as she glances first at Kepler and then Adelard. "Kep and Addy were there too, of course, but Gina had gone through it. Some people don't need that, but I really did. So, I sought out a sponsorship and was matched up with her."

I'm blown the fuck away. The way Flora talks about what she needed, with such clarity. The strength in that admission is mind-numbingly strong.

I squeeze Kepler's hand. "Gina sounds like an incredible woman."

"She is." Flora dips her head. "And I'm sure she'd help out with your fundraiser. An event like this could jump start her business, so it might work out perfectly."

"Absolutely." Kepler's thumb rolls over my knuckles. "I'll talk to her."

"Thank you." I glance over at him, intending to give him a quick smile and return to the conversation. But I'm caught. I stare at him, completely mesmerized by those dark-gray eyes. By the *warmth* in them. The way his thumb rolls over my knuckles, one at a time.

Heat rises behind my eyes.

There's such a deep kindness here. In this house, between these people. I don't know what it's like where Kepler lives now, but here—it's *family*. Made of people who don't share a drop of blood between them.

Christ. I take a ragged breath.

My mom is every bit my own blood, but I've never shared a meal with her like this. I hardly talk to Shin, and when we do, we always end up at odds. I see *Halmeoni*, but not nearly often enough.

And sometimes, even though I'll never admit it to anyone, the memory of my father hazes. His face, his voice, his manner. It's not as clear as it used to be.

I *miss* this. Like a big aching black hole in my gut. And I want it back. I want my mother and brother back.

If I have any hope of keeping Shin in my life, then we have to tell him now.

Even if it sucks. Even if it's hard.

Honestly? I *want* him to know. He's my brother, and I want him in my life.

"Jin?" Kepler leans closer.

"We have to tell Shin." I'm even more certain of it as I say the words. Maybe I should have waited until after dinner, but it's out there now. "We can't wait. We tell him tomorrow."

"Are you sure?" he asks, so much concern lacing through his eyes that I can feel it heating my skin.

"Yes."

"Then we tell him." He nods once, resolve streaming off him.

This is what it's like to have someone support you.

I swallow, heat still packed behind my eyes, and it's like the decision to tell Shin releases something in me. I lean over, my lips finding Kepler's. The kiss is awkward, with both of us in our seats, but it's still an instantly deep connection that vibrates through me. He kisses me back, zero hesitation, his hand coming up to palm my jaw, his tongue smoothing slowly across my bottom lip.

It's not until I lean back that I remember we're at the freaking dinner table, and I was pretty much just having a breakdown less than a minute ago. But when I look over, Adelard and Flora are smiling at each other. I can't imagine what it was like when Kepler's grandfather was here, with the three of them, it must have felt like the affection was spilling over.

"Sorry," I mumble. "It's just that this is . . ." I look around the table. Colors. Warmth. Kepler's fingers are locked around mine. If he lives alone, no wonder he feels like his life's empty. Compared to this. "I'm glad we came."

Flora leans over her plate. "You're always welcome here, Jae Jin."

"Thanks," I croak out. My voice is weighted with emotion, but I don't even try to hide it. "And, shit, I'm sorry I've been kinda up in my own head."

"No sorrys," Flora says. "We prefer to let everyone be whoever they are in this household."

Adelard grunts in agreement.

Kepler laughs softly.

I turn to him, brows going up. "What's funny?"

"Nothing. It's just that you're always up in your own head." He's smiling at me, a light tease that washes away all my lingering awkwardness in one swoop. "Sometimes I wish I was up there with you so I can eavesdrop on what's going on."

"You want to know what's in my head?"

"I do." He nods, leaning in closer. "I want to know something else too."

"Yeah?"

His smile expands. "Ever spend the night in a yurt?"

15

THE POSSIBILITIES of what we could do in a yurt make my head spin. We walk, hand in hand, down a winding path between the aspens, their golden leaves quivering above us.

Am I ready for this?

We've got no extra clothes, no plans. Nothing besides the next few hours to do . . . *something* . . .

"So . . ." I say, interrupting the easy silence. "I hear you're secretly into corporate responsibility in developing countries."

He laughs. "Not at all. Where did that come from?"

"Adelard said you read one of my essays."

His fingers tighten around mine. "Not *one*."

My steps slow. "How many?"

He shrugs a shoulder, eyes a dark gray in the low light. "I'm not sure. At least a dozen. Maybe two dozen. Whomever I've run into that has used your services."

"Two dozen," I repeat. "*Why?*"

"Because I like your words," he says simply. Like it's obvious. Like he's not completely blowing my mind. Like it's normal to read two dozen college essays just because you like someone's words.

"You're serious?"

"It was a way that I could get closer to you." He tugs my hand, and I keep walking, my thoughts scrambling to make sense of him, of us, of *everything*, when a small circular building comes into view, tucked in a grove of aspen.

The yurt is exactly as promised: traditional gently sloping roof crown, dome skylight, and single wooden door. I'm betting the inside is a lattice wall.

We start up the narrow, rocky path toward the front door. "Never in my life did I think I'd be staying in a yurt tonight."

He squeezes my hand. "What about getting your cock sucked in one?"

Holy shit.

I stumble over nothing, and he laughs softly, the sound so warm and easy and setting a line of goosebumps over my shoulders, my brain racing about what exactly is going to happen in the next few hours.

"Um, yeah." I clear my throat. "Didn't think that either when tonight first began."

He grabs keys from under a nearby rock and unlocks the door, and my stomach twists with nerves, my throat drying. Needless to say, my dick is already hard, but it's been that way ever since Kepler showed up at my apartment. I'm getting used to it.

He closes the door behind us, moonlight filtering through the open crown wheel skylight in the center of the roof. He clicks on a few lanterns hanging from the crown supports, the light swaying slightly, casting moving shadows across the lattice walls, the red-patterned rugs on the floor, the small table and chairs across from us, and the low bed covered in deep purple blankets in the center of the room.

"Christ," I mumble. It's romantic. Muted and deeply colored. "I didn't expect—"

I lose all train of thought as Kepler steps toward me.

We're alone.

Really, really, really alone. No one to hear. No one to walk in. Hours before we need to be anywhere else. No bad timing.

I'm pretty sure we don't even have to lock the door.

I wonder if he's thinking the same thing as he drags in a breath, eyes burning down to my lips before meeting my gaze again. "There's no electricity. The lights are solar powered. There's a bathhouse just outside with a pump for water, a stove in the middle here, and I can't even—"

He palms either side of my jaw, pulling me in for a deep, sudden kiss. He's flush against me, tongue flicking against mine, and *fuck*, I'm already grabbing at him, tugging up at the bottom hem of his button-down so that my fingers can smooth along the ridges of his abs.

"You like touching me there." He steps back, tugging open his shirt buttons, and I watch—spellbound as always—as he pulls apart the panels of his shirt, revealing a white tee underneath. He tosses his shirt toward the chair on the far side of the room and misses completely, but neither of us give a shit as he grabs his tee at the back of his neck, yanks it over his head, and deposits it somewhere on the floor too.

I get a first look at the skin my fingertips have been grazing across, the lean-cut, tightly compacted muscles that form his shoulders, pecs, abs, obliques, and the tight v that runs down into the jeans. My eyes are everywhere, soaking up the smooth skin, the way he stands before me.

I'm ready for this.

"More," I grate out.

Laughter flicks through his eyes as he fingers the button of his jeans, tugging them open, and then having to unhook his boxer briefs from his cock before he can shove both down and step out of them.

He does it all easily. No pause. No hesitation.

And then he's standing there.

He's really fucking beautiful. Head to toe. Brain to heart. *All of him.*

The tall, long length of him is perfection.

You'd think I'd be grabbing for him, and my hands are already trembling with desire, my mouth pooling with saliva, but we haven't had time for this. Just to pause, and feel this thing happening between us. *Linger* in it. Because I don't think there's gonna be much lingering later.

I do like he did and reach back to grab my tee, yanking it over the top of my head. I let out a long breath and drop it on the floor. I'm not as smooth and controlled as him. And definitely not as seemingly calm.

His gaze moves to the barbell through my nipple, his teeth scraping over his bottom lip. "I'm going to suck on that."

Holy shit, *yes*.

"Promise?" I ask gruffly.

"Absolutely."

I run a hand up over my pecs, the metal scraping lightly against my palm. "You don't mind the tatts?"

He laughs. "No, Jin. I'm going to suck on those too."

"You're making a lot of promises."

"I intend to fulfill any that you want."

I drag in a breath. "I'm thinking I pretty much want them all. The sucking ones at least. Maybe not the . . ." *Not the fucking ones?*

"The sucking ones sound perfect to me," he says quickly.

"Me too." My heart double-thumps in my chest.

His eyes drop to my jeans. "Then take those off too."

I'm grinning as I tug down my zipper, shove my jeans down, having to be careful with how hard my dick is, and step out. Kepler rubs his hand over his mouth, pulling in a breath that makes his chest expand to its fullest.

"Fuck me," he mumbles. "Turn around."

I blink, not expecting that, and my nerves jump up to a whole new level. But I do it, turning, listening to the groan he lets out when my ass is to him.

"Those galaxy tattoos along your spine . . ." he says when I'm facing him again. "Fucking hotty-pants."

I shake my head slightly. "You have us confused."

"Not a chance." His pupils flare. "You're the guy I've jacked off to."

My mouth drops open at that. My mind *spins* with that image.

"I want to see it." Christ. Did I just say that?

Fuck yeah, I did.

An amused smile flits around his face. It's like every smile gets easier for him, and damn, if that doesn't make my chest expand.

"Now?" he asks.

I drag my hand across my pec again, barbell snagging against my palm, a tingle shooting from my nipple to my navel. "Yeah, now. Jack off for me."

His smile widens into that genuine one that makes all my insides quiver.

"Thought you'd never ask," he says. His hand is on his chest, mirroring me, but he smooths it down to his abs, his breath catching as he slides lower, and my eyes just about fall out of my head as he slowly wraps those long fingers around his shaft and then takes a deliberately slow stroke of his dick, eyes still fixed on me.

It's sexy as fuck.

I'm spellbound as he strokes himself twice more. A bead of precum wells up, glistening in the low light, and I don't have the freaking willpower to stand across from him anymore. In two long strides, I grab the nape of his neck to pull him against me. His fist hits my stomach as his lips fit hard against mine, and then his fingers extend, wrapping both his dick and mine, and for a millisecond, my mind flashes back to him grabbing those two cups in that inferno of a kitchen. The flex of his long fingers. Christ, was *this* what I'd been really thinking about at the time?

But the memory rips out of my head, as his hand moves down our shafts. His palm is warm, and the feeling of his dick hard against mine is mind-blowing. My breath comes sharp, my eyes fixed on where he's gripping both of us.

"You like that?" he asks softly.

"Pretty much," I mumble, eyes transfixed.

He takes two more strong strokes and then releases us to shove me back. My ass hits the mattress, my dick bouncing eagerly.

I laugh. "We've never been on a bed before."

"First time for everything." He crawls over the top of me, his knees resting on either side of mine. I'm trapped under him.

I bite my bottom lip. "What's your plan, Quinn?"

He raises a brow. "Do you want to be in control again?"

"Uh, no. I don't think so. But first you gotta kiss me."

He does. A hard, bruising kiss that pushes me back into the mattress. A moan catches in my throat as he breaks from me, still trapping me with his thighs, his hair brushing my cheek before he moves lower. His lips skate over the ink along my pec, then his tongue flicks over the barbell in my nipple.

"Fuck," I mumble, arcing up against his mouth. "Yes. *That*, I like that too." My fingers shift into his hair, and he bites lightly on my nipple, his tongue roving around the barbell.

A louder moan passes my lips when his hand slides down to cup my balls, his tongue circling the piercing again before he scrapes his teeth lightly down to my sternum. His progress is slow. Unhurried. Like he's relishing every part of me. And I don't know, I've never thought much about myself before, but Kepler makes me feel sexy. Feel *good*. Like I'm worth the lingering attention he gives me. He kisses slowly lower, one long arm reaching up to flick my nipple as he shifts downwards and his breath heats my navel, then his tongue runs along the ridges of my abs.

"I could do this all night," I groan. "Just lie here and —*fuck*."

My curse is loud when his breath brushes over the head of my cock. I'm stupidly sensitive after being hard and stuffed in my jeans over the last hours, and he seems to guess that as he barely touches the crown with his tongue. Hardly even a touch at all, mostly breath, and my hips shift forward, my pelvis pitching up.

Fuck, fuck me, *fuck*. How does he do that to me? Every single touch is like lightning.

"You taste incredible," he mumbles as he licks me again, just the tip of his tongue, then one languidly expelled breath before he takes me deep into his mouth, slowly, all the way to the back of his throat. My eyes roll back, my cock leaking, my balls tightening.

I fist his hair as he sucks me down and then groan when he cups my balls, his fingers massaging lightly. I can't stop the noises shooting out of me. Half moans, half pleas, half curses. I full-on shout when he pulls off my cock and lowers farther, his tongue sliding over my sack before he sucks a ball into his mouth.

I'm about to lose it. Right there. Like a freaking geyser going off. I'm only able to hold back with a hard bite on my tongue, and right when I don't think I can take any more, his fingers slip lower, teasing across my taint.

"Widen your legs," he says, voice guttural and needy.

But I still, my stomach twisting into a knot, nerves spiking like shards of glass.

"I've, uh, never . . ." I blink, looking up at the slats across the ceiling. I have never, in my life, gone spread eagle for someone. *None* of my past partners have touched my taint or my ass. Hardly even my balls.

My dick has always been the main attraction. The *only* attraction, really.

But with Kepler, it turns out there's a whole amusement park full of attractions down there.

"I want to see you," he says, blowing a soft breath over my balls that shoots shivers up my spine. "Every sexy part of you."

"Yeah, okay." I'm gonna do this.

I open my thighs slowly. My abs tighten as I sit partway up, watching as he fists my cock, my legs sliding open. He takes unhurried, leisurely strokes as he drops to suck on my balls again, and then he moves lower, his shoulders shifting to get access, his tongue darting along my taint. My mouth opens, a soundless plea sticks in my throat as he continues to jack me, his tongue flicking even lower.

"So sexy," he mumbles. His breath hits nerve endings I didn't know *existed*. And apparently those nerve endings are connected to every single cell in my body because, with a light brush of his tongue, I can feel it *everywhere*. Zapping and zinging, lighting up parts of me I didn't even know were dark.

"Fuck," I breathe out.

"You're truly perfect," Kepler says, and when I look down through the haze that has become my vision, I *see* the truth of that on his face. His pupils are wide, lips parted and damp, fist starting to shake slightly as he jacks me.

I open my thighs wider, and he groans, sliding down between my legs, and then his tongue presses against me, firmer now that I've allowed him better access. I'm still propped up on my elbows, but my head rolls back when his tongue teases against my hole, and a whole new world opens up. Just that little tip of his tongue—it feels *huge*. So much that I hardly realize his hand has left my dick until I hear him rummaging for something on the floor, then a tear of a wrapper.

That wakes me the fuck up.

I tense, the precum from my cock wetting my navel. "I, uh . . . I don't know if I'm ready to fuck? I mean, I can't even think about it without my mind going berserk, but—"

"It's just a packet of lube." His lips expand into a smile as he holds up the packet pinched between his fingers. "Don't worry. I won't ever fuck you unless you ask, hotty-pants."

I scrub a hand over my face. "I'm sorry. I interrupted things. I just—"

"No, it's good." His warm palm settles on my thigh as he crawls back up on the bed. "I want to know what you're thinking. And we don't have to fuck. There's no shortage of other things we can do."

"Yeah." I nod, my eyes sailing down his lean, compactly muscled body to where his thick cock is achingly hard even though I haven't even touched him yet. "But you would? Fuck me, I mean. You would fuck me?"

I fight to figure out what the hell I'm trying to say, partly annoyed with myself for asking him to talk when his tongue could be back down there doing whatever it was doing a few minutes ago. But this feels like a conversation we should have.

And Kepler doesn't seem rushed, he just kneels over my legs, eyes like black smoke, dick resting against my lower thigh. "Absolutely, I would fuck you."

"That's hot," I groan.

He stretches over the top of me, lips coming close to mine, and I tip up into a kiss. When we break, he lingers over me, his lean frame above me.

"And just so you know," he says, an inch from my lips. "If you ever want to, you can fuck me. You don't even have to ask."

"Did you really just say that?" My fingers suddenly pick up a tremble as they clasp his obliques then slide down over his hips, tugging his pelvis closer to mine, our cocks brushing lightly.

"I mean it." His lips curl into a half-smile, and I'm about to respond when he shifts down to the bottom of the bed and pauses to squeeze out some lube onto his fingers.

I lose the ability to talk.

Keeping his gaze on me, he fists me with his other hand, taking a slow, steady stroke, and I'm instantly arching back against the mattress.

"Christ," I grind out. "How do you do that?"

"Do what?" He cups my sack, his lubed fingers sliding between my legs.

"Make me feel good," I mumble as I open my legs for

him, flinching just a little when he presses against my hole, his finger cool with lube this time.

He pauses, taking his hand off my dick and opening his mouth as if he's gonna ask a question, but I'm already nodding my head so hard it might fall off.

"Do it," I grate out. "Now."

A low pressure fills my abdomen, shooting zaps of electricity up into my navel and across my chest.

"Breathe," he says.

I didn't realize I wasn't breathing. Although it's a challenge to take a breath as the pressure doubles in intensity. His finger feels different from his tongue, harder.

I still at the sensation, startled, and not really sure what the fuck's going on down there.

It makes me want to grab my dick, and so I do, gripping my shaft and stroking as I explore the feeling of whatever the hell Kepler is doing. My thighs are parted, knees up. I'm exposed in a way I've never been before, and the fullness starts to pinch. I grind my teeth, pumping myself faster. I'm not sure I've ever been this hard before. And then I just need to . . . I groan out as I bare down on his finger.

"Fuck," Kepler mumbles, a bit of surprise flitting through his voice, and the pressure multiplies times a gazillion—pulsing through me, up into my stomach and down into my thighs and hitting every aching, taut muscle between. It's like this perfect pressure everywhere. I don't know if it feels good, but I'm *aching* for it.

"Kepler," I murmur, the world flashing a thousand different colors as I try to keep a hold on reality. But I can't. I'm pumping myself urgently, grinding down to get his finger deeper inside of me. I'm a beast that can't control itself, drumming, needing, shaking with the intensity.

"More?" Kepler's voice comes from somewhere. I nod,

then feel more electricity flicking out over me, like it's waking up every dormant cell in my body.

I'm guessing he's got two fingers in me, and then he's leaning over me, still working deeper in, and I tip up, struggling to get closer to him. To kiss him. But I can't reach him through my spread legs. Can't get close enough.

"Kepler," I groan. "*Yes*, more. I need more."

I need . . . *what?*

His lips, for starters.

With my free hand, I reach down and tangle my fingers in his hair, pulling him toward me, and he crawls up, guided by me. My lips crash against his as soon as I can reach them. My tongue carves into his mouth. Both of us groan into our kiss as his hands land on either side of my shoulders, his head dipping so he can kiss me. His thick cock is excruciatingly close to mine as it scrapes along the back of my knuckles.

This is what it would be like if he fucked me.

His body over mine, lips on mine. Except that low, needful pressure would be deep inside me as we suck each other's tongues.

Holy shit, I *want* that.

I tear away from the kiss. "I want your dick in me."

His nostrils flare. "You said you aren't ready."

"I think I was wrong." Shit, I wish I sounded more convinced.

I *am* convinced. I'm just nervous too.

He drags in a sharp breath. "Believe me, there's nothing I want to do more, but—"

"*Fuck me*, Kepler." This time, the conviction rings in my voice. I yank him down by the nape of his neck, and my tongue drags along his thinner bottom lip before it dives into his mouth. I let go of my dick and it grinds up against his. His skin is hot, both of us charged.

But he pulls back from me.

"You're sure," he says between heavy breaths. It's a statement, not a question.

I nod anyway. Because, yeah, I'm really freaking sure.

I'm ready for this. I'm ready for *us*. And however this changes things between us—because I know it will. I mean . . . he read my essays. For no other reason than to read my words. There's something so deeply humbling in that.

He wants me. Brain, body, and soul.

And I want him.

"I want you inside me," I say. "Now."

"*Fuck*, Jin." He groans as he leans in to quickly kiss me, and then he crawls down the bed, lithe muscles flexing as he reaches off the far end to snag his jeans. He produces another foil packet, tearing it open and sheathing himself in one fast motion before moving over the top of me again, his eyes locking on mine.

"Tell me if you want to stop," he says softly, and my stomach flexes, my chest pitches. "Or *anything* else. I'm listening to your words."

I nod, not believing that I could ever want to stop. Not a single bit of oxygen is in my lungs as he shifts back to his knees, dragging me down by my hips so I'm resting partly on his thighs. He starts with his fingers again, and I groan as soon as he presses into me, already lost to the feeling. He takes his time, and I don't rush him. He's doing what he thinks I need, and I trust him. I just go with it. Completely in his hands.

After a few minutes, his fingers leave me, and he pauses, his tongue wetting his bottom lip.

"Please," I say. "Just do it."

"Keep talking to me," he says. He hangs over me for a moment, eyes flicking around my face.

"Do it," I repeat, and a small smile tips his lip and he shifts to fist himself, one shoulder and bicep flexing from taking the bulk of his weight. My legs spread wider as he brushes the thick, broad head of his cock against my taint. Then he grazes against my hole, his eyes still fixed on mine. His cock is wider than his fingers, softer in a way. But not really soft at all when he brushes against me. He hasn't even pushed in yet, and already the broad head of his cock makes those sparks not just shoot but fly and zing all around me, then that low pressure resonates in my abdomen.

I grit my teeth, nerves spiking.

"Breathe." He licks his lips, his own breath coming sharp.

I nod, trying to relax into the mattress, but every one of my muscles is eagerly taut, and I *completely* stop breathing as he starts to press in, my eyes wanting to squeeze shut, but I force myself to keep looking at him because he's so fucking sexy it almost hurts.

I kick my legs out to the side, probably looking inelegant as hell, but like always, Kepler just seems turned on by me. His lips part, and a deep, masculine groan falls from him as the pressure intensifies. His head tips back slightly, but he seems to catch himself before giving into what he's feeling, and he looks down, jaw tightening, hardly moving.

He inhales sharply, nostrils flaring. "You good?"

"Yeah. *More.*"

This is it. This moment between us—it means something.

And I think he feels it too because a smile tips his lips,

but it vanishes as my pelvis tightens, verging on the edge of pain. My fingers grip onto the sheet.

He makes solid eye contact and pushes in deeper, giving me more. And *more*.

And more after that.

My mouth drops open.

"Fuck," he groans, leaning back on his knees, the change in angle making me moan. His gaze sails down to where he's inside me. "I wish you could see this."

My brain tries to pull up an image, but it short circuits.

It's overwhelming. *He's* overwhelming.

I reach out a hand, hovering it in the air between us as he slowly shifts forward so my palm can flatten against his sternum. The pressure edges on too much, my balls pressed between us in a way that's making my eyes roll back in my head.

"Are you ready?" he says, voice quiet.

"Ready for what?" I croak out. "We're pretty much already there, aren't we?"

It's impossible that there's more, but then he slowly pulls back his hips and a million sensations zing through me. I'm not fully sure if it's good or bad. At this point, it's just different.

I squeeze my eyes tight.

"Should I stop?" he asks.

I shake my head. "No."

"Stay with me." He pushes into me again, and the pressure's still there, but it's already morphing as he starts to slowly fuck me. Then without warning, it's like the deepest part of me scrapes against the edge of bliss. Like something racing through me, ebbing and hot, encompassing my abs, then chest, then shoulders, then arms, and every single muscle tightens with full-on *need* as Kepler fucks me. It's like with every pump into me, he's hitting something euphoric.

Holy shit, it's insane. And I'm suddenly groaning out pleas for him to fuck me harder. For him to fuck me deeper. I don't even know what I'm saying, just blurting things out.

Reality and fantasy crash together. From everything I've imagined to everything I've tried to avoid imagining. It all coalesces, shifting to something tangible and white-hot, slamming into me as he moves, and my eyes fly open to find him staring down at me, propped up on one hand again, his eyes hazed, lips damp.

He bends over me, his other hand gripping my jaw as he kisses me, but it's barely a kiss, more his breath against my lips, mouths open, tongues just tangling. The moment lingers between us.

I hook my hand around his neck, urgency coursing through me.

Holy fuck. I'm so freaking hard. My cock rubs against his upper abs as he fucks me. And that zinging doesn't stop, it just intensifies with every thrust.

It's mind-blowing heaven, and I'm cursing and groaning and begging for more as we grip onto each other, fucking harder, fighting to get deeper.

"Jin," he grits just above my mouth, thrusting with all his strength, shocking me with his eye-popping, breath-taking need.

And just when I think this can't get any better, he leans back and then shoves so deep into me I don't just see stars, I see planets and entire worlds. Colors and lights. I'm only half aware as he grabs my cock, stroking me at the same pace he's keeping, every thrust sending us both into a fervor that leaves us sweat-slick and gasping. Our movements become erratic, and then Kepler's hand on my dick becomes the focus of my entire existence, and I'm driving into his palm, my mouth opening, my abs tightening.

"*Kepler.*" I can't hold back anymore.

I come with a full-body force that wrecks me, wetting both our chests. He milks me through my climax, and I watch through my post-release haze, mesmerized, as his gray eyes darken, as his jaw clenches, shoulders contracting, all of him shifting into sharp clarity as he follows me, coming so hard that we shove up the mattress. I grab his ass, pulling him deep into me as he slows, my lips parting as he drags in a shaky breath.

"Jin," he mumbles as his weight sinks onto me. His forehead drops against my sweaty neck, our chests expanding together, my release plastered between us. His dick is still in me, twitching, which is so hot that my dick keeps leaking.

"Holy shit," I mumble, hardly able to speak with all of his weight on me. "When can we do that again?"

He laughs. "Give me a few minutes." His hands sneak under my back, making my spine bow as he wraps his arms around me, all of his warmth surrounding me.

A hug.

He's *hugging* me, and it makes this rush of heat simmer up my throat. *Simkung* to the max. I try to catch my breath as he slowly pulls back his hips and his dick slides out of me. My ass feels empty. But the rest of me . . . I'm not sure I've ever felt so full.

"Quinn," I push out, wrapping an arm around his shoulders, locking him on top of me. "What's your middle name?"

He laughs. "Please don't tell me you were thinking about that while we were fucking."

I'm grinning. "Nah. I was pretty much fixated on your dick inside me. But I figure if we're fucking, then I should know your middle name."

"Fair enough." His breath heats the top of my shoulder as he picks up his head. "Copernicus."

I laugh so hard that my chest aches, the weight of him making my breaths shallow. "Kepler Copernicus Quinn?"

"Yes." I feel his smile against my skin, just under my ear. "You don't have a middle name?"

"We don't really do that in Korea." I pause. "Why do you call me Jin instead of Jae or Jae Jin?"

He pulls back and meets my gaze, smoky gray eyes so close I can see the brown flecks. "It's not disrespectful?"

"Well, my *halmeoni* would never do it, but it's not something I've personally ever minded." I frown, not really wanting to talk about *Halmeoni* right now. "Just wondering. You've called me that since we were kids."

His teeth run over his bottom lip. "Because you once told me what the hangul meant."

I pause, trying to read everything I can on his face.

"Treasure," I say. "It means something like treasure."

He squeezes me tighter. "Exactly."

16

"Is Adelard okay?" The question is soft in the dead of the mountain night.

We're just outside the yurt, slowly swinging in a hammock stretched between two huge aspens, trunks pale white in the glow of the half moon.

My back is to Kepler's chest, my naked—sore—ass is pressed up against his dick, his legs wrapped around my thighs, his arms folded around my chest while my toes just drag on the ground.

No clue what time it is. We fucked again—and again—and since then, we've been out here, softly swinging and talking about everything from Kepler's summer in California last year to Dex's fundraiser to the essays I've been working on. But we haven't talked about anything overly serious.

Not until I ask that question, because I've been thinking about how Kepler had to fill in at the observatory. And the first question out of his mouth when he saw Adelard: *how are you feeling?*

Kepler drags in a deep breath, his chest solidifying against my back. "Prostate cancer."

"Shit."

"They found it early though." His arms tighten around me. "Treatment sucks, but he's going to be fine. It's just that they're both getting older. There will be other things. And top that off with me moving out of state, so I won't be here to help them."

A hard rock fists in my stomach at him talking about leaving, but he doesn't seem to notice, his lips feathering over the top of my shoulder, then he settles his chin on me saying, "You could come with me."

I freeze, stiffening against his chest. "That's insane."

"Is it?" He twists his head, his chin digging into me just a fraction, slightly rough with stubble. "Honestly, I don't really care if it's insane or not. It's still the truth. You could, in fact, come with me."

"You're fucking with me," I say lowly.

"No." He tips his head to kiss my neck, then just under my ear, his lips igniting a wave that rolls down my chest and instantly stiffens my always eager dick.

I lean my head back against his shoulder, looking at the aspen leaves quaking above us, pale yellow in the moon. "You like to say things that set me off kilter."

"That's not why I said it." He pauses. "That's not the *only* reason I said it. Just think about it. Let it roll around in that smarty-pants brain of yours for a while. See what falls out."

"You haven't even gotten the job yet," I say, although I know he will. They'd be stupid not to offer it to him.

"No," he says quietly. "But I have hope. About a lot of things."

His arms tighten around me, and I'm at a complete loss for what to say, so we swing, the silent forest around us.

Just the two of us. *Alone.*

We're a million miles away from anyone else. From all the things that are waiting for us back in Indigo Falls.

Is this what it could be like?

Moments like this. Swinging on a hammock, his arms wrapped around me, his chin resting on my shoulder, his chest expanding against my back.

I could get used to this.

Especially the way he kisses me here, in the open, languidly and like we have all the time in the world, his hand sliding around to cup my dick under the blanket like he knows what I'm thinking.

He nibbles my earlobe. "How do you feel?"

"A bit sore in certain places," I admit. "Not sure I'm up for being fucked again. But I'm pretty sure I've got other working parts."

"Good," he says, his hand deliciously familiar on my cock. Already stroking in a rhythm that makes my head spin. I groan and twist to face him as his other hand cups my jaw, our lips fighting to be on each other.

Christ. I want him inside me again. I don't care how damn sore I am. He can fuck me until—

My thoughts stop, and I grumble at a far-off sound.

He pulls back from me. "Something wrong?"

"No." I sigh. "It's just my phone."

He frowns. "I don't hear it."

"It rang earlier too. Twice." I drag a hand over my face. "I should probably see what it is, considering it's three in the morning. It's probably Dex, sending a check-in text. I never told him I was staying the night, and he'll worry if I don't respond."

The air feels cold and sharp as I slip from our warm cocoon of blankets. I jog down the dirt path to the yurt,

Kepler following me at a slower pace with the blankets bundled under his arm. I brush my feet off on the mat before going inside. A moment later, Kepler steps in and closes the door behind him, the lanterns casting a warm glow over his skin. He turns to fold the blankets, long arms outstretched, tight ass flexing, and I'm half-gawking at him as I find my jeans crumpled in front of the bed.

I snake my phone out of the pocket just as it rings again.

Shin.

"Shit." I pause, staring down at my brother's name. Reality floods back in. "It's Shin."

Kepler finishes with the first blanket and gets started folding the second. "Then you should probably answer."

"Yeah." I clear my throat and click on the call. "Hey, bro. What's up?"

"About time you answered."

"Yeah, I've been busy," I say.

Kepler tosses the second blanket on the folded pile, completely naked and entirely distracting. Those intelligent, smoky eyes land on me as he turns, and then an arduously slow, teasing brow rises when he finds me gawking at him.

He tilts his head, that teasing brow falling, and I wonder what he's reading in my face. Then he nods toward the phone.

Oh, yeah.

I'm talking to my brother.

His best friend.

"So, if you don't get here," Shin's saying, "then she's asking to call Fender."

"Wait, what?" My voice is thick, and I clear my throat. "Can you repeat that?"

Shin grinds out a curse. His radio crackles in the background, and it sounds like he's got a million other things demanding his attention.

"She's asking to call Fender," he says.

"I heard that part." I pivot away from Kepler, focusing on my brother. "Can you repeat everything else?"

"Fuck, Jae Jin." His voice drops. "What's going on? Are you good?"

"Yeah, fine. What's up with Mom?"

"Didn't you hear anything I said?" His annoyance with me is loud and clear. "She took a piss in the middle of an intersection and then got into an altercation with a driver who was waiting for the stoplight to change."

"Seriously?" I scrub a hand over my face, my stomach sinking. Why the fuck would she take a piss in the middle of an intersection? "Where is she?"

"She's at the hospital. Nothing serious, just a couple stitches. Hold on." He muffles the phone and responds to someone in the background before coming back on the line. In that time, I tugged on my jeans and started looking around for my tee.

"That's not all though," he says when he's back. "There's an older bruise along her ribs. She made up an excuse. First about slipping in the bathroom, then later about tripping over a chair."

The sinking of my stomach turns to a full-on clench. "Fender?"

"I don't know. She wouldn't talk about it. But the hospital wants someone to check her out, and if one of us doesn't do it, then it's going to be him. We need to let her live her own life, but..."

He doesn't have to say it.

I know that feeling. Responsibility. Guilt. Frustration. Worry.

"You're working?" I ask.

"Shift began an hour ago and there's a multi-car accident over on Snake River Road. I was needed there five minutes ago. So, can you just get over to the hospital? We can figure shit out later."

I twist back to look at Kepler. He's only a few feet from me now, and I don't know if he can hear Shin, but his forehead lines as he mouths, "Whatever you need."

Need.

That's a big word.

What I *want* is to end this call, crawl back in bed with him, and see just how sore my ass can get. I want to keep shutting out the world for just a few more hours and pretend that this fantasy can actually exist for longer than half a night.

"I've got to go, Jae," Shin says. A car door ding echoes in the background.

"I'm a ninety-minute drive away," I tell him.

"Where are you?"

"Um, just visiting this observatory."

"An observatory?" A pause. "*Kepler's?*"

"That's actually something I wanted to talk to you about."

More radio chatter in the background. Then the sound of far-off sirens.

This is a bad time to tell him about Kepler.

"I've got to go," he says sharply.

The phone goes dead. I stare down at it.

"Jin." Kepler takes a few long steps toward me. "What's going on?"

"It's my mom." My voice is suddenly thick, the words sticking in my throat. "I need to get her."

He nods. "Now?"

I shake my head. "I don't know."

I feel heavy, like all my bones just doubled in weight. It's not the first time I've had to pick her up in the middle of the night, but it is the first time that I've been with someone when I've gotten the call.

And not just someone.

But Kepler.

And *here*.

"Fuck." I toss my phone on the bed. "I don't want to go. I mean, we just... I like being here with you."

He takes a long stride forward, not touching me, but close enough that either of us could reach out. "I like it too. And we can come back. As much as you want."

I drag in a breath, needing that full-on support that he gives me. "Fucking kiss me."

He does. Instantly. No questions, just hooking an arm around my shoulders and pulling me against him, his chest and stomach and lips all so warm. Afterwards, I squeeze my eyes as he wraps me into a hug, feeling his breath on my cheek, his arms around me. One of his hands clasps my neck, the other resting on my hip.

"I don't know what the fuck to do." The confession tumbles out of me. Words that I've never admitted to anyone. His long fingers squeeze the nape of my neck lightly, and I know he's listening. He's always listening.

"Am I supposed to just let her sink?" I continue. "Date this Fender asshole? Stop paying the bills? Am I supposed to watch her take herself down? I can't do that, but what else am I supposed to do?"

His fingers smooth along the back of my neck, his breath steady against my cheek. "You've been fighting this battle your entire life."

"I have." *And it's never changed.*

It's a cold thought.

What if it *never* changes? What if she never wants help?

I shake my head, my stomach a rock. "I don't know what the fuck to do. I just . . ." My words trail off, heat racing up my throat.

"You're not alone." His low voice anchors me, and I let out the ragged breath I'd been holding, heat building behind my eyes as I grip onto him.

"I'm here," he mumbles against my ear. "Always have been."

Something in me folds. Something that's been held up tenuously for the last nine years after having my father die and then watching my mother shatter apart over and over. I don't know how to pick up any of the pieces.

I need help.

I nod against his shoulder, forcing words past the boulder-sized knot in my throat. "I don't know what to do, but I know I need to go get her."

His fingers stroke the back of my neck. "Then we'll go."

17

WE TALK.

For the ninety-minute drive back to Indigo Falls, I just open my mouth and let it all fall out.

I tell him the true shit, the honest shit, the embarrassing shit. The shit I've never told anyone. He knows some of it, but a lot he doesn't. Like finding her passed out with her pants down next to the toilet. Or the times when she's so drunk she can hardly remember my name and she thinks that I'm Dad.

I tell him shit that Shin doesn't know. Not that I was intentionally keeping things from my brother, but I didn't tell him every time that I found her in her own vomit. Or picked her up from some guy's house with her shirt on inside out.

"Shin doesn't know a lot," Kepler says quietly as we turn onto the main highway that will eventually wind into Indigo Falls.

I settle back against the leather seat with a sigh, extending my legs as far as they'll go in the front seat of the

Jeep and itching at the leather band around my wrist. "Guess not."

I suck in a breath, feeling that hard clamp around my chest when I think about the future. "I don't know what's going to happen to her when I go."

He side-glances me, long fingers wrapping over the top of the steering wheel. "Can you get her in some kind of rehab?"

"She's been there." I shake my head. "More than once. It just doesn't work. Besides, it's like a reunion when she heads into rehab here. Half the people there are people she drinks with."

"Have you tried sending her somewhere farther away?" he asks. "Somewhere unfamiliar?"

I blow out a breath. "That costs money. Lots of it. I get by with the essay job, but it's not enough for that. I don't know if Shin would help, but cops aren't exactly rolling in cash."

"What if money didn't matter?"

I frown. "Nice dream. But it *does* matter. There's no getting around that. I got information from this place in Ohio that seems like it could be a good place for her, but once I saw the cost . . ." I shake my head, staring out the window at the trees zipping past. "I started a savings account for it. I toss what I can in there, but it'll take years."

My reflection stares at me from the window, brow piercing glinting, black hair in windy chaos. "I could get a night job somewhere. I'm usually awake anyway."

Maybe I'm a selfish asshole. Going to college. Wasting the money on who-the-fuck-knows. I try to drag in a breath, my throat tightening, the weight of it all pressing on me.

Kepler taps his long fingers against the steering wheel, the tie from the leather cord knotted around his wrist swaying. "What if I helped? What if I paid for it?"

"You would pay to send my mom to rehab?"

"Yes." He nods, fingers quieting. "Spending it on something like that is more important than a new Jeep."

"You're serious," I croak out.

"Dead."

I swallow, trying to ease my throat, and lean back against the headrest. "I could never ask you to do that."

"You're not asking." He glances at me quickly before returning his attention to driving. It's still dark out, the time of night when deer dart into the road. "I'm offering."

I shake my head again, not even sure how to sort out my thoughts on that one. "Where'd your money come from?"

"My grandfather was an inventor," he says. "He's got quite a few licenses that still bring in royalties. Some interesting stuff, actually. I'll show you sometime. But the point is that most of the money just sits in an account, doing nothing." He glances at me again. "It could do something."

"You don't even know how much money we're talking about."

"I don't have to." He shrugs. "Say *yes*."

"No." My stomach clenches. I can't take this from him.

Can I? A little spark of hope lights in my chest, but I stomp it out, and all that's left is this growing heat. My lungs feel *hot*.

I can't take his money.

It's too much. It's not right.

Ahead the sign for Indigo Falls comes into view. Nine miles away, and my throat tightens even more. That heat in my chest burns up my esophagus. I cough, but that feels like it tightens my throat even more.

This damn road is so familiar. The rock outcropping ahead that looks like a frying pan on its side. The old, falling-apart water tower that someone spray painted a gigantic dick on recently. Three little spurts of cum shooting out the top.

It's all painfully familiar.

I just . . . don't want to go back. An image of Kepler turning the Jeep around and driving off skips through my head. Going somewhere—anywhere—maybe a beach. I can picture Kepler at a beach, the sun highlighting the blond in his hair, his forearms tanned as he reaches a hand out toward me. Maybe we could rent a sailboat.

I've never been on a boat.

I shake my head.

It's a fucking fantasy that'll never happen.

I make some kind of choking noise, the heat and tightness binding down so hard that I'm suddenly having a hard time breathing. I lean toward the open window, trying to suck in the night air.

I can smell the air, thick with the scent of evergreen. But I can't breathe it in.

"Jin?" Alarm rings through Kepler's voice, but I'm not looking at him, just staring out at the trees and trying to suck in air.

The Jeep swerves off the road, tilting as it leaves the pavement and veers onto the dirt embankment on the side.

"Jin?" He grips my shoulder, turning my chin so that I'm looking at him.

My breath cages even harder as I blink at him, tears gathering at the corners of my eyes, hardly able to see in the dark interior of the Jeep.

I try to respond, but I can't suck in enough air to say anything. I'm just shaking my head, panic welling up. I jab at the button on my seatbelt, not able to still my hands enough to work it.

Kepler clicks it off for me.

"Breathe, Jin." His hand cups my jaw. "Try to relax."

As if relaxing's possible.

I try to tell him that I can't. His widened pupils dart around my face.

"Don't try to talk," he says. "Just follow my breath."

He leans close, his cheek against mine, his breath feathering my ear. One slow drag in and then a long exhale. Another, then another.

On his third breath, I focus on my own, able to open my throat just enough to pull in a shaky half-breath.

"Good," he breathes out. "Now let it out."

I nod—my cheek moving against his, his low stubble scraping—and push out the breath.

"In." He inhales, and I try to mimic him, still not able to breathe in as fully as him, but I get enough air to stop the flare of panic. Enough to halfway fill my chest.

I listen as he tells me to breathe out. In. Out. I don't know how long he guides me. Until I'm finally able to take a long, full breath that seems to fill most of my lungs.

"Fuck," I mumble, the words rasping out of my throat. "That scared the shit out of me."

"Me too." His forehead lines, his hand still cupped softly on my jaw. "Are you good?"

"I guess so." I look down to find my hands clamped around his wrists. My fingertips are white from gripping him so hard. Shit. I release him. "Did I hurt you?"

"I didn't even feel it." He doesn't take his eyes off me, dark gray and so full of concern that it floors me.

"Kepler," I mumble.

He leans in, slowly, seeming to know that I need him, his lips just brushing mine. A soft, barely-there kiss, and then his arms go around me, and we stay there, for long minutes, on the dirt shoulder of the road, just holding onto each other.

I don't want to let go.

But I finally do because we can't stay here forever. And we can't turn the Jeep around and drive off to a beach somewhere and sail away.

We need to go back to Indigo Falls.

"Jin." Kepler's thumb smooths over the solar system inked across my forearm. "Do you think we should talk about what just happened?"

I clear my throat. "It was a panic attack."

"Have you had one before?"

"I used to get them right after my dad died."

His jaw tightens. "I didn't know that."

"Now you do." I catch his hand in mine, thumb rubbing along the leather cord wrapped around his wrist and then along that vein. "Why do you wear this?"

"Flora gave it to me." He watches me trace along his vein. "When I came out."

"When was that?"

"About five years ago." He studies me for a moment, like he's thinking I should connect something, but I'm still only half in my head. "Do you still want to go get your mom?"

"Yeah." I click on my seatbelt. "I need to get her home."

His Adam's apple bobs as he studies me for a second longer. Then he nods and pulls back on the highway.

THE HOSPITAL CENTER is on the far side of town. We drive through stoplights that are all flashing yellow at this time of night, the sky just starting to lighten behind the eastern peaks. There's still snow up there—it never melts completely—high up on the jagged summits in the shadows of the peaks.

I slide a hand over to Kepler's thigh and set my palm just above his knee. He covers my hand with his, warming my knuckles.

Last night, he was mine.

We drive silently through town. Hardly any lights are on. No other traffic. There's no music in the Jeep right now, just the sound of the engine and the tires on the pavement.

He taps his thumb against the top of the steering wheel, his leg shifting under my hand to touch on the brake as the speed limit falls, but he doesn't let go of my hand.

I could do this—for a long, long time.

But what would that even look like?

He's leaving.

Whether it's for the NASA job or something else. He's too smart to stay in Indigo Falls. He's too capable. Too determined.

All the things that I like about him. They're the same things that are going to take him out of here.

And what about me?

What the hell am I going to do with my life?

It's a question I should have answered long ago. But then, the answers depend on other things.

He pulls into the hospital center and parks. The long, brick building is lit up despite the hour, red emergency sign bright. I suppose it always is.

Kepler turns off the ignition, looking down at my hand resting under his. "How do you want to do this?"

I swallow. I'd been thinking about that on the way back. "Come in with me."

He nods. "Will Shin be there?"

I shake my head. "He had a call that will take a while."

I slip my hand out from under his and get out of the Jeep.

We walk up to the front doors, and they slide open. As we step in, we're greeted by security.

"A security checkpoint isn't how I wanted this night to end," I mumble before we step through.

"It's fine," Kepler says quietly after we retrieve our phones, wallets, and keys.

I scrub a hand through my hair, feeling it sticking out in every direction. "I'll make it up to you."

He shakes his head slightly. "Nothing to make up."

I head up to the counter and ask after my mom. The nurse behind the desk tells me to wait, that she's with a financial officer.

I sigh, glancing down the hallway at the line of individual little alcoves, all with glass doors. My mom's in the second office, her back to the hallway, a sling over her shoulder, and she's talking quickly. Even though I can't see the finance officer, I can tell that Mom's trying to explain something to them.

Probably that she doesn't have any money.

Sighing again, I take a step forward but stop when Mom suddenly stands and exits the office. She's in jeans and a turquoise tank top, and mascara is smeared under her drooping eyes. Her right arm is in the sling, and a couple of cuts mar her cheek. She stops just outside the doorway, digging in her purse. With it still open, she glances around, not noticing us yet.

Then she slips a green pill into her mouth and dry swallows.

Fuck.

I'm already crossing toward her, jaw locking hard.

When she sees me, she smiles tiredly, reaching out to give me a one-armed hug. I don't let her hug me yet.

"Give them to me." I stare down at her. I'm starting to be at my wits' end with this.

Maybe this is how Shin feels. And he doesn't just have her to deal with. He's got a million things coming at him as a cop, and then he gets off work and has to deal with this shit too.

Mom looks up at me. "Give you what?"

"Cut the shit, Mom."

Her lips tighten, and then she reaches into her bag, grabs the pills—in the same kind of blue prescription bottle with the label scratched off—and hands them to me. I pocket them and then steer her toward the main door.

"Thanks for the ride, nugget," she says casually, as if that exchange didn't just happen.

I have to wrap my arm around her to keep her upright as we ease toward Kepler. I glance over her head at him, and she swivels, seeming to notice him for the first time.

"Kepler?" She squints blearily at him. "Is that you? I haven't seen you in forever."

He nods, lips in a line. "Hello, Lilah."

"Hi," she says again as she sweeps him. Head to toe. "It's so good to see you."

Her lips part in a tired, coy smile, and she leans toward him enough that she stumbles, her hand reaching out to brace on his forearm, her fingers lingering there even as I pull her along toward the exit.

Shit.

No way is she checking him out. I have to be imagining things, right?

She wouldn't do that.

I wrap my arm more firmly around her waist. "Let's go, Mom."

My voice is sharp, and Mom flinches. "Why so grumpy?"

"I'm not grumpy." I guide her through the security checkpoint and the wide sliding front door.

I'm totally grumpy.

But she's still not listening to me. She's still smiling at Kepler, who steps up on the other side of her as we stop in the front circle drive, his shoulders stiff.

"I'll pull up the Jeep," he says.

Mom's smile widens. "Thanks." She brushes her fingertips over his forearm again, and he stiffens even more.

Fuck this.

I can't let it happen.

"Stop, Mom." I open my mouth to say that he's Shin's best friend. That he's the same age as her sons. All these reasons that I could use to tell her to back off. "Just stop. He's *mine*."

I say it. Right there. The real truth.

Or what I want to be the truth.

Regardless, that felt good.

And when I look across at Kepler, he arches a brow, eyes a warm gray. Then they flit behind me and stay fixed there.

The sliding door closes behind me with a gust of air, and the breath hardens in my lungs because I know —*know* from the look on Kepler's face—who's standing there.

I scrub my free hand over my mouth and then turn around, still gripping Mom's waist so that she turns partly with me.

Shin stands there, uniform neatly pressed, feet shoulder width apart, lips parting as he stares directly at Kepler with this look on his face like he's just seen a ghost.

"Shin," I grit out and then stop because I've got no clue what comes after.

"Look at the three of you together again," Mom says brightly. And apparently completely oblivious to the tension that's bounding around her. "It's just like old times."

"Not the way I remember." A hardness builds across Shin's face, closing his features, setting his chin, focus drilling into Kepler, flipping to me, and then back to his best friend. "What the *fuck*?"

Kepler raises his hands. "I'll tell you everything."

"Everything?" Shin shoves a finger toward me. "How long has this been going on?"

Kepler stills. "I don't know how to answer that question."

"Did you tell him?" Shin's voice rises. "About me?"

Kepler nods slowly. "Yes."

In a flash, Shin snaps, one quick step forward, fist coming up, and it pounds into Kepler's jaw.

One hit.

Silence after.

Kepler doesn't move from his spot, jaw already darkening with a bruise, a trace of blood on his upper lip. He spits on the sidewalk and then nods at Shin. "I deserve that, but it's not going to change anything. Shin—"

"Don't even *start*." Shin takes another step toward Kepler and then pauses, glancing down and shoving a fist hard against his bulletproof vest. "I *hit* you. What the hell am I doing? Not only that, I'm in uniform. I just punched a guy while in uniform"—his glare darts to the door behind us—"in a place where there's goddamn cameras."

"Then let's just talk, man," Kepler says, hands still up. "Let's go somewhere we can talk."

The look that my brother settles on Kepler chills me to the bone. It's ice cold. Anger vibrating underneath.

"Shin," I whisper, but my brother doesn't look at me, just shakes his head and keeps that cold stare on Kepler.

"*Now* you want to talk?" Shin's nostrils flare. "Are you going to tell me in detail what you're doing with my brother?"

"I'll tell you whatever you want to know." Kepler steps toward him, voice steady, but a swallow moves his Adam's apple, tension tightening his shoulders. "We were going to tell you."

"*We*?" Shin spits out. "Screw this. I honestly don't want to know." He turns and stalks toward the parking lot, shaking his head, his hands sinking to his belt, strides long and focused.

I stare after him, torn right down the middle. "Go after him."

"Jin." Kepler reaches out for me, hand cupping the back of my neck. I can tell he doesn't want to leave me, but one of us needs to go after Shin. And I can't leave Kepler to deal with my mom.

"Go after him," I say again. I know what their friendship means—to *both* of them. And something tells me that if Kepler doesn't go, then we'll never get to the other side of this.

"Fuck," he breathes out, glancing after my brother. "Can I come over later?"

"You better."

He nods, digs out his Jeep fob, and drops it in my extended hand, and then he jogs after Shin.

18

Velocity
Noun
1. the rate of change in an object's position

"Are you in love with him?" Mom asks.

I freeze, a glass of water in my hand, my head still spinning with what happened with Shin. We're in the kitchen, the contents of her purse all over the counter because I just made her dump it out to show me she doesn't have anything else in there.

I've never made her do that before.

I sigh, set the water down on the counter, and slide it toward her. "That's a complicated question."

She nods, picking up her wallet and some tissues and stuffing them back in her purse. Along with some makeup and a tampon. Then she picks up a keychain, with a plastic-coated picture dangling off the end. It's all four of us—back when Shin and I weren't even old enough to be in school yet. She stops on that, mouth tightening as she looks down at it.

"Are you gay?"

I blink at her. "That's not the only option, Mom. And what's with the questions?"

She drags in a breath. "I just . . . realized that we never talk about you. I mean, you've been going through stuff, and I . . ."

"Was drunk?" I shake my head, all the frustration from the past years brushing against the surface.

She pinches her eyes shut. "Yes."

I freeze, surprised. She's never admitted it so clearly. It's always been responses like *it's not a problem* or *it's no big deal*.

"Do you want to be?" I ask. It's a weird question, but she seems to understand my meaning.

She shakes her head no, then nods, then answers, "Sometimes."

I drag in a breath. That's more than I've gotten from her in a long, long time.

"I just miss him," she whispers, biting hard on her bottom lip and clutching onto her keys. "So much. I miss him so much." She shakes her head, staring at the sea blue walls. "And it never gets better. It just hurts so much to know that he wanted to be here for you, and he can't be. For graduations and birthdays and all the small stuff between. And all the really big stuff, like falling in love. He would have wanted to see you fall in love."

She's crying now, tears cresting over, and I'm watching her, not even able to talk, feeling like all the air is leaving my lungs again, like there's nothing left, like we're folding down into nothing, just an empty black hole that's never going to get filled up again because Dad's never coming back.

I stare down at my hands, flat on the countertop. The hands of a man. They belonged to a boy when he died.

"I'm sorry," she sniffles, dropping her keys and setting her thin fingers over the top of mine. "I'm so sorry, Jae. I can't seem to pull it together, and now it's too late." Her voice breaks. "I know it's too late with Shin. He's only here because of you now."

"That's not true." I swallow hard, struggling to talk around the lump in my throat. "But things have to change, Mom. If we're going to stay and help you, then things have to change. *Right now*."

"Okay." She whispers her answer. There's no conviction in the word. It's timid and scared. But for the first time, it hints that she knows how big of an answer it is. What it means. How hard it'll be. And how important it is to all of us.

I DON'T MAKE it home until sometime the next afternoon. I was supposed to go to *Halmeoni*'s, but I'm so exhausted I wouldn't even be able to hold a conversation, and she seems to hear that in my voice when I call her and reschedule.

"*Jal jayo*, Jae Jin," she orders before hanging up. *Sleep well.*

I don't know if that's possible, but I flop back on my bed, sweatpants itchy, hair damp from the shower.

I dumped out all of Mom's liquor while she slept. I went through all the cabinets, all the drawers, and the boxes in the garage that she said didn't have anything in them but clinked like glass when I moved them.

I wasn't sure about leaving her today, but she seemed

fine, cleaning around the house. And I couldn't stay there forever.

I need to talk with Shin about getting her into a program again. But I don't think the program over at Sunrise Crossing is going to help her.

What if I helped? What if I paid for it? Kepler's voice rings in my head.

No, Kepler. Absolutely fucking not.

I don't think he's stopped to think about what that would really mean.

What if she drops out? Would he want that money back?

What if she makes it through, but then she relapses two weeks later?

What if it comes between us? *Exactly* like it's come between me and Shin.

I glare at the ceiling, my stomach twisting into a hard knot.

What if it's her only real chance?

What if something like this could finally change everything?

I groan, drop a forearm over my forehead, and squeeze my eyes shut.

Hope.

It quivers like a tiny flame. Hesitant and wavering, but still there. Flickering like it wants to catch.

But a tiny flame can also start a whole freaking forest fire that burns everything down.

The knock on my door has me sitting up.

"Come in," I grate out, expecting it to be Dex since I haven't seen him since yesterday.

The door pushes open.

Kepler.

His jaw has a deep bruise on it now, eyes sunken, lips in a firm line.

I'm off the bed in two seconds, my heart thumping up into my throat. I pull him to me, and his forehead sinks against my shoulder. His tee is cool against my skin as his arms wrap around me.

We stand like that for a long minute, clasped together, just breathing each other in.

"Shin?" I ask quietly.

He shakes his head against my shoulder. "He listened to me talk for awhile, but he didn't want to talk."

"He will."

"Maybe to you." He drags in a breath and picks his head up, focusing on me. He's got dark patches under his eyes, lips slack. "Maybe in a day or two. After he calms down, I don't know. I knew that he would be angry, but I haven't ever seen him like this. I didn't expect . . ." He sighs. "I think I misjudged things."

I lace my fingers with his and pull him toward the bed. "Come on. Lie down with me."

His face softens, jaw releasing as we crawl onto the bed together. I tug up on his tee and he slips it off, then his arms go around me, his bare chest cool against mine. Our legs thread and, tucked together in our own little world, we sleep.

19

I PEER down at my phone, completely baffled by the random address that Kepler just texted me. It's quickly followed by a time: seven p.m.

This a date? I text him.

No. I won't be there.

I get a snippet of disappointment, but I quelch it. He can't be taking me off to observatories and yurts all the time.

Shin? My throat tightens as I send the text. A full week and my brother still hasn't returned any of my calls or texts. He's avoiding Kepler too.

Although Kepler and I are all over each other every chance we get, crammed around essays and dissertations, we attempt to be good on campus, but there *might* have been another bj in his office and maybe a small make-out session in the back stacks of the library. But it's the nights with him that I look forward to the most, talking quietly until we finally drift asleep, wrapped around each other, not an inch of space between our damp skin.

It's real. I hear it every time he says my name, feel it when he pushes into me with that perfect control, learn it when he talks—for hours—telling me all the things I didn't know about his life. He answers my questions. He holds nothing back.

No, he texts. *I don't think Shin will be there. It's a meeting.*

I frown. *A meeting?*

It's a support group for families who are dealing with addiction.

I stare at his text, unease flicking down my spine. *I don't know, man.*

Why not?

I hesitate, thumb hovering over my phone. *I don't know that either.*

It's just a thought. I found out about it, and I'm passing it on. If you want to go, go. If not, cool.

Did you look this up for me?

Yes.

I scrub a hand over my mouth and stare at that one word. Warmth clogs my throat and heats the back of my eyes. The fact that he looked up this meeting means that he was thinking of me. He cares about me.

For so long, I've felt alone when it comes to dealing with my mom. But I'm not alone. I never have been. I just didn't let anyone else in. Somehow Kepler climbed over that wall I'd kept locked around me, and he reminded me that I can rely on people. That he's there.

Thanks, I text. I hope he has even a glimmer of how deeply I mean it. *Whether I decide to go or not.*

A COUPLE OF HOURS LATER, I park my shitter car outside a low, brick building. It looks like an old laundromat, but the windows have been half boarded up, and the other half is covered with flyers for jobs and missing pets and all kinds of shit.

I turn off the ignition and stare at the door.

I don't know why my heart is thumping so damn hard in my chest. I pull out my phone.

I'm here. I text to Kepler.

His response is fast. *Are you going inside?*

Not sure.

Do you want me to come over?

I shake my head, like he can see me. *No.*

He's busy, and I'm capable of doing this myself.

Another car pulls up, and a woman gets out. She fixes her red hair back into a ponytail as she goes up to unlock the door on the building. She turns when the door is open, smiles at me, and waves before she ducks inside. She seems nice. Low pressure. Her manner sets me at ease—partly, at least.

Okay, I text. *I'm gonna go.*

I need to try. Kepler's right: things can't stay like they are.

My phone buzzes, and I glance down.

Do you want to call me when it's over?

A smile jumps to my lips. *Yeah, man. I do.*

I'll be waiting.

It takes me another ten minutes of watching people show up and calming my nerves before I get out of the car. But I do get out, and I tell myself that I can handle this—that I'm as strong as Flora—as I step inside the sparse room. There's a bookshelf along one wall, half full of old books, and a circle of metal folding chairs in the center of the room. Past the circle is a table with coffee and water bottles. Most everyone lingers around the table, talking in quiet voices.

Overall, it looks like I expected. I stuff my hands deep in

my pockets and step farther into the room, not sure what to do with myself.

The red-haired woman leaves the group and walks over to me. "Are you here for the meeting?"

"Yes," I say stiffly. It feels like there's a piece of rebar shoved down my spine.

She nods. "There's coffee, tea, and water. Sometimes snacks too, but I don't think anyone brought them today."

"Okay."

She smiles at me. "We're glad you're here."

"Thanks." My focus flits to the door. It's hot in here with a musky smell that doesn't sit well in my stomach. I don't know if I can sit and listen to people talking about what it's like to love an addict. I can't even read shit on the internet.

Chairs scrape on the floor, and I guess we're all supposed to sit in a circle. I itch at my forehead and glance at the door again, feeling like I missed the moment to escape.

No. I need to try this. It's not just Mom who has to do the hard work.

We all have to do it.

The door opens again, and a girl in a blue sequined hoodie steps in. She's focused on her phone, her curly hair up in a tumble on the top of her head.

It takes me a minute to place her. Partly because this is never a place I'd thought she'd be.

She's halfway across to the circle, still focused on her phone.

"Michela," I say, and her head darts up as she passes me, her eyes widening.

"Jae?"

I nod, still not really believing it's her. I never would

have guessed that her life has been touched by an addict. But then, we never really talked either.

She stops and tucks her phone into her hoodie pocket. "I've never seen you here before."

"I've never been here." I glance around. Everyone's sitting down, still chatting, but the woman who came up to me earlier is watching us. She waves to Michela, and Michela waves back, giving her a smile.

"I'm here every other week." Michela points toward two empty seats on the side of the circle closest to the door.

I nod and sit down next to her. "Someone you know is..."

Shit, I don't know if I'm supposed to ask that question.

"My sibling." Michela tilts her head. "Hey, do you want to get a coffee or something after this?"

I blink at her. "A coffee?"

"We can chat, if you want." She leans in closer, dropping her voice as the red-headed woman begins the meeting by welcoming everyone. "Not anything else. I'm just thinking that if you're here, then maybe you need someone to talk to? We don't have to talk about why you're here, but I don't mind telling you about why I am."

I swallow hard. Maybe it wouldn't be so bad to hear others talk about what it's like for them.

Maybe I need this.

"Yeah," I say. "I'd like that."

The meeting sucks. I mean, it doesn't *suck*, it's just difficult to sit through. Everyone here is different: in age, in gender, in background, in ethnicity, in experiences. And, yet, when anyone talks, I hear things that I've thought. Words that I've used. About how every good memory you have gets tinged with something bad. How every other relationship you have starts to revolve around addiction—like Shin and me. The endless guilt, the worry, the frustration. And the anger. There were times that I didn't think I could sit there anymore. That I might just tumble apart.

Somehow, I don't.

I don't talk either, so my throat is dry and my words gravely by the time I step out into the parking lot with Michela. My stomach aches from clenching so many times, but somehow, I also feel a bit lighter. Like a small weight has been lifted off my shoulders.

Michela takes one look at my shitter car and then gestures toward her slick black SUV. "Can I drive? I'll drop you back here after."

I hold back a laugh. "Yeah, that's fine. I've just got to make a call first."

"Cool." She shrugs, pulls out her own phone, and jumps up in the driver's seat.

I step around the corner and tug out my phone.

"How was it?" Kepler's low voice fills my ear.

"It sucked."

"Are you going to go back?"

"At least once or twice. The person who runs the program, Nell, said to try the group a few times before deciding if it's right for me. And that maybe I can work up to actually talking."

"That makes sense."

"But it was . . . helpful," I say. "Just hearing other people talking about how confusing life with an addict can be. How it's constantly hard to know if you're making the right decisions." I suck in a shaky breath. "It was nice to feel like I'm not alone."

"You're not alone," he says strongly. "You'll never be alone."

There's so much promise in his words. He makes me feel like there's solid ground under my feet.

Shit, the man's going to make me tear up.

I clear my throat and wipe at my eyes. "And I kinda know someone here too." I stop, realizing that it's not cool to tell him who. Everyone is supposed to be anonymous if they want.

"That's good," he says, voice so warm I could bask in it.

"I was gonna go get a coffee with them," I say. "Maybe talk about some stuff."

"That's good too. Very good."

"The thing is . . ." Am I really discussing this with him now? But I don't want to risk a misunderstanding considering that Kepler saw me kissing Michela. There's not a chance on this earth that I want to jeopardize what's growing between Kepler and me. "It's a person I sorta hooked up with in the past. I mean, not really. It didn't go anywhere." *Because I was too busy fantasizing about you.* "And there's nothing with them now. I just wanted to ask because . . . you know."

I spin on my heel, looking up at the dark clouds that cover half the sky tonight.

"You never need to ask permission. That's not what we're —" Kepler's breath catches on the other end of the line. "Wait, are we having the relationship conversation?"

I huff out a laugh. "I know it's probably better to do it in person."

"I don't feel the need to be with anyone else." His voice is soft, and it sends shivers skittering down my spine.

"You don't?" I ask.

"Not at all."

"Me neither." Hell, I'm not sure I really had the desire to be with anyone else *before* we hooked up. I've never really dated anyone for a length of time because no one ever held a candle to the man on the phone with me right now. "So then . . . we're boyfriends?"

"Yes." There's a smile in his voice. It's the same one I feel in mine, expanding across my face at record speed.

"Shit, I like that."

"Good." His voice gravels. "Then I'm going to call you that the next time I'm fucking you."

Every single cell in my body is smiling now. "Promise?"

"Absolutely."

20

Dex clasps my shoulder as he steps around the table in the student union and takes the seat across from me. "Hey, man. What's up?"

I glance up from the physics textbook I've been absorbed in for the last couple hours. "Just learning more than any liberal arts major should know about physics."

He laughs. "London here yet?"

"Nope." I tap the color-coded notes sitting next to me. "He was supposed to meet to go over these notes, but he didn't show."

I wouldn't say that physics is my favorite subject, although I do like the astronomy applications, of course, but I will say this: I don't want to give Kepler any reason to doubt the grade he's gonna give me. I'll earn that A so clearly that it's a no-brainer.

In fact, I don't think I've ever studied so much for a class.

"Well, he'll have to get the good news later." Dex is practically beaming, dimple on display since he finally shaved, olive green eyes crinkling. "You wouldn't believe the conversation I just had."

"Yeah?"

"I was gonna wait until London was around, but I guess I can tell you first." He grabs the bag of chips I've been munching on over the last hour. "It has to do with your boyfriend, actually."

"*Dude*," I hiss, glancing around quickly, although no one's paying attention to us. And the tables are packed in here—voices carrying everywhere. But still, Dex isn't exactly stealthy.

I flip my physics book closed. "Kinda trying to keep that quiet considering the circumstances."

"Oh, sure, sorry." He shrugs. "It's just that you're not exactly secretive around the apartment. I guess I got used to seeing you together. Or *hearing* you together. You guys get loud."

"Uh, yeah. Sorry about that." Honestly, it's not like Kepler and I are especially good at being stealthy either. We've been better over the last weeks, even though it's been torture watching him in the lecture well, glasses on, a pen pressed firmly against his bottom lip as he reads over the lab reports. Or the last lab when London and I were diligently working, and he passed behind us, the scent of him prickling across my shoulders as he leaned over our lab work, his breath catching slightly as he checked our results, his fingers brushing quickly against my hip.

I clear my throat. "In a couple of months, you can scream it from the rooftops."

"Will do." Dex upnods behind me, and I turn to see London weaving his way between the tables, giving us a grin when he sees us.

"S'up?" I ask when he stops at the table and drops his bag on the floor.

"Not much." He takes the seat next to me and groans

when he sees the textbook. "Crap, I forgot we were meeting to study for the midterm."

I shrug. "We can do it later."

"Thanks." He reaches down to grab his pen, but he doesn't take off the cap, just twirls it between his fingers and nods at Dex. "So, I hear you've got some good news."

"Fuck, yeah, I do." Dex reaches into the bag and grabs a chip. "You ready for this?"

I laugh at Dex's need to get us excited. It's good though. Cool to see him upbeat.

Dex opens his mouth to speak, but then he hesitates, confusion flashing in his eyes as he glances at London.

Who isn't paying attention to either of us. *At all.*

London's staring toward the food court, pen motionless in his hand, lips slightly parted, and this look on his face like he's been captured by something—hook, line, and sinker.

I follow his line of sight toward the food court, and there is no question who he's staring at.

Vain picks a green apple out of a fruit basket and rubs it on the sleeve of his t-shirt before he takes a tremendous bite. He's surrounded by the usual tight-knit group of his teammates and a couple of puck bunnies.

No, London's not just staring.

It's more than that. It's like he's picking Vain apart, from his tight IFU hockey tee that's like a second skin over thickly muscled shoulders to his grace of step as he leans forward and gives the girl behind the counter a cocky smile before pulling his wallet out of the pocket of his joggers.

I look between them, my brain connecting up about a thousand different things.

"London?" I ask.

He rotates toward me, eyes widening when he catches both Dex and I watching him curiously. "Sorry, what?"

I nod toward Vain. "Do you know him?"

It occurs to me that I've been hanging out with London. And I've occasionally been helping Vain with his classes at night. But I've never seen them at the same time before. In fact, the other night when I texted London to say we were heading to a party, he'd been keen to go until I mentioned it was at Vain's. Then he quickly texted a "no thanks". I hadn't thought about it at the time, figured he was just busy or something else had come up, but I'm thinking about it now.

London frowns. "I don't know him any more than anyone else." His pen taps the table. "So, the good news, Dex?"

We both blink at him for a minute. But then Dex shrugs and that familiar grin darts across his face.

"You ready for this?"

"Christ, man." I lean back in my chair, shaking my head, still a bit fixed on London and that look he was giving Vain, but pushing it aside for the moment to focus on my roommate. "Just tell us already."

Dex's smile expands so far that it might split his face. "Thanks to your boyfriend, we've got a venue for the fundraiser."

Simkung whacks me hard, and Kepler's not even here. "Seriously?"

"Apparently, he's friends with the manager at that new coffee shop over on Culvert," he continues. I nod. Dex must be talking about Gina, the woman Flora mentioned. "They've got the space, and they're down with the fundraiser. Kepler must have talked me up because they can't *wait* to see me this afternoon."

"Holy shit." I'm grinning. "This is big."

Dex nods. "Kepler called me an hour ago to tell me the news."

Even London's smiling, seeming to have forgotten about Vain. "So, we're on, then? It's a go?"

"Definitely a go. But"—he knocks a fist on the table—"we're gonna have to get to work. Turns out the weekend we tentatively planned is booked for a dog breed convention or something, so we moved it up two weeks earlier. Which means this weekend, I need all hands on deck."

"Absolutely, man," I say. No hesitation.

"We're in." London holds up his fist, pen sticking out to the side, and I bump him.

"Cool." Dex pulls out the now notorious fundraiser binder from his bag. "J, I'll get you a to-do list this afternoon. London, can you look at these things? Tell me if it's doable?"

I slip out my phone as Dex and London go over details, half listening as I fire off a text to Kepler. *You didn't tell me about the coffee house.*

Figured Dex would want to tell you.

My heart does a hard thump. *Thanks.*

No need to thank me. It's a good cause.

I'm thanking you anyway.

I look up, glancing around, the tables all full, the food court packed. I'd bet Kepler is on campus somewhere. Not far from here. My stomach tightens at the thought, my breath catching. We've both been busy with work the last couple of nights, and I haven't seen him other than in lecture and lab for a few days now.

Feels like eternity.

Where are you? I type.

Physics building. Getting lab ready. You?

Student center with Dex and London.

Send a picture.

What?

A picture.

I shake my head, a smile touching my lips. *Kinda weird to snap a picture right now.*

Is it?

His response makes my smile grow even more because he knows that I'll do it. I hold up my phone, quickly snap a picture of myself, then send it over.

It's a second before he responds, and then I blink down at it in confusion.

Why is Smith looking at you?

I stiffen, scanning around me. Sure enough, just over my shoulder is a table full of TAs including Smith, the damn finger-toucher, sitting on the far end.

He's not looking at me now. A soda cup and a phone are in front of him, and he's chatting with the other people at the table.

Shit. Was he staring when I snapped the picture?

I pull it up, my stomach roiling as I find him there, eyes fixed on me. With a kind of focus that makes me shiver uncomfortably.

Another text comes through. *Jin? Is he still there? You good?*

Yeah, I'm fine. I don't know why he was staring at me.

Why would he?

I wait a beat and then text again. *Does he know?*

My phone rings. I stare at Kepler's name for a heart-thumping moment. I'll hardly be able to hear him here.

I lift the phone up toward Dex. "Can I—"

"Go." He waves me away. "This part has nothing to do with you."

I'm up and across the room in a second, diving into the little alcove just across the hallway.

"You shouldn't be calling me," I say as soon as I answer.

"Why not? I always call you."

I sigh, turning so my back hits the recessed wall. "Not in the presence of the finger-toucher."

"He doesn't know," Kepler says.

"You positive?" I shake my head. "Dex was just talking about us at full volume. I just don't want shit to go bad."

"It won't."

"You never should have convinced me to take your freaking class."

He laughs softly. "Maybe I just wanted to get you close to me. And, honestly, I never in a million years thought I had a chance with you."

My mouth falls open. "Seriously?"

"Desperately." There's a low breathiness to his voice, the kind that he has when he's pushing into me, and damn . . .

I clear my throat, adjust my ready-to-go dick. "Fuck, now I'm hard."

"Right now?"

"You have no idea."

"I might have a clue."

There's a long pause, both of us breathing. Not going to lie, the thought of hightailing it over to the physics building and locking ourselves in his office for a few minutes passes through my mind, but it's way too big of a risk during the day. We've only slipped in there after most everyone's gone. Besides, there's not enough time for me to get all the way over there before his next lab section.

"Find somewhere alone," he says.

"I'm at the student union. There's nowhere to be alone."

"There are private study rooms upstairs. Go there."

"You're insane."

"Does that mean you're not going to go?"

"Shit." I glance back toward the tables. Dex and London are hunkered over the binder. The finger-toucher is still chatting with the other TAs. Hell, maybe he wasn't really staring at me in that picture, just happened to be glancing over at the exact right time.

Or he saw some dude randomly snapping selfies in the café and had to look. I'd look at that too.

"What's your decision?" Kepler asks.

"Not going," I say, even as I find myself jogging up the stairs, dick bouncing in my athletic shorts, pulse thumping.

"You're already walking there, aren't you?"

I roll my eyes. "You think you know me so well."

"I do. Find an empty room."

I groan. "What are we doing, Kepler?"

"Getting you off. Now find an empty room."

It's quiet up here—just some university offices that are rarely used. And private study rooms that you can rent. But no one does because the library is so much easier and it's free.

I slip into the room farthest down the hall, closing the door behind me and flipping the lock. Inside, there's a table with four chairs. Just a bit of natural light from the high rectangular windows. No cameras, no anything except the square room and long table.

"Shit," I mumble. "This is a bad idea. Dex and London are downstairs waiting for me."

"You can leave at any time."

"Yeah, I know." But I don't. I stand there. "Shit, this is awkward."

"Unzip your jeans."

I laugh. "I'm not wearing jeans. And that's not making me feel less awkward."

"How about this . . . I'm in my office now. Door locked. Shade down."

"You're what?" I croak out. The picture of him in his tiny office, phone pressed to his ear, cock hardening against his zipper—it all just about pushes me over a cliff.

"You heard me." His voice is low again, sexy as fuck. "I'm sliding down to the floor behind my desk, so no one can see me, and I'm unzipping."

I hold my breath and listen with everything I have. I don't think I can hear his zipper, but just the thought of it makes me reach down and adjust myself.

I glance around. I'm solidly alone.

Am I really gonna do this?

I take a breath and stroke my hand over the outside of my slick shorts again, a low groan rolling out.

"I love the sounds you make," Kepler says softly. "Now fist yourself."

"*Dude.* Just like that? Don't I get a lead-up first?"

"Fine." He laughs. "What are you wearing?"

"What am I *wearing*? Do you seriously give a shit?"

"Yes, I do. I'm curious since you said you aren't wearing jeans."

I groan. "Athletic shorts, a black tee, and a freaking beanie because I haven't showered yet today. What the fuck are you wearing?"

"Jeans. Hoodie. No beanie. Okay, you ready to jack off now?"

I'm laughing, smiling so hard that my face hurts. "I suppose. My hand has been on my dick this entire conversation."

His breath catches. "Same."

Fuuuck.

That changes the mood. I glance at the door—locked.

The windows—high up. I'm standing next to the table, one hand holding the phone, the other palming myself.

I swallow, saliva pooling in the back of my mouth. "So, your hand is on your dick?"

"Yes."

Fuck me. *Fuck me.*

My fingers tug at the elastic of my shorts, pulling them down an inch. I'm free-balling it today, so there's nothing else between. "Are you stroking yourself?"

"Not until you do."

Christ. That's hot.

I reach under the elastic hem of my shorts and slowly grab my dick, sure that he can hear my breath stagger as I take a long, deliberate stroke—the way he strokes me—the fabric slick against my knuckles.

"Oh fuck," I push out. "I just did it."

"Then I am too." He lets out a gravel-throated groan, and it's so hot that I could probably get off just listening to him. Which I guess is what's happening.

"Keep talking," I say.

"Do you want to know what I'm thinking about?"

"Yeah," I mumble, rolling my thumb over my cockhead as I pick up the pace. Hearing his voice makes it so fucking good. Way better than jacking off by myself.

"I'm thinking about the last time you were in my office." He's breathing heavier, voice becoming even more gritty. "Your cock in my mouth. So sexy looking down at me."

I grip my shaft harder, listening to that voice of his.

"You were fucking my mouth so deep that I could throat-swallow," he continues. "I can almost taste it now. Slick and salty, running down the back of my throat."

Shit.

I pump harder, balls tightening, forearm taut. "I want you here."

"You'll see me tonight."

I squeeze my eyes shut. "*Fuck.* Quinn, fuck. I want you to fuck me."

"Tell me," he says, the command in his voice tightening my balls further.

I jack faster, picturing it, trying to keep a grasp on reality. My knees half buckle, and I stumble forward, bracing my forehead against the wall, hand still deep in my shorts.

My wrist loosens as I stroke faster, messier, forgetting everything except for his voice and breath on the other end of the phone, images welling in my brain. I let them spill out, talking but not even really thinking about it. I imagine him gripping onto my shoulders as he pounds me, both of us sweat-slicked and groaning, until we flip and . . . *I push into you.*

"Jin." Kepler's low, breathy voice curls around me. "Is that what you want?"

My hand pauses on my dick.

I just said that out loud?

The image is so vivid in my mind.

Just go with it, J.

"Yes." I'm breathing hard, and I start stroking again, pulled into the thought of what it would be like, my dick inside him. I squeeze my eyes. "Christ, you'd be so tight. Sexy as fuck on my dick." My orgasm zaps out of me suddenly, a shout welling up in my chest that I can't cage.

As I'm milking it out, I hear him follow, cursing in a low, tight voice, and I close my eyes to picture how he must look, spurting his release, hand still on his beautiful dick.

Fuck me. Fuck me.

We're silent for a long minute, other than our breaths rasping over the phone.

"Shit," I mumble as I return to planet Earth. "I made a mess."

His laugh is warm. "Me too."

"Dude, I came all over my hand." I look around for a tissue or a paper towel.

"Was it worth it?"

"So much." I drag in a breath, feeling the expansion of my chest and the release of my abs and pelvis. "We need to do this again."

"Anytime you want," Kepler says. "See you tonight?"

"You better, after that." I wipe off my dick with my palm, then pull my hand out from under the elastic of my shorts because I'm already getting hard again as my mind spirals over what we just did. And what we *will* do. But I hesitate.

"I'm not quite ready," I find myself saying. "To fuck you, I mean. I know we just, uh, fantasized about it together? But I'm not..."

"Relax," he says easily. "There's no rush."

"Yeah, okay." I inhale a relieved breath, and my nose wrinkles. I smell like jizz, and both my hands are a mess. I'm definitely gonna need to stop by the bathroom.

"And, Jin?" Kepler's voice is throaty. "We'll get through this. Eight little weeks. And then I'll fuck you myself on that study table, and I don't care who sees."

"I want that." A smile grows across my face. "Okay, maybe not people watching, but I want to be out." I swallow hard, all the things I deeply want vibrating in my chest. "I want to be out with you."

He drags in a sharp breath. "We will be."

"Promise?"

"*Yes.*" The conviction in his voice grounds me, and I'm

grinning ear to ear as we hang up. I step out of the study room, focused on the men's room across the hall.

"Hey, aren't you in Lacher's class?"

Shit.

The voice comes out of nowhere, and I just about jump out of my skin.

I turn, and my stomach drops to the floor.

Smith leers at me, waiting for an answer. I've never been this close to him before, and he's got a really long nose, a slight sneer on his chunky lips, and not a spec of friendliness in his glare.

"Yeah." I stand up to my full height, which is an inch taller than him. "I've seen you, I think. You're a TA."

"I am." He holds out his hand. "Name's Egan Smith."

I stare down at the extended hand. *Shit.*

"Sorry, I don't shake hands. But I'm Jae Jin." I hook a thumb toward the bathroom. It's glistening with my cum. "Gotta take a piss. Good to meet you."

"You too," he says, but I'm already halfway across the hall.

I head to the sink, shoving my hands into the water, glancing up in the mirror to find myself wide-eyed, hair askew, face flushed.

Shit, shit, *shit.*

I don't think Kepler's right on this one.

I'm pretty sure Smith knows.

21

I THROW myself headfirst into the fundraiser for the next two weeks. I'm barely keeping up. I have essays that I've got to finish, the hour that I'm spending at Mom's every day, and a tutor session with Vain; although, he doesn't need my help anymore. The dude is definitely not dumb.

I don't see Kepler much. He's out of town for part of it anyway, flying out to Virginia for his last interview.

Which meant that Smith took over his lab section for a week, and he had no problem assigning London and me extra cleanup duty for our "shoddy, pathetic work."

He's a fucking asshole, and a bitter taste grows in my mouth every time I see him.

Kepler still doesn't think he knows about us. But the sight of him standing across from me—hand extended for a handshake—sticks in my head. There's still something vaguely familiar about him.

And I think he knows. Or he guesses.

If so, why hasn't he done something about it? Maybe he doesn't plan to? Or maybe he's waiting for something?

The question is *what*?

I'm still fixed on the answer to that question when Kepler's name darts across my phone Saturday night, and I answer in a split second, practically tripping over myself.

"Come over." Kepler's voice is husky, and so sexy I about swallow my own tongue. He must have just gotten back from the airport.

"To your place?" I ask.

"Yes."

"Your gray-walled secret hideaway?"

He laughs. "Yes."

"You're ready for that? I mean, we're *finally* at that point in our relationship?"

"Absolutely."

I'm grinning, clutching the phone against my ear as I complete a last scan for typos over a paper on property law in *Pride and Prejudice* for a graduate lit class. "How did the interview go?"

He pauses. "I'll tell you when you get here. I'll pick you up?"

I lean back and run a palm across my bare chest. "I can drive. Shitter car's still working like a charm."

"Roads will be difficult for a small car," he says, concern heavy in his voice. "Especially with snow on the ground. And there aren't street signs."

"It's only a few miles, right?"

"Three. Up to the west behind your apartment."

"I'll make it." I flip my iPad closed. "I'll call if I have problems."

"Then I'll text directions." He sighs. "Just get here, Jin. I can't believe I haven't seen you in a week."

My car moves slowly down the dirt roads to Kepler's house, back tires sliding on the one-inch layer of snow. True to his word, none of the streets are labeled. The directions are more like *turn right at the two fallen logs shaped like an X*. But I find my way, headlights crawling over a narrow road framed by pines, snow floating softly down, and the engine struggling when the road hairpins up.

The house must be on a ridge, and it takes me at least twenty minutes to traverse the three miles between my apartment and his place.

No wonder he owns that Jeep.

When I finally break through the trees, my breath catches.

Fucking *Christ*.

I'd expected something a bit crazy—it's obvious that he's got money. But I didn't expect it to be one of *those* houses. The kind owned by out-of-staters who buy these secluded mountain homes to live in a month or two out of the year with high, wide windows and beamed ceilings and antler chandeliers.

I swallow, park on the gravel circle drive, and just *stare* at the house.

What he must think of Dex and my crappy apartment with its scratched vinyl flooring, single bathroom, and duct tape sealing up the windows.

All this time, he's lived here.

My eyes grow into saucers as I step up to the double front door with copper entryway lights and take in the solar system carved into the thick wood.

No way it'll be him who answers when I knock.

But there he is opening the door, a light smile curling his lips. Gorgeous as always as those smoky eyes flick down me. His hair is askew, swept back but sticking up just slightly on the side, jeans and a lavender tee, bare feet sliding on the wood floor as he steps back to let me in.

"You're shitting me," I say, shaking my head. "This is not where you live."

"It's home," he says softly.

"Then why do we fuck at my place with the constant drone of gas station traffic and the loud water pipes and Dex singing his head off in the shower?"

He grabs my hoodie between his long fingers, pulling me closer to him. And suddenly I'm not looking at the high arching windows or the stone fireplace or the open concept kitchen with a huge rack for pans over the equally huge island. I'm just looking at him, my breath lodging in my throat.

I want to ask about the interview. And yet, I really, really don't.

I just want a few minutes before the confirmation that he's leaving sets in.

"We can stay here anytime you want," he says, but as soon as he gets the sentence out, I'm kissing him, one hand grasping at the nape of his neck to bring him closer, the other sliding down his back, smoothing over the hard ridges and planes, a desperate groan as his warm tongue slips into my mouth, backing me up until my shoulders hit the wall.

All thoughts of the future fly out of my head.

We're combustible. This instant pull between us, filling up my veins, and I can feel it racing his pulse as he sweeps his hands down to palm my ass.

Seven days without him was an eternity. And on top of that, just being here warms something deep in me. He's letting me in. Fully. Completely. Even though I suspect it's sometimes hard for him.

I don't know how long we kiss like that, him gripping my

ass, my shoulders against the wall. We finally break to breathe, the snow that had been in my hair long melted.

"Jin," he mumbles, his forehead falling against my shoulder, his hands still cupping my ass. "Can I show you something?"

"Now?" I groan out, my voice thick with the need to have his cock in my mouth. "Is it your dick?"

"No." He laughs as he steps back. "Later. Come on."

He leads me through the house. Which, compared to the one I grew up in, is a freaking palace. Up some stairs and down a hallway that's glassed on one side, there's nothing but evergreen trees and nighttime sky to our left, and I get what he means about *empty*. It's quiet here, the space cavernous, the silence deep.

I side-glance him as we walk down the hall. I wonder if he has a lot of memories here from before his grandfather died. During those long nights, he told me a lot about his grandfather and growing up, but not much about this house.

He steps aside at an open doorway at the end of the hall, letting me through first. The lights are off, the bedroom in shadows, but there's enough moonlight through the wide balcony doors to see that it's all simple lines. A bed, a desk, a reading chair with a utilitarian light to one side.

I scan the room. "You've got the whole house, but it looks like you mostly live in here."

"I don't need the rest of the space." He nods toward the glass doors. "Through here."

I step out onto the wide balcony, thick beams coming down on the sides, mostly empty except for a small table and one chair set up by the railing.

But, shit, the *view*.

I was right; the house is on a ridge, the lights of Indigo

Falls below. Close enough that I can still distinguish the streets. Including the gas station and the apartments across from it.

"You have a view of my place," I murmur.

"Yes." A snowflake falls on his lashes, and he blinks it away.

"Can you see my window?"

He laughs softly. "It's too far to see anything except for the light. But I can see that, and sometimes I just stand here, knowing you're over there."

A smile expands across my face as I rest my forearms on the railing, brushing off the thin layer of snow. "That's stalkerish of you."

"It is." He drags in a slow breath, stepping behind me, hands landing on either side of the railing, lips close to my ear, his chest to my back. "I'm absolutely guilty of looking for that light. Just to know you're there."

I full-on shiver.

I don't know how he does that to me. No one else ever has. It's like he's got a special superpower that annihilates me specifically. Turns me inside out and flays me open.

Not that I'm complaining. Especially as one of his hands leaves the railing to settle on my hip, fingers digging into my jeans just hard enough to make me pull in a sharp breath, my mind already flashing to all the places I want him to fuck me.

Or all the places I want to fuck him?

Nerves bubble up in my chest.

"Do you want to go inside?" His warm breath raises goosebumps, but the snowflakes on my face are pinpricks of cold.

"Nah." So much blood rushes to my dick that my head spins. "I want you to fuck me right here."

His fingers tighten on my hip, his groan close to the nape of my neck as his lips fall there, and then in one quick zip, he's fisting my cock, stroking me as his own hard dick rakes against my ass. Our breathing becomes fractured, visible as white puffs of air, and he builds me up, fast and hard, only easing back as I shove my jeans down. The cold air startles me, and I twist to see him step inside to grab a packet of lube and tear off the edge with his teeth as he returns to me. He's quick to lube his fingers before they slide down my crease.

I'm always tight as hell, but I relax quicker now, anticipation building like a storm.

When his second finger slips inside, I'm already impatient, grinding back for him. I rip off my tee, and the cold air hardens my nipples, causing the barbell to pinch in a way that makes my balls tighten.

"More," I push out, the word that always comes to my lips when I'm with him. More, more, *more*. I'll never get enough of him.

I cover his hand that's fisting my dick and take over his rhythm, his hand slipping out from underneath mine. A brush of cold air kisses my back, and I turn to see him stroking himself, a condom packet he must have grabbed earlier pinched between the fingers of his free hand.

I watch as he sheaths himself, always mesmerized by the roll of the condom over his shaft.

When he's done, he looks up, his gaze playing over me, head to toe. His eyes heat as he steps behind me, his palm settling between my shoulder blades and then smoothing down my spine as his dick grazes my ass cheek. Anticipation sucker punches me.

His brow hitches as he lines himself up. "Hotty-pants is too tame a word for you."

I groan as the fat head of his cock presses against my taint. "I told you, you're the hotty-pants in this relationship."

"I'm not." His words strangle as he starts to push in. The feeling of him consumes me as I stretch to fit him, all that pressure mounting low in my pelvis. "That's you, Jin."

I suck in a breath, relaxing to take him. "What if we both are? Because I know *you* are hot as fuck. And when we're together . . ." I moan as he slides in deeper, then lean forward against the railing so I can feel him bury himself to the hilt.

"Jin," he breathes. "Finish your thought."

I had a thought?

I try to focus on speaking. "You just make me feel so *good* about myself. No matter how fucked up my life is."

He pauses, deep inside of me. Usually we'd be fucking hard by now. Instead, he grabs my shoulders and pulls me so my back presses against his chest. He's warm against the cold breeze, holding me flush against him. His lips graze my ear.

"I missed you," he says softly. "So much."

I squeeze my eyes, emotion heavy in my throat. My dick and ass want to race forward to the part where he fucks me hard against the railing, but my mind aches to linger in this moment, to draw it out. To simmer in this deep, warm feeling that grows in my chest every time Kepler is near. He kisses along my neck as he starts to move, thrusting deeply and steadily, still holding me against his chest. It's different than usual—quieter.

"Kepler," I say between heavy breaths, not even sure what I want to say as we grip onto each other like our lives depend on it.

He slows his strokes. "Do you want to fuck me?"

"*Yes*." God fucking *yes*. Now, here. With lights spread out above and below, and the slow drift of snow falling. And how did he know that? But I don't want to stop to question it.

"I want you to come first," I say.

It feels like less pressure that way. Like if I mess things up somehow, or if I can't go through with it, it's not as big of a deal.

He nods against my shoulder, burying himself deep in me and pushing me forward. The railing is cold against my chest, and in a few strokes, his breath starts to come sharp and fast. It's like I'm on the edge of the world, the lights of the city blurring as he slams into me, a guttural "*Jin*" on his lips with his orgasm. I let him simmer in his release, until he eases out of me, forehead falling down between my sweat-drenched shoulder blades.

We still for a long moment, his breath warm on my shoulder, my thoughts starting to spin.

I'm going to fuck him.

"Are you sure about this?" I ask him.

"Absolutely." He grips my jaw, pulling me back and twisting me into a kiss. My tongue delves into his mouth, and I turn, my hands smoothing down his back to cup his ass, my fingers playing in his crease. And then *he* turns, switching us so his chest is against the railing, my fingers already sliding across his taint as I stand behind him.

My breath catches in my throat as I brush against his hole, fingers shaking. I didn't expect touching him there to be so hot.

"*Christ*," I mumble, my dick twitching as I feather a finger over him. "What if I mess up somehow?"

He looks over his shoulder, dark-gray eyes evaluating me. "That's impossible."

"I could hurt you?"

He shakes his head. "No. I'll tell you if there's anything I need."

I pause. I'm still touching him, but I'm nervous as hell.

"Jin," he says, voice dropping low, his hand coming back to grab my wrist. "I want you to fuck me."

I groan, his words resonating low in my gut. I reach for what's left of the lube packet, squeezing some out into my palm. My entire body trembles as I slowly slide a finger into him, watching as best I can in the dim light, snowflakes clustering on my lashes. He takes me easily, grinding back with a moan on first one finger, then two.

It's so hot that I could stand there for hours, just touching him and watching him. But my dick is throbbing, and the urge to bury it deep inside of him swamps me.

"Desk drawer," he says.

"What?"

"Condoms."

I reluctantly leave him to retrieve a second condom, my stomach knotting with so many damn emotions that I can't sort them out. Desire. Need. Nerves. Anticipation. Eagerness.

Did I say nerves? Because they need to be counted twice.

I return to him before rolling the condom on, pinching the tip, my hands still shaking.

"I, uh . . ." I swallow hard. "Think we need more lube."

"Here." He reaches down, and I hear the snap of his condom.

My eyes bug out as he hands it back to me, and then I groan as I tip the condom, letting his cum dribble out, using his own release to cover my dick.

"This is so fuckin' dirty," I mumble as I stroke his release onto me. "In the best possible way." I toss his condom to the side, my nerves spiking to new heights as I meet his gaze.

"Ready?" he asks. His voice is steady, and I latch onto that.

"Yeah, I'm ready." I feel it in my bones as I line my dick up, and then, with the same slowness that he used with me that first time, I push in. Just the crown of my cock at first, and I'm overtaken by his moan and initial tightness before he relaxes enough to take me. And I finally—*finally*—get to see how it looks as my dick fills him, inch by gradual inch, disappearing into him.

Fuck me. Fuck me. *Fuck me.*

He grips me so tight. And he's so beautiful splayed out before me, leaning against that railing—the spread of his shoulders, delts taut, muscles curving down his back to narrow hips that I clasp with both hands, snow melting on his hot skin as my dick buries to the hilt, my thumbs rolling over those dimples above his ass.

"Fuuuuck," I breathe out. "This is the best sex I've ever had, and it hasn't even really started yet."

He twists at the waist, spine curving, smoky eyes finding mine, and I lean forward with the need to have his mouth on mine, groaning and eyes almost rolling back at the change of angle that squeezes my dick even more. Since he's taller than me, I can't really kiss him from here, but our lips brush, our tongues dancing open-mouthed before he makes a circle with his hips, and it's like I'm hit by a freaking avalanche.

"*Holy fuck*, that's incredible," I mumble. And I don't know if I'm just talking about the sex, or if I'm talking about everything. What we have. This link between us shimmers and sparks, constantly growing, getting bigger until it's almost overwhelming.

The sky's the limit.

I didn't know that being with someone could be like this.

"Jin," he says in that low voice, and that's all it takes before we're lost together, my fingers gripping hard into his hips, both of us possessed by the feeling of each other—our breath, our movements, the heat of our skin, and tenor of our groans—until I can't distinguish between his breath and mine, between his movement and mine.

And for the first time in my life, holding onto Kepler Quinn—with Indigo Falls spread far-off below, city lights blending into the stars and the snow—I couldn't want anything more.

"Are you cold?" Kepler steps out of the balcony door, a plate of eggs and toast in each hand, his gaze flicking over me—just like it always does—before coming to land on my face.

I shake my head. "Feels good."

The balcony is cold under my bare feet, and I'm buck-ass naked. It's a nice respite considering we fucked until we were overheated and sweat drenched.

And starving.

Hence the three-in-the-morning eggs and buttered toast.

Kepler sets the plates on the table, forks propped on the side. He ducks back into his room to grab a chair from his desk and sits across from me, hair falling into his eyes, just as naked as me as he tucks into his eggs.

I do the same.

I'm famished. I must eat for a solid two minutes before looking back up, and when I do, I find Kepler looking across the table at me, the light of his bedroom illuminating his face as snowflakes tumble softly around us.

"You didn't tell me about the interview," I say.

"No, I didn't."

I smile. "You got it, didn't you?"

His eyes spark. "I did."

I recline, the seatback freezing my spine, eggs forgotten. "That's truly incredible. Congratulations."

"Thank you." He watches me across our eggs, the excitement I'd expected doesn't cross his face. I mean this is *big*. Why isn't he acting like it?

He sets down his fork and taps his thumb on the edge of the wood table, making a soft clunking noise. "Have you thought about coming with me?"

I set down my fork too. "I've *thought* about it a lot."

"And?"

I scrub a hand through my mess of hair, glancing off toward the street and building lights below. "I just don't know."

"How about a weekend?" he asks, leaning forward and placing his elbows on the small table. That corded leather is tied around his wrist, sexy-as-fuck vein running underneath. "There's an air and space museum and a couple of lighthouses. Or we can rent a boat."

A tingle radiates through my chest. "A sailboat?"

"Sure. Do you sail?"

I laugh. "Not at all, man. I've never been on a boat. Never even left Colorado except for once."

His brows rise. "Where'd you go?"

"Carlsbad Caverns with my dad."

"My grandfather and Flora and Adelard took me there once." Kepler smiles. "That place is freaking awesome."

"Yeah, it is."

Silence. His thumb rolls along the edge of the table.

I tilt my head. "Kepler Quinn wants to give me another first."

He hums softly. "I like the sound of that."

"I do too." I inhale slowly. "I wish I could return the favor."

He huffs out a laugh that becomes a white cloud. "You don't know how many firsts you've given me."

"Name one," I challenge him.

He picks up his toast, bites the corner, chews slowly, then swallows. "Love."

I still. He doesn't say *I love you*. And I don't say it back. It doesn't feel like the right time yet. Not with Shin still angry, and not with having to keep so much of ourselves hidden.

But it's there, hovering all around us, and it feels like we could reach out and catch it, if we wanted, like softly falling snowflakes. We could snag it with our fingertips and make it real.

So I nod, reach for my toast, and hold it above the plate. "A weekend. I'm in."

His smile is perfect.

22

Free fall
Noun
1. downward movement under the force of gravity only

"This place looks *fantastic*." I'm standing in the front entry of the coffee house, my mouth slightly open as I stare around me. I mean, I *knew* the fundraiser was coming together, but I had no idea it would look this good.

There's artwork *everywhere*. Every conceivable bit of wall space is covered to the point it's almost overwhelming. So many colors and styles. And I can see some of Dex's work on the far wall by the patio door.

The coffee house is in an old industrial building—high, deep-red walls and exposed pipes—it was like this place was made to show off an event like this.

Dex's green eyes scan the room, too focused on everything that needs to be done to stop and take it all in. "Can you check that all the correct auction cards are lined up with the right artwork?"

"You bet." I throw myself at the task, just like I have over the last couple weeks, working hard with London. But everyone's been donating time when they can, Kepler too.

The amount of artist support that Dex's friend, Eli, brings in is crazy. The fundraiser's way bigger than Dex ever expected. Turns out there's a thriving artist community spread out over all these little mountain towns, and I'm pretty sure this place will be packed tonight.

But right now, it's just Dex, London and me—along with Gina, the coffee shop owner, and a couple of employees.

The hours go fast with London and me plowing through every task that Dex sets in front of us, and before we can blink, some of the artists start showing up, and then guests, and then the freaking mayor and university president. I'm pretty sure the entire town of Indigo Falls turns out for this event, and the auction cards fill up with so many bids that I have to rush over to the campus printshop and make some additional pages.

"Holy crap," Dex whispers in my ear after I get back. He was just shaking hands with the over-ecstatic principal who works at his school. "We're gonna make more for these kids than I ever expected."

I nod toward the principal, who is talking excitedly with Dex's supervising teacher. "And I'm betting you've probably got a job offer for after graduation too."

He laughs. "I didn't think about that."

Of course he didn't. Because he's *Dex*. He did this for the kids, throwing himself in without even thinking of himself. London couldn't be more right about him: he's a good man.

I pull him in for a half-hug. "You did it, man. You pulled this off."

His smile widens. "You helped me."

"Yeah, barely."

"Nah. You came through in the end." He hugs me back. "Like you always do."

When we release each other, we're both smiling. Hell, even London has been smiling tonight, and I haven't seen him do that much in recent weeks.

I tried to talk to him a few times about whatever happened in the café with Vain, but he always ducks out of the conversation with an excuse. A legitimate excuse about listening in lecture or needing to get to class. But still ... an excuse.

So, when he slides up next to us with a broad smile on his face, I instantly return it.

He leans in closer to me and whispers, "Saw our physics TA here."

And, of course, every cell in my body heats and vibrates. I don't think that'll ever stop when it comes to Kepler Quinn.

But I just nod. "He said he'd be here."

I try to keep my gaze from flicking around the room, but it doesn't work. If Kepler's here, then I can't not look for him. It's as simple as that.

But when I glance toward the door, someone else catches my eye.

Shin.

He stands there, taking in the room, hands in his pockets, wearing slacks, a button-down, and a sharp wool coat. I can't remember the last time I saw him out of uniform.

I drag in a breath and cross to him, stopping a few feet away. "Thanks for coming."

His head jerks in a nod. "I wouldn't miss it. It looks like you and Dex have been working hard."

"Mostly Dex," I say. "Can we talk?"

Maybe not the best place, but he hasn't answered a single text I've sent over the last weeks, and I'll take any chance I can get to fix this.

His lips press as he glances around. "You sure that's a good idea?"

"Yeah, I am. I miss you, bro." I point toward the patio doors. "Let's go outside."

I turn and head that way, hoping like hell that he's following. When I step out into the cold night and turn, he's there. Three steps behind me. Looking pissed and stubborn as always, but still there.

I cross through the patio, which is crowded with people, and take the steps down to a wide, cracked sidewalk that looks like it's been here for as long as the warehouses. The snow has melted, a brief respite before we get hit by the first official storm that's expected any day now, and the sky above us is a dark roll of clouds. I stop at the end of the sidewalk.

Shin stops across from me.

"So . . . you're fucking," he says.

Okay, right into it then.

"No." I frown. "Well, yes. But not in the way you just implied."

"And how did I imply?" He crosses his arms over his chest. Looking every bit like a cop, even out of uniform.

"You implied that it's only about the fucking. It's not." I dig my toes into the cement. "Why is it an issue for you, Shin? Really? I know that it's weird and that finding out that way was shitty, but it's been *weeks* now, and I've never seen you this angry. Not even at some of the assholes Mom's dated over the last years."

His arms fall from across his chest, his coat falling open. "You don't know."

"That's why I'm asking." I itch at my jaw, trying to figure my brother out. "Tell me what's going on. If you won't talk to Kepler, then talk to me."

He shakes his head, cracking his neck in a way that makes my gut knot. "Are you sure you really want to hear it?"

"Of course, I do." I swallow hard. "Do you have feelings for Kepler?"

"No." He shakes his head. "Not like you're thinking."

"Then explain it to me."

He groans in annoyance. "It was a long time ago, and it's not like I'm harboring a torch for the guy. I mean, we're best friends, and that's how I think about him, but . . ." His lips tighten. "He's the only one."

"The only guy you've been with?"

"It seems so easy for you." His hands swing up in frustration. "You didn't even really come out, just you *were* suddenly. It was the same with Kepler a few years ago. It hasn't been so easy for me, and I don't even fully know why. I'm broken about it. Really fucking broken."

"You're not broken," I cut in.

"The fuck I'm *not*," he snaps, his voice rising. "I *hit* him, and I've got no clue how to apologize for that. I hit him, not because I'm jealous of him, but because I'm jealous of what the two of you have. And that I'm *never* going to fucking have it."

"Shin," I start again, but he snorts and plants his hands on his head, walking in a tight circle. I watch him for a moment, letting him calm.

When he finally stops before me again, his chin is still rigid, but his eyes are marginally softer.

I start slowly. "I don't believe for a second that you won't find what you're looking for."

"How is that possible when I can't even manage to come out?" He snorts. "You know, a gay cop. Who would want that?"

"A very lucky man would." My forehead lines. "Hell, I think a lot of people would. And if someone can't see who you are—a person who's dedicated his life to helping others, who's strong and caring and annoyingly stubborn, and who just happens to be gay—then they have the problem, not you."

He huffs out a low laugh. "See, I know that. In my brain. But when I go to tell someone, even you, it just doesn't come out. Even after all these years, I'm still not ready. And that frustrates the hell out of me."

"Then be patient with yourself."

"*Patient?*"

"Yeah." I nod. "You can be out around me. And out around Kepler. Dex, too, if you're feeling comfortable. Let that be enough for now. And then maybe there's a next step after that, but you don't need to take it today."

"Patient," he scoffs. But he's looking at me steadily. "I guess I could give that a try. I don't know. It's just . . . frustrating."

"Have you ever talked to Kepler about it?"

His frown deepens. "It's awkward, with him being the only guy I've been with. I don't know that he would even want to talk about—"

"Of course he would." I lean back on my heels, my breath coming out in white puffs. "You should talk to him."

He stiffens. "I don't even know what to say. I don't know how to talk about anything with him right now."

"You've been friends for twenty years. Don't give that up." I shake my head. "Not for anything."

He drags in a breath, hand coming up to itch under his wool collar. "Since when did you become so damn smart?"

"I've always been this way, *hyeong*."

He snorts. "Guess I should hang out with you more."

My smile falls. "You really should."

"What about after my shift on Monday, maybe?" He shrugs one shoulder stiffly. "We could go get a beer. At that one bar?"

I blink at him. He's asking me to hang out? "You mean, at Taverns?"

He nods. "If you're up that late. I don't know if—"

"Hell, yeah," I say, grinning. "I'd like that."

"Maybe Dex can come too." He eyes me. "Are you still doing that two-drink limit?"

"Yeah." I nod. "You?

"Every time." A half-smile curves up his lips as he reaches out and smacks me on the shoulder. "Love you, bro."

I tip my chin at him. "You too."

Shin upnods at me. "And I know you've been heading over to Mom's a lot. I see your car in the driveway."

"You drive by?"

"Beginning and end of every shift. I always have."

"She's doing good. She should be here tonight. She'd be excited if you talked to her for a bit too."

He inhales through his nose, looking over my shoulder toward the packed coffee house. "I'll try. But no promises."

TWENTY MINUTES LATER, after chatting for a bit more, Shin and I head back in, stopping in front of Dex's work. There are some newer ones of me, which feels kinda odd considering they're for auction, but I told Dex it was cool.

The one of Shin, Kepler, and I in front of the treehouse is there too. Not for auction.

We wander over to look at some of the other artwork, which isn't easy because of the crowd. Servers cut through the throng, carrying trays of miniature coffees garnished with peppermint sticks. Or teas with fresh lemon and sprigs of thyme.

Dex is over at the coffee bar talking to a tall man with colorful tattoos sleeving both arms and bleach blond hair. The man must be Eli Reynolds, the artist who helped him out. And the one responsible for that naked guy-in-the-water portrait.

Christ, that feels like ages ago.

I look for Kepler, who I still haven't seen. We're definitely not gonna be able to be around each other much here, but that doesn't preclude an aching glance from across the room.

Shin and I head over to talk with Flora and Adelard for a bit, which could be awkward, but Flora has a way of smoothing things. And then I excuse myself because I'm getting uneasy about not seeing Kepler.

I pull out my phone as I cut through the crowd toward the patio door, but there isn't a single text from him. I turn and head around the back of the building where it's all asphalt and brick walls, then stop.

Two men stand at the farthest edge of the building.

Kepler and another man.

My body jolts awake like it always does, and a wash of relief rolls over me, but it fades as I stand there a second longer.

Standing across from him is the freaking finger-toucher.

Kepler's in that sleek leather jacket, shaking his head, and Smith is saying something to him.

No, they're arguing?

I frown, hesitating, not sure what I should do. Go to him?

Probably a bad choice.

Smith steps closer to Kepler, his voice rising so that I can almost hear it, and then in the blink of an eye, Smith's hands dart up and shove Kepler back. He stumbles, barely catching himself.

Christ.

Did that really happen?

I'm moving before I can answer my own question. Before Kepler even responds, my pulse throbbing in my throat, tension spiking down my spine. Bad choice or not, there is no way I'm not going to my boyfriend.

I'm halfway down the sidewalk when Kepler's words reach me.

"Don't ever touch me again." His tone is low and resolute, winding back toward me as I'm barreling forward. "I didn't steal your job."

Smith shoves a finger in Kepler's chest. "It's only because of Lacher. I'm tired of always being—"

"Get the fuck away from him." My voice echoes against the brick and asphalt, and the finger-toucher's gaze snaps to me. He blinks, confusion lacing his features for a split second before he leers at me.

"I *knew* it," he spits out.

Kepler swivels toward me, surprise darting through his eyes before they soften.

"Admit it," Smith hisses. "The two of you are fucking."

Kepler drags in a breath, turning back toward Smith, a

slight twitching in his fingers is the only evidence of what's going on under the surface. "So what if we are?"

I slam to a stop.

Holy shit. Did Kepler really just say that?

Smith wipes his hand over his lips and spits on the ground, his sneer curling up as he takes in Kepler. Maybe Smith's just as surprised by what Kepler said as I am.

Kepler stands stiffly, arms at his side as he looms over Smith. "And you won't say a single thing about it. Not to me. Not to Lacher. And you definitely won't fuck with Jin."

My stomach twists so hard I might get sick.

We're *screwed*.

This guy does not like Kepler. He doesn't like me. There's no reason for him to keep this secret.

Smith scoffs. "Are you crazy?" He shoves an index finger at me. "And your boyfriend here isn't any better. I know he sells essays."

"You will not do a fucking thing to Jin." The heat in Kepler's voice makes me flinch. I've never heard him speak in that tone. He steps directly in front of Smith. "Do you hear me?"

Smith stiffens. "Are you threatening me?"

Kepler's eyes narrow. "I'm telling you how it is."

Smith glares at Kepler, and I get a flash of memory—from years ago. I *know* Smith. It was always in the back of my head that he looked vaguely familiar, but I couldn't place it.

"Egan Smith," I say stiffly, trying to tamp down the sick feeling in my stomach. "You're one of my past clients."

Smith stills.

I don't remember what I wrote for him, but the knowledge that I remember who he is seems to chill him enough. And now that I've hit upon the truth, it won't take me that long to sort through past essays and find whatever I wrote for him.

"Are you willing to risk yourself too?" I ask Smith, stepping next to Kepler, heart thumping up in my throat.

He pales. "A couple of essays is *nothing* compared to what the two of you are doing." He wipes at his nose with the back of his hand and then spits on the ground again. "I'll find proof."

He turns and barrels toward the building before disappearing around the corner.

"This is bad," I murmur as soon as he's gone. "This is really bad, Kepler."

"He's just pissed right now." His fingers reach out to brush against my forearm. "He's mad I got the NASA job. But he'll get over it."

"Are you sure?" I scrub a hand over my face, my nose cold against my palm. The weight of all that we're risking settles deep into my bones. "This is so fucked up. You could lose *everything*. The job. Your chance to defend your dissertation. Would they even let you earn your doctorate? And for what?"

"For us," he says urgently, stepping closer. "I pick *you*. No question in my mind. I'm not scared of writing another dissertation or finding another job. But the thought of losing you? It's like standing on the edge of that roof, it *terrifies* me."

I suck in a breath, staring into those gray eyes that are lit with something so fierce that it might burn me.

Then I let out a groan and step back. "We can wait."

He stills. "No. I want this time with you."

"We can't keep risking this." I shove a finger toward the packed coffee house. "Even right here, where that fucking finger-toucher could come back. Where Lacher could walk around the corner. The university dean. Hell, *anyone*. We're pretty much incapable of holding back, Quinn, and it's gonna destroy us."

He sucks in an uneven breath. "What if we just came out with it? What if we just own up to it?"

I stare at him wide-eyed. "Are you *crazy*?"

"Probably." He blows out a breath, hand coming up to palm the back of his neck. "You want us to stop seeing each other. And that sounds even crazier to me."

"Just until the end of the semester." Am I really saying this?

But we *have* to stop. I won't let him risk his entire life for me. Even though just thinking about walking away from him makes me feel like I'm going to vibrate apart.

He's worth more.

He's worth so damn much. My eyes heat, but my resolve firms.

"We have to stop," I push out. "We're stupid if we don't."

Kepler hesitates, a million thoughts flashing through his eyes as they darken. "I don't like it."

"Tell me that I'm wrong. Tell me that we won't get found out. We've been stepping on the stupid side of the line way too much." I shake my head, my own words cutting me to the core. "I can't do this. I can't let you risk yourself for me."

A long step forward and he's right in front of me. "Then say you'll come with me after the year ends."

I *want* to. So deeply that *yes* is on the tip of my tongue.

Why can't I say yes?

I run a hand over my mouth, trying to hold back that sick feeling crawling up my throat. "We're just gonna have to trust that this thing between us won't fade."

His jaw binds. "It won't."

I squeeze my eyes. I want to believe him.

More than anything.

But the fear that's been lurking in the back of my mind explodes to the surface, hot and sudden, tumbling out, and my throat tightens, and I will myself to keep breathing.

What if this is all over when he leaves?

A sudden bolt darts through his eyes. "Will it fade for you?"

"*No.* That's not possible." My voice wavers, the truth simmering to the surface. "I'll always want you."

Vulnerability. Right out there, on display.

His lips part, and I can tell he wants to rush toward me, but he holds his position.

One second longer, I won't be able to stop myself from going to him. If there's anything I've learned recently, it's that, when it comes to Kepler Quinn, I've got zero restraint.

But I have to believe that we can come back together at the end of this, and that I'm doing the right thing. If Smith finds the proof he needs, who knows what he will do. And I won't let Kepler risk himself any more than he already has.

So, I turn and walk away.

23

I DON'T KNOW what happens after that.

I'm on autopilot when I step back inside. Dex's hand falls on my shoulder, and he's asking me to pick up the auction sheets, but he has to say it three times.

I nod, answering the way I'm supposed to, and then slide up next to London who takes over whatever we're doing, giving me a side-look with a lined forehead. I'm really glad that he doesn't ask why I can't seem to concentrate on anything because I've got no clue what I would say.

Are Kepler and I over?

Kepler will leave at the end of the semester, and Langley is *1,900 miles* away from Indigo Falls. That's the length of India from north to south. It's longer than the Great Barrier Reef. I can't drive that far in a day. Hell, I doubt my shitter car would make it there at all.

And why can't I agree to go with him? I drag in a breath and try to concentrate on the canvas that I'm helping London pack up.

Thank fuck he knows what he's doing because I've got no clue. Even if I was fully functioning. It's all I can do to focus enough to fit on the cardboard corners to protect the frame, my fingers picking up a slight tremble.

I glance up.

Kepler's across the room.

I didn't even know that he came back inside. But he's saying something to Lacher, nodding in response. And then he glances over her head at me.

Gray eyes settle on me. Just for a moment. Then he pivots, heading toward the door.

And I'm wrecked.

Right here. In a crowd of people. One cardboard corner held up over the top of the frame. My throat binding, my chest pitching so hard that I can hardly breathe. My life feels like it's closing in.

I don't want to do this without Kepler.

And shit, I'm going to have a panic attack.

The realization doesn't make it better, it just makes it worse.

I can't do this here. I can't—

A warm hand falls on my shoulder, London's voice close to my ear. "Set this down for a moment."

His fingers wrap my hand, and then we're moving through the crowd. Somehow, my feet are falling one after the other until we're sliding down a hallway, and London tugs open an "employees only" door.

I don't even look around, just follow him.

"Jae?" His palm is cool on my cheek. "What's going on?"

I shake my head, dragging in a slow breath. It's easier here. Less crowded. I can focus on London, dark eyes warming me with concern, fauxhawk at full attention tonight.

Another breath. And another. After a third, I realize we're in a supply closet. Coffee cups and tiny stirrer straws and napkins surround us. There's one overhead bulb without a cover, a harsh light beaming down.

"Kepler and I . . ." I shake my head. Even just the thought of finishing that sentence binds my chest down again. "I can't say it," I manage to push out, the words tripping over each other, eyes burning.

"I'm sorry." He grabs my forearm. "I know what it's like to want a man so desperately that you can't breathe."

"For your entire life?" I mumble, my eyes burning, my words garbled. And that's so desperately true that it scares the shit out of me.

It creates a crater in my chest.

I don't know how I'm gonna survive in Indigo Falls without Kepler.

I squeeze my hand into a fist, feeling my cuff cut into my wrist. "I've got to be with him."

London wrinkles his nose, moving the piercing. "I know that feeling too."

The conviction on his face is clear.

"Yeah, it seems like you do." My voice is still rough, but I push the words out, studying him as I do. "Can you just . . . talk? About anything, man. I just need to clear my freaking head."

He nods, hand releasing mine as he steps back to lean against the shelf. "The fundraiser was good. Did you know we auctioned every single piece of artwork?"

I swallow through my tight throat and scrub a hand over my face. "Dex is gonna be ecstatic."

"I, uh . . ." He itches at his hawk. "I don't know what else to talk about."

I suck in a partial breath. "Anything. This is helping. I can almost—"

"I'm stalking Vain Henley," he blurts suddenly.

I freeze, a half-cough stuck in my throat. "Wait . . . what?"

Apparently that distraction works because as soon as I get the cough out, I drag in a huge breath of air. "You're doing *what*? Like stalking-*stalking*?"

He bites his bottom lip, letting out a frustrated groan. "I can't believe I said that."

"Well, it's out now."

He shakes his head, gritting his teeth. "You know who he is?"

"Everyone knows who he is." I think back to that moment Vain was in the café, chewing on that green apple, surrounded by his hockey entourage. "What exactly do you mean by stalking?"

He sighs, closing his eyes. "I, uh . . . *Shit*. It's more like I need to know that he's okay." His eyes flash open, a desperate light in them. "And he doesn't know who I am, so I can't really ask him. I just . . . check in on him." He winces. "Damn, this sounds even more messed up than I thought it would."

He's not entirely wrong about that. But he's also *London*. He's a good guy, and he's obviously torn by all this. Doesn't mean that stalking the guy is cool, but like usual with London, I'm not sure I understand the full picture.

I frown, chewing on everything he's said. "Why do you need to know he's okay?"

He stills, eyeing me. "Do you know what happened to his older brother?"

"No," I say. Vain mentioned his father a few times, but never a brother. "He has a brother?"

He swallows. "He did."

"Shit."

He nods. "He was an Army Ranger. Killed in a friendly fire incident. And you know I was a military kid?"

"Yeah, I remember that."

He shakes his head, his hands balling into fists in his pockets, his teeth gritting again. "It was my father who killed him."

"Holy shit." I'm staring at him, at a complete loss. "I'm so sorry, man."

"I am too." He closes his eyes, standing there breathing for a moment. "It's jacked. I *know* it is. But you don't have to worry, because it's ending. I need to get away from him. Just let the past be the past."

I nod, reaching out to clasp his shoulder in my hand. It feels like a really lame attempt to comfort him, but I'm not sure what else to do. "I'm here. If you need to talk about it. Or, hell, hang out with Dex and me more. Maybe we'll head out to the bars, and the two of you can meet some guys. Get your mind off him."

He sighs. "That actually sounds like a good idea."

"Fuck, yeah, it is." I squeeze his shoulder. I don't know that I understand all that he just told me, but I've started to understand something lately.

"You're not alone," I tell him. "None of us are."

"Alright, dude." Dex flops onto the couch next to me. "Tell me what's going on."

I frown. "I'm working."

He points at the iPad propped on my lap. "Screen's off."

Shit. I wake it up with a swipe of my finger. "Well, I *was* working. Like two seconds ago."

"Nope." He shakes his head. "You were staring at nothing. I watched you from the doorway for like a solid five minutes."

"Alright, you caught me." I sigh and flip my iPad closed, setting it on the arm of the couch. "I've been staring at the same page for an hour." Maybe two hours, but who's counting?

Dex grabs an Xbox controller and holds it out to me. "Wanna drop in on some *Call of Duty*?"

I glance at my phone. "I've got time for one round."

"Good enough." Dex starts the Xbox. "You also canceled on *Halmeoni* again last weekend. Isn't that like six weeks in a row?"

I groan. "Yeah."

Three weeks since the fundraiser, and it's like I've slipped back into a dark pit.

Every time I step on campus, the world closes in. I haven't exchanged more than a couple of words with Kepler. No texts, no boring photos, no calls.

Nothing.

Cold turkey.

And it sucks.

The only real news I've gotten is from Shin, who texted to say that he and Kepler talked.

I'm glad for that, at least.

But lab has been the worst. It's physically painful to sit there, knowing Kepler's so close but having zero idea what's going on in his head.

I freaking miss him.

Dex gestures toward the screen with his controller. "Ready up, dude."

"Shit, sorry." We drop in on a map, and it's chaos from the start. Dex gets a solid killstreak going, but I'm not much help, even with a decent loadout. My mind's not really into it.

Dex can probably guess that, but he doesn't hassle me about it.

"I've got to get going." I say after our team gets demolished. I haul myself up and head toward the door. I've got lab in an hour. Even if it's painful to go, I won't miss it. I still get to see Kepler, and I won't turn that opportunity down. "Want a ride to campus?"

"Nah, I'm gonna work on stuff here." Dex drops his controller and reaches for his fundraising binder, which has now turned into his project planning binder. He's pretty much a hero at our old middle school after that fundraiser. "We should go out this weekend. I hear Vain's having a party."

"Vain's always having a party." I grab my coat off the hook. I know that Dex is trying to bring me back to the living again, figuring that *Call of Duty* and a couple beers will help. I don't think he's right, but I appreciate what he's doing, so I shrug. "Sure. I'll go."

"Cool. Text London too."

"Okay," I say vaguely, letting that one slide by.

Dex nods. "Or if you need to talk . . . that's what friends are for, right?"

I pause with my coat halfway on. Dex's olive green eyes are fixed on me, but instead of his usual grin, his lips are in a line. He's worried about me. He's also the best damn friend anyone could ask for. I know I've said that before, but I'll say it a thousand times over.

I'm lucky to have a friend like him. Lucky to have London. Lucky to have my brother.

"Yeah," I say. And I'd be a better friend if I'd asked him the same. "Hey, how are things going with Brady?"

He rolls his shoulders. "Still not. But after thinking back on it, I'm not sure he's really my type anyway."

I try to piece together what Dex's type *is* from who he's dated over the years. There's nothing they all have in common—other than Dex. "What's your type?"

He laughs and flips open his binder. "No clue. I feel like I haven't met them yet."

"Fair enough."

He waves at me. "Get out of here, dude. I've got work to do."

"Later." I step out, defrost my car, and brave the icy roads to campus. I'm halfway there, freezing my ass off because of the crappy heater in my car, when my phone buzzes from its spot on the passenger seat. I freaking hate the sound now. It's never Kepler.

I flip the phone over, and my stomach damn near falls out.

It's mom.

She never texts.

I pull over, hard on the brakes and sliding a touch on the ice, and then grab my phone.

I don't know where I am.

I bite back a string of curse words. *Are you at a bar?*

No. A house somewhere.

Are you sober?

I tried to say no.

I stare down at the message. Fuck.

I hate the cycles of loving someone who's an addict. The constant up-and-down of it. The way things always turn so suddenly. The way you're always trying to keep up with the sober periods and relapses. Trying to understand *why*.

I thought she was going to try. Anger punches me hard, but I shake it off for the moment.

What happened? I type out.

He just kept at me, Jae. I'm sorry.

I let my head fall back against the cold headrest. She's been doing good. For *weeks*. She's been the mom I remember flashes of from years ago, when Shin and I were jumping our bikes off the front sidewalk and she set up a make-shift ramp for us. Or when she'd let us sleep out in the backyard, wrapped in old sleeping bags, with a splay of stars overhead.

I clutch my phone hard. *Did you text Shin?*

No.

Text him. He can GPS track her cell. Whether she's relapsed or not, the first thing is to find her.

Okay. But Jae?

Yeah?

I'm scared.

My mouth dries as I read the message. I don't know if she's scared about texting Shin or about where she is, but I've got the overwhelming need to find her.

Tell me what you see, I type.

I'm in a bedroom. Voices outside. Lots of them. Men.

Is there a window?

Yes.

Look outside. Having to lead her through the most basic steps makes me feel like she's probably on something.

There's a street sign. Bauder Drive.

I slam a palm against the steering wheel and curse so loud it echoes off the windshield. Then I focus back on the phone.

Have you ever been to Fender's house?

No. He never let me.

I shake my head, not sure what to think. But I do know one thing. I type, *I'm coming to get you.*

I check for traffic and pull out, hooking a U-turn to head

toward East Lake. I remember that freaking street name when Shin drove us over there.

Shin.

I need my brother.

I call him, cursing when it goes to voicemail, and leave him a message telling him about every single text.

When I hang up, I shove my foot down on the gas, hightailing it across Indigo Falls as fast as I can considering the thin layer of ice over everything.

This is going to be one of those moments that I'll want to forget. I know it. The kind I told Kepler about on the drive back from the observatory—the painful ones. The embarrassing ones. The ones that make us all feel lost and ashamed.

I'm so angry by the time that I get over to East Lake that my hands are shaking, my stomach is in knots. I just want to get her out of there, then we can figure out what happened, and if she's drinking again, Shin can get her admitted, even if it'll only be for seventy-two hours.

And I could keep better tabs on her. Go over there more.

Move in.

No. I slam a hand on the steering wheel as I turn into the neighborhood. A moment later, I'm pulling up across the street from Fender's house. Two trucks are in the driveway, a couple of guys are standing just out front, the front door wide open.

I push out of my car, flipping up the hood of my coat and fisting my phone, fixed on my destination, my chest binding harder with every damn step.

If she's in there, I'm gonna get her out.

I cross the street, stopping at the edge of the yard.

"Is Lilah here?" I call up to the guys.

"Who the fuck are you?" One calls back to me, but I'm already not paying attention.

Mom. I see her through the open door, wearing fuzzy aqua pajama bottoms and an old Rockies tee that used to belong to Dad. She's running toward the open door, then she's yanked back, *hard.*

Fender has her by the wrist, and she turns and smacks him across the jaw, but he doesn't let her go. Not until he sees me.

Then he smiles.

She jerks her wrist from his grip and stumbles to the matted carpet. I'm already running toward the house, my Chucks slipping on ice as I fly up the front steps, phone gripped in one hand, the other reaching for her.

"Let's go," I grit out as soon as I clench her thin fingers in mine. Her wrist bruised from how hard he was holding her.

"Fine, she can go." Fender glowers at me from his spot in the middle of the room. Big, meaty hands that were fisted at his sides now cross over his chest. "You're the fucker I want to have a few words with anyway."

"Mom," I say, keeping my glare on Fender. "Go wait in the car."

Fender leers at me, and every one of my muscles binds like a taut spring. My awareness increases tenfold, taking in the dingy carpet and the television along one wall and the open door behind me, ice covered sidewalks beyond that, the heavy boot step that Fender takes toward me.

"Jae." My mom grabs my forearm, tugging on me and shaking her head. Her face is so ashen that it's almost translucent. I have never in my life seen her look like that. I've seen her through depression, regret, grief. But never fear. Not like this.

"We have to go." She keeps tugging on my arm.

That's exactly what I want to do. But this asshole has also messed with my mom again and again. We need him out of our lives. Enough is enough. And I need to make it clear he's not welcome.

I unloop my arm from her hands and bend down, kissing her quickly on the top of her head, dragging in a faint scent of lavender shampoo.

"Go," I say, pressing my phone into her hand. "Call Shin."

"Who the fuck is Shin?" Fender snarls.

Well, that's interesting. Mom must have never told him her other son is a cop.

I glare at him, an inferno of anger hardening my shoulders, my hands trembling hard. "You're not allowed at her house anymore. I'm going to get a restraining order, and if I even see you at the gas station across the street, I'm gonna call the cops on you."

Mom keeps standing there, and fuck, I just need her to *go*.

Fender snorts. "Fucking call the cops. I'll tell them you broke into my house." Three boot steps and he's within arm's distance. "Because that's exactly what happened. I was minding my own fucking business, and you bust in the goddamn door."

"You're not very smart, are you?" I steel myself, eyeing his fat fists.

His eyes narrow. "You think I'm stupid? Always making fun of me. Talking like you think you're better than me."

"Jae." Mom says, blue eyes filling with tears. She slips around me, trying to put herself between me and Fender. "This is my fault. This is—" She's shaking so hard she can hardly speak. She keeps trying to get in front of me, but I wrap a hand around her thin bicep and pull her behind me.

Honestly, I don't know what I'm feeling toward her right now. There's worry and concern. There's also a well of anger rolling up from deep in my gut. But none of that matters right now.

We need to get safe. And then we'll deal with the fact that she relapsed *again*. That every time I start to feel a touch of hope, everything falls apart.

But for now, we need to get out of this house.

"Let's go," I say to her, turning toward the exit, eyeing the guy who's standing in the doorframe. I take one step, and something grabs my coat hood, yanking me back.

The world tips. Mom grabs my arm, but I'm twisting away from her, focused on Fender who's clutching onto my hood. I take a swing, catching him hard on the jaw before I stumble down.

It's the only hit I'll get. So I make it count.

Then I'm down. A thick boot slams into my stomach, and I cough hard. I try to push myself up, but a kick to my obliques shoves me right back down.

I crawl up again and get a kick to the ribs. It's not just Fender. I peer up at the guy who was in the door and get another hit. There's another one too. I'm surrounded.

Mom screams from somewhere behind them.

Fuck, we have to get out of here. I crawl up to my knees and get a kick to the stomach so hard that my knees are lifted an inch off the floor. I cough again, blood speckling the carpet.

The kicks come from all sides. Every time I try to get up. There's at least three of them. And one of me.

I squeeze my eyes, trying to hold onto any sense of reality as a boot slams hard into my ribs.

Kepler.

I think of him, holding onto him when there's nothing

else to hold onto. I picture his gray eyes lit with so many thoughts. Lips curving when I make him smile. Arms strongly hooked around me.

That feeling I have pounding against the inside of my chest every time he's around. *Simkung.* Possibility. Hope.

Love.

I squeeze my eyes tighter and hold onto him. His strength, his control. His words.

You're not alone. I'm here. Always have been.

This is rock bottom.

It has to be. If it's not, then there's no hope for any of us.

A kick to the jaw knocks my head back sharply, forcing my eyes open. I look up as best I can.

Mom screams and jumps onto Fender, clutching onto his back. He twists, trying to get her off. And, shit, this is the moment I need. I roll forward and wrap myself around his ankles.

It's a weird move, but it's one I learned about for a self-defense essay. It traps whoever is coming after you, and it can make them panic.

Which Fender does. He curses, trying to stumble back, and then he lands on his ass, Mom somewhere behind him. She yanks on his hair, hard. She's *fighting.*

And maybe it's too little. And maybe it's too late. I don't know, but I scramble up and throw a punch at the guy who was in the door, and then I'm reaching down to grab her wrist. I pull her up, and I don't know how we do it, but we're sprinting toward the door. Out into the ice and the snow, my Chucks slipping and sliding.

And, just faintly, off in the distance, I hear the sirens.

24

Snow soaks into my jeans, and I sink into Mom's arms. She's saying something, talking to me in a soft voice like she used to do when I was a kid. Even though I'm not a kid anymore, I still latch onto her words.

Everything hurts. But I'm breathing and I'm still *here*.

I flinch at someone looming above us, but the man squats, his hand cupping my shoulder, the familiar scent of cotton and soap and my brother.

Shin. I practically cry with relief.

"Jae." Shin's voice cracks as he leans over me. There's *fear* in his tone, and relief floods his eyes as I push out a croaking sound that's supposed to be "*What?*"

"Jesus," he mumbles. "Stay there. EMTs are coming."

I nod, feeling Mom release me. My head's swimming. "Where's Fender?"

Shin's face hardens. "We're taking care of that."

I squeeze my eyes as I reach out and clutch onto his forearm. "Kepler?"

Shin frowns. "Was he here?"

"No." *Yes, but only in my brain.*

He never left my thoughts. Not even for a second.

Shin twists and waves to someone. "Over here."

He moves out of the way as a paramedic kneels next to me, asking me questions and feeling over my neck, shoulders, and hands.

It's a blur after that. I'm pushed from one place to another, paramedics to ambulance to hospital. X-Rays and doctors telling me that my ribs are bruised, my wrist sprained, my face busted up a bit. But it's nothing that time won't fix.

I'm lucky, they say.

And I believe them. It could have been a hell of a lot worse.

And the entire time, I hold onto one echoing thought —*Kepler, Kepler,* Kepler.

I fucking *love* him.

I think I have for a long time. And I need to tell him.

Although I've got no clue where my phone ended up. Probably kicked somewhere in Fender's house.

I swallow and sit up in the white-sheeted hospital bed when Shin steps into the room a couple hours later. I've been slowly eating some green Jell-O even though food is the last thing on my mind.

"You look better." Shin frowns as he crosses the room, looking me up and down. "You still look like shit, but you look better."

"Thanks." I toss down my spoon and push the little rolling table away.

He laughs. "Yeah—"

"No, I really mean it." I catch his eyes. "I don't know what would have happened if you hadn't been there."

"I didn't get there fast enough."

"I don't know." I shake my head and wince at the

stinging cut above my brow. "He might have followed us out there. It might have been worse."

"Maybe." He nods sharply, crossing his arms over his chest and standing stiffly next to the bed. "I don't even want to think about that."

"What happened to Mom?" The question sticks in my throat, my hand picking up a low shake. I can't even start to sort out the mass of feelings I've got right now, but it feels a lot like anger that's heating in my chest.

And like I can't keep doing this.

Shin pulls out his baton so he can sit in a brown vinyl chair next to the bed. "She's over at Sunrise Crossing for a couple of days."

My brows go up. "You admitted her again?"

"No." He shakes his head slowly. "She admitted herself." He pauses. I squint at him, trying to see past the steady cop exterior. "I've never seen her like that. Not even after Dad died. She wouldn't stop crying, and as much as she wanted to be here to see you, it was like she knew she had to go."

I take in a slow breath. "It's the first time she's admitted herself."

"And she wants an inpatient program." He itches at his bulletproof vest. "She asked me to put the house on the market."

I blink at him. "She's never even been willing to consider that." To her, it's like leaving him.

He nods. "I think today she realized she can't keep living in the past anymore. That all she's doing is hurting herself. And you. And me. And the memory of Dad too. I mean . . ." He pauses. "Look at yourself, Jae. What happened to you today."

I press my lips, taking all of that in. Anger still beats a

steady pulse, but something else is peeking through: *is she really willing to try?*

Hope is like this tiny flower bud in my palm. I don't know if I'm ready to let it bloom yet. It's been smashed and obliterated so many times. But maybe...

I shake my head. "The house won't be enough. There's a reverse mortgage on it from Dad's medical—"

"Enough for what?" The low voice from the door makes my head snap toward it.

I already know who is standing there. Just like I know when it's him behind me in lab or who's texting before I even pick up my phone.

I'm so attuned to him that it's instinctual.

"Kepler," I utter his name in an expelled breath as I take him in, gray eyes so fixed on me that it feels like he sees nothing else. He crosses to me in long strides that don't stop until he's at my bedside; his hands clasp my jaw softly. His fingers are shaking, his breath coming sharp as he leans over me, that spicy omija scent of him, the low timbre of his voice close to my ear.

"Jin."

He whispers my name.

That's all.

And it's like he's read me an entire book. I hear so much in that one syllable. Worry and fear. Ache and need. So many emotions spill out in one whispered syllable. He once told me that he's not calm on the inside. Not even a little fucking bit. And I feel it now, rushing over me, overwhelming me.

He turns his head so his lips brush against mine, his warm hands cupping my jaw. Our lips meet softly, less of a kiss, and more just *breathing* together. And even though my heart hits that hard beat against my ribcage with his nearness, I still sink into a peace that I only find with him. My hand comes up to fold over the nape of his neck, my fingers scratching into his hair.

He's mine. He's *here*.

"Are you good?" he mumbles, pulling back just slightly, still only millimeters between us.

"Mostly." My voice is choked. Fuck, I've missed him. I *love* him. "I'll tell you about it later. Everything. I just can't... now."

"What's the prognosis of your ribs?"

Shin must have told him about the X-rays.

"Bruised," I say. "Not broken."

He nods, hands still shaking as he feathers a kiss along my jaw, over to my ear, and then against my temple.

"I was so damn scared, Jin," he whispers so quietly that I can hardly hear him. "*Terrified.*"

A throat clears.

I jump. I'd forgotten where we were. Forgotten there was anyone else in the room.

But when I turn toward Shin, I can't ignore how my brother is staring at us with a slightly open mouth. Like he can't believe what he sees. His gaze flashes from Kepler to me and back again.

Then his eyes narrow on Kepler. "Do you always kiss my brother like that?"

"Yes." Kepler takes a seat on the bed, his hand reaching for mine, his attention still fixed on me, pausing when my tongue slides along my bottom lip. His pupils flare slightly, even though he sits resolutely on the edge of my hospital bed.

Shin mumbles something under his breath, but he doesn't seem angry or annoyed. Just still slightly surprised.

He didn't know that I'm absolutely head over heels in love with his best friend.

Kepler looks between us. "I get the feeling I interrupted a conversation."

I clear my throat. "I've gotta ask you a favor."

He squeezes my fingers. "Anything."

Shit, I *feel* how deeply he means that.

"That place in Ohio," I start. That little flower bud of hope in my palm? I won't let it get squashed. Not this time. "The inpatient facility we talked about? I want to take you up on your offer. If it still stands, I mean. Even if we sell the house, that would probably only pay for a place here. But I understand if—"

"It's already paid for," he says quietly. "Ninety days at the inpatient facility and then six months at a nearby extended sober living home."

There's a hush in the room. "You're serious?"

He nods. "I set it up right after we talked about it. I didn't want you to think that offer was ever tied to anything. I set it in a trust to be paid out upon the condition that Lilah ever began the program." He glances over at Shin. "It won't be easy for her. There will be therapy and regular testing and requirements. She's got to really want it."

"She does," Shin says quietly. "But Kep, man. This is a big ask. This kind of favor is—"

"It doesn't feel like a favor to me." Kepler's lips arc softly. "Shin, you've been my best friend for my entire life. And Jin . . ." His gray eyes settle on me. "You've been my constant. For longer than you can possibly guess. You're as bright as starlight for me. *Brighter.*"

My eyes heat, my throat closing, so many emotions flooding me that I can't even start to sort them out. Kepler squeezes my fingers again, like he can feel what his words do to me.

Maybe he can.

"What did I tell you before?" He leans in toward me, as if drawn forward. "It's not any kind of exchange. If I can do anything to help a person who you both love, then I will."

My lips part, but I can't even explain what this means to me. And to Shin.

The jarring ring of Kepler's phone cuts into the room, and Shin and I flinch. Kepler sighs and yanks his phone out of his back pocket, muting it.

My forehead lines as concern tickles in the back of my thoughts. "Who's that?"

Kepler shakes his head stiffly, his jaw tightening. "It's nothing for you to worry about now."

I frown. "Well, that's ominous. Tell me."

Kepler shakes his head again. "You should worry about resting—"

"Tell me." I clutch his hand in mine, a low panic starting to fizzle in my chest. "Just fucking tell me."

His jaw ticks. "I was in lab when I got Shin's messages. I called him back in a panic, not even thinking about what I was saying. I just . . . had to get to you. I didn't care how or about anything else."

I stiffen. "Someone overheard you talking about me?"

He nods. "Lacher."

Holy shit.

"They know?" A coldness darts down my spine. "They know about *us*?"

His lips press. "I told her."

"You *told* her?"

"They were hours away from finding out the truth. Between Smith and that call . . ." Kepler's shoulders bind, all of him rigid. "I couldn't lie when she asked, Jin. I *wouldn't*. You're the—" He shakes his head, seeming to change tracks mid-sentence. I'm about to ask him to explain when he continues. "Anyway, the department's calling an emergency meeting to discuss what will happen."

"Fuck," I mumble, blinking at him. "When's the meeting?"

"Two hours from now."

"Two *hours*?" I let go of his hand and swing my feet over the side, grunting from the pain that shoots down my side when my toes hit the cold tile. "Then we need to go."

Kepler shakes his head. "You're in no condition to—"

"I'm going," I said firmly. I push myself up with a groan, my hospital gown flapping open awkwardly, but I don't give a shit. There is no freaking way that I'm not going to be there with Kepler when he faces this. "We're going together. End of discussion, Quinn."

25

Cohesion
Noun
1. the force that holds together atoms or molecules

KEPLER TAKES my hand just before the steps that lead up to the main STEM admin building.

My hand. Right there. At the bottom of the steps. Where anyone can see.

I close my eyes for a moment before ascending the stairs, just feeling his warm fingers around mine, in broad daylight. My shoulders loosen, my steps are surer. I'm still reeling from the knowledge of what we're about to walk into, but I need his hand in mine.

We need this.

This is one seriously fucked up day, and we haven't even finished dealing with it yet.

I grit my teeth after the first three steps, my free hand

settling on the frozen railing. I keep climbing, but hell if my ribs don't scream with every step. I got a reluctant okay from the doctor to leave. Mostly because I didn't give her much of a choice but to discharge me.

"Are you good?" he whispers as he pulls open the door for me, the heat of the building welling out into the wintry afternoon.

"*No*," I say. "You?"

"No, but we will be." He squeezes my hand, cognizant of my injuries, and then he lets it fall. I miss the touch, but it's probably better for both of us if we're not walking around hand in hand. That little moment on the step will have to be enough for now.

But Kepler pauses. "Maybe you should wait here."

I flinch back. "Fuck that."

He drags in breath. "I don't want to see you hurt by this, Jin. I deserve whatever happens. I broke a university ethics code, pure and simple. But you—"

I turn and head down the narrow, quiet hallway toward the room number provided for us. I'm fucking going.

There's nothing that Kepler can say to change my mind.

He follows after me, about to say something else when we get to the door, but Professor Lacher steps out. Her red suit is impossibly bright, her long braids pulled back over one shoulder.

Kepler's shoulders stiffen, his lips pressing. I know that he admires her and that she's the one who helped him get the position at Langley. This must be hard for him.

"We're ready for you, Mr. Quinn," she says stiffly. She turns to look at me and pauses, a flash of concern darkening her eyes. "This looks like a bad time, Mr. Lee."

"I'll be fine." I rake my hand through my still damp hair

and hiss at the bite of pain flaring along my obliques at the movement. I'd only had a chance for a quick shower, the hot water hurting like hell on my face. And I haven't been trying to think about what I look like.

Or about what happened at Fender's. I take a deep breath, focusing on the doorway before us, not the demons in my head. Kepler's hand falls low on my back almost immediately, warm and firm.

He's always paying attention to me. Always aware.

He raises a brow in silent question, asking if I'm okay, and I nod before he turns to Lacher.

"Professor." His voice is soft. "I'm sorry for whatever weight this has put on you. I very much regret that."

Shit, I *feel* those words. They're a simple apology, but so much weight hangs in them.

"I do too, Mr. Quinn." The pinch in her face doesn't release as she turns to me. "You can wait outside, Mr. Lee."

I shake my head. "Nope, I'm going in."

Kepler frowns, leaning close to my ear. "Please think about this. I don't want them to think for one second that you've caused any of this. If you're with me, then—"

I step in front of him, my palm settling on his chest. "I've already said that I'm going in with you."

He shakes his head. "They'll be more inclined to take disciplinary action against you if you go in with me."

"Fucking let them." My voice rises slightly as I stare across at him. "We're in this *together*. You and me. I'm not going to let you go in alone."

Kepler stares back at me. Then, slowly, a hint of a smile feathers over his lips, something deep and certain passing through his unfathomable smoky eyes. In an instant, I'm zapped awake by him, my breath catching, my heart hammering. He wakes me up, just like always.

His smile falls as he tips forward onto his toes, like he's going to kiss me, but then he stops. "You fill up so much of me. And no matter what happens, no matter what the consequence, I'd make all the same choices again."

Holy fuck. I need to tell this man that I love him. I'm one breath away from letting it spill out.

But not here. Not now with Professor Lacher eyeballing us in a hallway that's starting to crowd as the lecture hall door opens. When I say it the first time, I want it to be just the two of us.

I turn to Professor Lacher. "I'm going in."

She frowns, considering me. "I suppose there are no regulations against Mr. Lee being present. As long as the board agrees, and they already agreed to your witnesses."

Witnesses?

"Witnesses?" Kepler voices the same question.

Lacher gestures us into the room. "They said that you asked for them to be here."

I crash to a stop just inside the doorway. "*Shin?*"

My mouth drops open. Shin's standing to the side near a tall window, in full uniform, with his hands clasped behind his back like he's standing at attention. Then my eyes swing to the man next to him—Dex. His eyes grow wide, probably at the bruises on my face.

I'm about to walk over and ask what they're doing here when Lacher calls our attention up front.

Both Kepler and I stiffen at the panel in front of us. Lacher sits at the end. Next to her is Professor Manford, the professor I was going to switch to. Next to him is the university president and Dean Preston, neither of whom I really know. And then a man Lacher introduces as the head of the university ethics committee.

They sit at a long table, faces severe, lips drawn, and my

steps almost falter as we walk toward them. *Fuck.* They wouldn't have pulled together a panel like this unless they're serious. My stomach knots hard.

What if we lose? What if they kick Kepler out? His entire doctorate just up in smoke because of me. I know he said he'd make the same choice, but would he? *Really?*

Their heads swivel toward us as we stop before the table.

Lacher starts. "We have questions for you, Mr. Quinn."

Kepler looks them dead-on, like he's staring down an oncoming train. "I'd like a chance to speak first."

"No," she says, no room for argument in her voice. "You can speak after we've asked our questions."

He nods stiffly. "Fine."

Professor Manford grunts and tosses a notepad filled with sharply scribbled words on the long table. "Is your argument the same that Officer Lee put forward?"

We both turn to look over at Shin, who hooks his arms over his chest. Dex stands resolutely next to him, not illuminating the situation either.

What the fuck is happening?

But Kepler just turns back to the panel. "Yes. That's our argument."

I've got a feeling he doesn't know either.

But he trusts Shin. And so do I.

The panel stares at us, all of them with notepads and folders before them. Pens in their hands and—

I still.

Holy fuck.

"Kepler," I whisper, reaching for his hand.

Spread out across the table are at least twenty of Dex's pencil drawings. The image of us at the treehouse is on top of a scattered pile. There's more—all four of us at a lake,

Dex is pushing me in, Shin yelling something, and Kepler with a broad smile. There's one I've never seen before with Kepler and I huddled over that old telescope.

And, holy fuck, the way he's *looking* at me in Dex's drawing.

How did I never see it? Even with the way he's so enigmatic and baffling, I should have *seen* it.

Our history is laid out before them.

All that we are in Dex's smooth, detailed pencil strokes. So lifelike that they could be photographs.

Shin and Dex must have brought them here. They must have told them that what we have began long before this semester.

Does that matter? My brain flips through the ethics code Kepler had mentioned on the way over. I've never read it—never had reason to before now—but would it matter *when* our relationship started?

I mean, yeah, the *sex* started this semester.

But Kepler and I are so much more than that.

Manford jabs a finger at the top drawing of the treehouse, and I've got the urge to snatch it up and protect it from that glower he's giving.

"You can't tell me that this really makes a difference." Manford's voice rises as he looks up and down the panel.

It's the same question I had.

"The university ethics code says it does," Lacher says calmly, addressing both the panel and tilting her chin at us. "There's a significant difference between a teaching assistant beginning a sexual relationship with a student *during* the semester compared to a teaching assistant having a prior relationship with a student and failing to notify their observing professor of the conflict of interest."

I glance over at Shin, who gives me a tiny head tilt.

Christ. He's saving us. And Dex is saving us too.

Lacher continues calmly. "In the first situation, it's grounds for expulsion and possible revocation of past degrees." She lets the weight of that sink in, and trust me, it does. Kepler could lose *everything*.

"In the other situation," she continues, "when the relationship began prior to the semester, the university response is more in line with simply removing the teaching assistant from their current assignment to prevent further conflict of interest." She focuses on Kepler. "So, Mr. Quinn, did this relationship start before this semester?"

My heart pounds, my hand becoming clammy clutched with Kepler's.

Manford guffaws before Kepler can respond. "You're leading the question, Lacher. You're getting emotional because he's your assistant, and it's—"

"*Enough.*" The dean sets her palm down flat on the table, an inch away from the drawing of us at the treehouse. She's been quiet this entire time, watching thoughtfully, but now she leans forward, and it's pretty obvious who's actually in charge here. I blow out a breath of relief that it's not Manford.

"Let him answer the question," the dean says. "That's why he's here. Then we'll make our decision."

Manford shakes his head, picking up his notebook and scribbling something on it.

They're planning to vote, I realize. They'll vote and then supply their decision to the ethics committee, but I doubt the committee would ever go against the president and dean. Our hope is right here, in this room.

Manford is clearly against us.

The others? I have no clue.

Dean Preston points to our linked hands. "You don't seem to debate that there *is* a relationship?"

"No," Kepler says strongly.

She nods. "So then, Mr. Quinn, how long has it been going on?"

Kepler looks over at me, a warmth lighting up his eyes, one that I share so deeply, and my throat tightens. His lips part slowly, and he takes a full breath before continuing.

"I could explain to you all the years of our history." His voice is soft and warm and full of so much emotion that it hits me low in the gut. "I could tell you about the treehouse and the telescope, the way that this man lives in my soul, that first moment I saw him on the Quad five years ago, how he's my constant, how he fills me up. But you can see all that because it's spread out on the table before you. It speaks for itself. So, 'how long has it been going on?' I'll just distill it down to one word." His eyes warm to a light gray. "*Always*."

"Kiss me," I say, shivering as Kepler's lips just brush against the outer shell of my ear. His fingers tighten around mine as he does what I ask, leaning in to take my lips.

Now.

Here.

In public, on the Quad, not holding back. We're lounging on a park bench under a thick-trunked boxelder as we wait for a decision from the panel that could alter the course of both our lives. Branches covered in tiny icicles shimmer above us, sparkling white as they slowly drip water.

When he pulls back from our kiss, he studies me. "How are you feeling?"

"Like I got hammered by Thor."

He feathers fingers over my swollen knuckles, barely touching them. "We should put some ice on it after this."

I groan. "I haven't thought about what comes after this."

His brow hitches. "I think about it all the time."

The future.

For once he doesn't ask about me coming with him to Virginia. I guess that's up in the air too.

Is it, J?

We're silent for a moment, sinking into each other, watching people hurry past. I slide a palm over his coat, resting over the top of his stomach, feeling the rise and fall of his breath, replaying that word he said before the panel.

Always.

It sticks in my throat. It makes me think about the past. And the present.

And the future.

He tugs me tighter against him, and when his phone finally rings, it's like a storm breaking into our heaven.

He sighs, twists to pull it out of his back pocket, brings it up to his ear, and listens, expression fixed. I'm hardly breathing. Hardly thinking. Just waiting. I can't hear a single damn thing they're saying.

"What did they say?" I ask as soon as he hangs up.

He clears his throat, blinking like he's surprised. "They believe the bulk of our relationship began before the semester. That I'm guilty of not admitting a bias about a current student."

"And?"

His jaw tenses. "I lost the TA position."

"Christ, Kepler, fuck."

He shakes his head. "I expected that. But . . . you'll have to retake your lab requirement."

"I can do that." That's the smallest of my concerns. "What else? NASA?"

"Lacher already contacted them to explain the situation." He frowns, glancing down at his phone. "She said that her recommendation for me is stronger than ever. That I made a mistake, but strength in character is owning up to it. And . . . that's it."

"That's it?" I breathe out the words, hardly believing them.

His lips part slightly, a surprised laugh slipping out. "That's it."

"You get to defend your dissertation?" I ask, just as surprised as him. "Graduate? *Both* of us graduate? And you keep the NASA job?"

"Yes." He stares across at me, the weight of everything still not hitting me.

We're gonna make it.

We're gonna survive this.

I don't have the words to express what that means to me. Or what he does.

But I also know that losing that TA position had to hurt. I watch his thumb track over the dark screen of his phone. "I'm really sorry about your TA position."

He nods. "I am too. But I think it was a fair decision. It's the same one I would have made if I were on that panel."

"Doesn't make it any easier."

"No, it doesn't. And Smith . . ." He groans and leans back against the bench. "He's going to gloat so much. He'll be taking over my sections." He shakes his head and tucks his phone in his pocket. "But I'll deal."

"You will."

He nods. "Do you want to head back to your place? Or mine. We could—"

"I need to go see someone," I say. "It's important. Come with me?"

He stands and extends a hand down to me. "Absolutely."

I SLIP off my shoes just inside the door. Kepler does the same, and I'm about to ask if he wants some house slippers when I'm wrapped in a hug. My *halmeoni* is tiny, and I loom over her, hugging her back as she speaks a million miles an hour in Korean.

She pulls back and touches my face lightly. "*Gwenchani?*"

"I'm fine, *Halmeoni*," I assure her. "It's not as bad as it looks."

I'm not ready to speak about what happened yet. I just want to be here, in her too-warm house that always smells like lavender and eucalyptus.

She turns to the door where Kepler's standing in his gray socks.

"Kepler," she says, accent heavy, reaching out to squeeze his forearm. "Good to see you."

"You too, *Halmeoni*," he says, reminding me how many times he's been here with Shin. Which might make this weird for her, I don't know.

I take a breath and reach out for Kepler's hand, lacing his fingers with mine. "Sorry we didn't call first."

"Never have to call, Jae Jin." Her gaze falls to our hands, but darts back up to my face quickly, her eyes widening just a touch. "Glad you came. That you both came."

And, shit. I just came out to my *halmeoni*.

She gives Kepler's forearm another squeeze. "You boys hungry?" Then she shakes her head and turns, heading toward the kitchen.

"What am I asking?" she mumbles in Korean as she goes. "Of course you are."

She disappears around the corner, still talking to herself.

Kepler squeezes my hand. "Did that go okay? I can't ever really tell with her."

It's not just about gender. *Halmeoni* used to argue endlessly with my father about not marrying a Korean woman. That one hundred percent Korean bloodline was always important to her, but that was years ago, and she's never said anything since.

But it doesn't matter. She'll have to be okay with Kepler and me.

"It'll be fine," I say as I lead him into the kitchen.

Halmeoni's already tisking around the kitchen, opening Tupperware and pulling short ribs out of the refrigerator.

"No time to marinate," she says. "But I know what you like, Kepler."

Kepler laughs. "Yes, you've got me."

"Good." She frowns at us. "Get to work."

I reach for a knife and cutting board. "Garlic?"

"No. No. No." She shakes her head sharply. "Kepler does garlic. You peel pear."

She ushers us to our workstations, instructing in Korean the entire time. Kepler seems to puzzle through it pretty well, although I help translate a few times, and once she's got us organized, she preps the meat, asking about school and Shin and Dex.

When there's a moment of silence, Kepler tells her about Virginia, his eyes lighting.

Halmeoni leans over closer to me. "*Neoneun?*" she asks quietly.

"I don't know," I answer. Kepler glances over me, raising a brow.

Halmeoni nods once, gives me a knowing look, and then goes back to her work. Once the ribs are cooking and the dishwasher is stacked, I lean a hip against the counter.

"*Halmeoni*, do you remember that old telescope?"

"Upstairs." She points up at the ceiling. "Empty bedroom. You go see."

I wave for Kepler to follow me, and he climbs behind me up the narrow stairway, family pictures posted along the wall, both from the States and from Korea.

"What did she ask you earlier?" he asks as we crest the stairs. "You said that you didn't know."

I pause, hands sinking into my pockets. "She asked if I was going with you."

He nods, face passive, but I know that a thousand thoughts are going on in that brain of his.

They're going on in mine too.

I turn toward the empty bedroom and stop dead in the door frame.

The old telescope sits over by a single window that looks directly out to the small, fenced backyard. It's *exactly* like I remember. A refractor telescope with a white casing, sitting on a black stand. A couple of scratches run along the casing from years of use.

"It's been forever since I've seen this thing." Kepler squeezes past me. He leans down to look through the viewfinder and then tinkers with the focus knob.

I follow after him, then smooth my hand down the top of the casing. "It seems smaller."

He laughs. "Well, we were smaller."

"Yeah, I guess." I tug on the plastic bag taped to the leg. It's another *Halmeoni* thing: always put the manual in a bag and tape it to whatever it belongs to. Even if that's the ceiling fan and you have to see that bag swiveling around and around. I flip it over in my hand and then still.

"What's wrong?" Kepler asks, straightening up from where he'd been adjusting the eyepiece.

I hold up the manual. "This says '*Kepler Quinn*'."

He hitches a brow. "I suppose it might."

I blink, shaking my head. "Why would it say that?"

"Because it was mine," he says with a shrug. "My grandfather bought it for me. And then I gave it to you because it seemed like you needed it more."

I'm staring across at him, manual held loosely in my hands, my mouth hanging open. "You gave me your telescope?"

"You didn't have one," he says simply, going back to fidgeting with the focus knob. "I think this is jammed."

"Wait, step back a minute." I'm staring at him, heat racing up my throat. "I didn't have one, so you *gave* me yours?"

"I did." He glances up, his brow lining, like he's not sure why I'm reacting like I am. Like giving me this telescope was the simplest thing in the world.

To him, maybe it was.

A hum starts deep in my bones, branching out over my chest and trembling in my fingers as I tape the manual back on the telescope and then lick my lips, not sure that I can keep my voice steady. "I want to go with you."

He stills, fingers on the knob, chest expanding with an inhale. "To Virginia?"

"Yeah." I swallow hard, emotion crowding my throat. "I

mean, I have to finish up a semester here. But after that, yeah."

"You're really coming?" He breathes out the words, gray eyes flicking around my face as his hand falls from the telescope.

I nod. "Yeah, man." I can't hardly talk, so I step forward and brush his lips lightly with mine. He brings me into him instantly, our chests melding as he returns my kiss.

I'm going with him.

"I want to go," I whisper after breaking from him. "And..."

All I can think is *one* thing. One simple, true thing that has fluttered in my heart for so long that it's become a part of me. I squeeze my eyes and lean closer to his ear to let it out. "I love you. I always have."

He drags in a breath, his fingers warm on the back of my neck, his heart pounding against mine.

I lean back to settle a palm over his sternum, flatting it right over that thumping heart.

He's staring at me, eyes reddened. I've never seen so much emotion on his face.

Ever.

And I'm pretty sure I've left him speechless.

That's probably a first for Kepler Quinn.

"*Simkung*," I nod to my hand flat over his heart. "You have it too."

"What does that mean?" His voice cracks, his heart hammering even harder like it's going to rocket right out of his body.

"I hope it means," I begin, my own eyes heating, "that you love me too."

"Jin." A half-smile tugs at his lips as his eyes soften. "You're my universal constant. Something that will *never* change." That genuine smile expands over his face, the one I'll never get tired of. "I love you to the depth of my ability to love."

I laugh. "Shit, that was a good '*I love you*'."

"It's my first." His smile falls as he tips forward, his forehead pressing against mine. "If you want to hear it simpler, then here it is: I love you too. *Always*."

EPILOGUE

Three months later...

I sink my hands in my pockets and lean my ass back against the driver's side of Kepler's Jeep, glancing up at the Ohio evening sky, which seems to extend forever compared to Colorado. No mountains to cut the view, just endless sky that meets the far-off horizon.

Kepler's not here, but for a second, I can almost smell that spicy, warm scent of his when I focus on Andromeda. Hear his low voice, feel his thumb brushing over the back of my hand.

He's five hundred miles away, but I'm barreling toward him.

Always barreling toward him.

I shift my attention back to the front doors of the rehab facility. It's late for visitors, but my mom's therapist allowed for an exception since I only got in this afternoon.

Nine weeks she's been there.

Nine weeks sober.

Nine weeks of not walking out.

It hasn't been easy. She called me or Shin every day for the first two weeks crying, but she stuck it out.

We all have.

This last therapy session was brutal for both Mom and me. For the first time, I talked about what happened that night with Fender and the anger that I feel about it—toward both him and her. And I told her the truth of how I've felt over the last decade.

It was hard for her to hear. It was hard for me to say.

But it needed to be said.

We talked about Dad too. How every morning she still wakes up crying. And I think: what if that were Kepler? What if I lost him like that?

Christ. I can't even think about it. Even just the vague thought makes my eyes heat.

I take in a full breath, rip my gaze off Andromeda and Pegasus and Pisces, and tug open the door to the Jeep. Kepler asked me to drive it out when I came, which is good because I doubt my shitter car would have made it. I lent it to London since he's staying at Dex and my apartment for the summer. Maybe I'll just give it to him when Kepler and I go back in a couple months.

Kepler needs to go back to complete the paperwork for transferring his house to Flora and Adelard. He just... gave it to them. To live in or to sell and pay for medical bills. And even though he's probably paying some hefty taxes on the transfer, he did it with a casual shrug. His simple generosity for the people he loves never fails to amaze me.

And I need to go head back to finish up my physics credit. Professor Lacher was nice enough to let me do an independent study to finish up my physics credit, but I do need to give a presentation and complete some of the lab work.

And then graduation. Because of everything that happened, it'll be a full year from now. Kepler hates the delay—that there was any fallout from our dating. But, honestly, I don't care all that much. I was never in it for the diploma. I just wanted a different view.

I turn on the ignition and glance over my shoulder at all my shit packed into the back.

I'm seven hours away from Kepler Quinn.

I should probably pull into a hotel room and spend the night. Get some sleep and leave first thing in the morning.

Yeah. Except I don't do that.

THE HOUSE KEPLER rented is pale gray. I feel the need to tease him about that as I pull up in front of the little house in Hampton, Virginia, not far off Interstate 64, close to both his work and also the tutoring job I'd picked up until I can figure out what to do with myself. I'd expected him to rent something bigger, but he said this one was perfect. A compact two-level with a garage and some kind of weird squat palm tree growing out front.

I don't care what it looks like. I care about the man inside.

Nerves twine through me as I push out of the Jeep and drag in a breath of humid air, heavier in my lungs than the air in Colorado. The grass under my shoes is thick as I walk around the side of the silent, dark-windowed house.

Once past the house, I smash to a stop, *breathless*.

There's a dock. Straight down from the house that extends onto the Chesapeake Bay. And there's a fucking *sail-*

boat tied to the dock. A small one with one mast. It's a sloop, which I know from research papers. But I've never actually seen one.

I walk down to the dock, the slow lap of the water just reaching my ears. The wood shifts under my feet as I step onto it.

Holy fuck, Kepler. He did this for me.

The night is quiet. The bay is filled with sailboats, their masts extending up into the slowly lightening horizon as they bob silently.

This view is like nothing I've ever seen.

Somewhere new. Somewhere *different*.

"There's a shooting star."

My heart launches up into my throat, my abs tightening at the low roll of his voice, every cell zinging awake. Heat races down my spine.

Just like always.

I turn, and he's *there*. Kepler steps down from the porch, feet bare, and dark lounge pants low on his hips. He runs a hand through mussed hair as if he's worried about how he looks.

As if he should ever worry.

Kepler Quinn is fuckin' hot. Through and through. And it doesn't have to do with his mussed-up hair or his sleek abs glowing in the moonlight or that mole or even those smoky gray eyes that are focused on me.

It's his strength, his intelligence, his humor, his determination.

His kindness.

I'm moving toward him before I make the decision. We're drawn together, his skin is warm under my cold palms, and his lips veer to my ear.

"I missed you," he says, and all I can do is swallow, push

out a mangled *"me too"* and hold onto him so hard that my biceps ache.

I'd ask about the sailboat, but I'm too choked up.

"Jin." He leans back. "You good?"

"Yeah," I grate through my tight throat.

Whatever he reads on my face, it makes him smile one of those effervescent, genuine smiles.

"Want to see our house?" He tips his head behind him toward the long, wooden porch.

Our house.

Him and me.

Now I'm smiling too. So big that it definitely will crack my face this time.

"Come on." He arches a brow, reaching a hand toward me, long fingers extended, palm open. It's like he's asking me to step into a new future. New *life*. One that's so packed with possibility and hope and love that it crowds everything else out.

How can I say no to that?

THANK YOU FOR READING ALWAYS

I hope you enjoyed it!

If you're wondering what's happening between London & Vain, sign up for my newsletter for teasers and release dates for their book, *Never*:

www.lorenleighbooks.com/lorens-vips

Or join Loren's Starlights, my Facebook Readers Group:
www.facebook.com/groups/lorenstarlights/

Finally, if you enjoyed going on this journey with Kepler and Jin, please let your friends know and lend this book to them! And if you leave a review for *Always*, I'd love to read it! Email me the link at loren@lorenleighbooks.com

ABOUT ALWAYS

Always has had a long and winding journey. When it began, it was a very different novel. It was first drafted in 2011 and while some readers enjoyed it, something didn't sit right with me. I set it aside, wrote other novels, and pulled it out again around 2017. It was revised and edited, and even read by a few—but it still didn't feel quite right, and it definitely wasn't the story that it is today. So I hid it away again and moved on, not sure what to do with it, but continually feeling a burning need to return.

Then in 2021, I re-wrote it from a scratch in a three week flurry. Many of the current scenes are an echo from that first story—like Kepler's speech in the library, the struggles with Jin's mother, the observatory and telescope. But it essentially became a very different story, and one that feels like it finally answers the questions I set out to ask in 2011.

Now it's finally done, and Kepler and Jin have found their happily ever after. I suppose from my perspective, I've been waiting for that to happen for over a decade—just like they have.

Thank you so much for taking this journey with Kepler and Jin.

ABOUT LOREN

Loren Leigh writes contemporary m/m romance, spanning from college romance to romantic suspense, with characters who jump off the page and chemistry that's burning hot.

Her characters want nothing more than to fall in love —*wholeheartedly, deeply and wildly*—and they're ready to take you on the journey with them.

Always is her first book, but not her last.

Want to know more? For updates, sneak peeks and freebies, sign up for her newsletter here:

www.lorenleighbooks.com/lorens-vips

A LAST 'THANK YOU'

Thank you for reading. Without you, Jin and Kepler are just characters in my head. But as soon as you read, they become so much more—real and vibrant.

I couldn't do it without you.

To Laura, Immy, Steph, Cass and Renee . . . what do I say? Whatever words I write here are too small, and what you have done for me, too big. So I'll leave it at a glorious and obnoxiously loud THANK YOU and the hope that, someday, I'll be able to shout it in person.

To Cassie, my eagle-eyed editor who not only cleaned up all the details, but also gave me inspiration to keep chugging along. This book is better because of you, and I can't wait to get started on the next one.

To The Raven's Touch, who designed the most beautiful paperback cover I could ever hope for. Thank you for artwork that not only perfectly fits the story, but warms my heart every time I see it.

To Jessica and Brona, who read this novel when it was an early draft and provided priceless thoughts and more kind words than I deserved. You saw the glitter hiding in the dust and helped me bring it out.

To everyone who read this book when it was not this book at all. Back when it was another book entirely, I've carried your thoughts and advice with me for all these years, and I feel like I finally got to implement your counsel. I hope you love this newly re-written version of Indigo Falls as much as I do.

And, finally, to my family. I'm grateful for each and every moment, each and every day.

Printed in Great Britain
by Amazon